डRAFTED

DRAFTED
PARA-MILITARY RECRUITER™ BOOK 01

RENÉE JAGGÉR
MICHAEL ANDERLE

DISRUPTIVE IMAGINATION

THE DRAFTED TEAM

Thanks to the Beta Readers
Malyssa Brannon, Rachel Beckford, Larry Omans, John Ashmore, Kelly O'Donnell, Mary Morris, David Laughlin

Thanks to the JIT Readers
Peter Manis
Wendy L Bonell
Jeff Goode
Diane L. Smith
Jan Hunnicutt
Dave Hicks
Paul Westman
Dorothy Lloyd
Zacc Pelter

If We've missed anyone, please let us know!

Editor
The SkyFyre Editing Team

This book is a work of fiction. All of the characters, organizations, and events portrayed in this novel are either products of the author's imagination or are used fictitiously. Sometimes both.

Copyright © 2022 by LMBPN Publishing
Cover by Mihaela Voicu http://www.mihaelavoicu.com/
Cover copyright © LMBPN Publishing
A Michael Anderle Production

LMBPN Publishing supports the right to free expression and the value of copyright. The purpose of copyright is to encourage writers and artists to produce the creative works that enrich our culture.

The distribution of this book without permission is a theft of the author's intellectual property. If you would like permission to use material from the book (other than for review purposes), please contact support@lmbpn.com. Thank you for your support of the author's rights.

LMBPN Publishing
PMB 196, 2540 South Maryland Pkwy
Las Vegas, NV 89109

Version 1.00, November 2022
ebook ISBN: 979-8-88541-962-8
Print ISBN: 979-8-88541-963-5

DEDICATION

*To Family, Friends and
Those Who Love
to Read.
May We All Enjoy Grace
to Live the Life We Are
Called.*

— Michael

CHAPTER ONE

It was going so well until the check came.

Julie would almost say she liked Sam when he made his way to her through the bar, which was crowded for a Wednesday night. She clutched the stem of her wineglass for fortitude as she watched him approach. He looked like his profile pic on the dating website she'd used: tall, slender, fussily combed black hair. Not smoking hot, but when you were a nobody looking for love in the big city, adequate would have to do, and he was.

He paused a short distance from the bar and glanced up and down. His eyes eventually fixed on her. "Julie? Julie Meadows?"

"That's me." Julia slipped off the bar stool and extended a hand.

"Don't get up." He gripped her outstretched hand and, instead of shaking it, gave it a strange little nod as though he wanted to kiss it. "I'm Sam."

"It's nice to meet you." Julie cursed inwardly. *Way to go, Julie. Excellent choice of words.* "Uh... you want a drink?"

"That's okay. I was hoping we'd get straight to dinner." He smiled.

Well, why offer to meet me at a bar, then? Julie pushed the testy thought aside and ensured her chirpy smile stayed in place. "Okay! Sounds good. Where did you want to go?"

"How about La Rose Dansante?"

Julie almost choked on a sip of her wine. She set it down slowly, eyeing Sam. "You like seafood?"

"It has the best lobster thermidor in the city." He smiled, and two adorable dimples appeared on his cheeks.

Those dimples. They made Julie want to forget that, while she might like lobster thermidor as much as anyone, her budget would argue ramen noodles were more her speed.

"We'll go in my car," Sam offered, his smile widening. "My treat."

In that case, Julie wasn't in a position to give up free food. She grinned. "Sounds good to me."

He extended a gallant arm to her as though it was the nineteenth century, and Julie permitted herself a small giggle as she threaded her arm through his and allowed herself to be escorted across the bar. She liked the feeling of Sam's sleeve under her fingers. His suit was well-cut, and the fabric had a rich, expensive thickness.

When they stepped into the warm summer night, a constellation of city lights above their heads, Sam's car was waiting by the curb. It was a sleek, low thing, purring with speed even when it wasn't moving. Sam led her to the passenger side and opened the door.

"Well, I'm getting the royal treatment tonight," Julie joked, then immediately cursed herself again.

He gave her another dimply smile. "Just being a gentleman."

It *did* seem like he was a gentleman. He played quiet classical music on the drive to La Rose Dansante and talked about travel and the weather. When they reached the restaurant—complete with red carpets, crystal chandeliers, and free breadsticks—Sam held the door and pulled out her chair. Julie did her best to play the part of the elegant little date, too. The conversation flowed (as did the wine), the lobster thermidor was excellent as far as she could tell, and everything seemed boring but fine.

Until Julie stared at Sam across the table with the check lying between them.

"Excuse me?" she managed in a strangled whisper.

"I said, should I ask him to bring a card machine?" Sam raised an eyebrow at her. "I've got cash for my half."

She gaped from him to the check and back. Then the total at the bottom, a sum so large the lobster thermidor in her stomach threatened to reappear.

"You don't mind splitting the check, do you?" Sam prompted.

"I...guess I don't." Not usually, but if she'd known they'd split the check, she would never have agreed to come here.

"Great." Sam grinned. "I'm all for people paying their way. So, cash or card?"

"Card," Julie croaked. She hadn't carried that much cash since she'd left home. *Ugh, home.* Her mom was going to have a field day when she learned about this.

Dry-mouthed, she unlocked her phone under the table and checked if she had enough money in her account to cover half of the bill. The digits glowing cheerfully on the screen would be just enough.

The waiter accepted their payments, and Sam offered her his arm to lead her from the warm restaurant with a now-queasy bellyful of lobster. "So..." he began as they stepped outside. "Would you, uh, like to head to my place?"

Julie stared up at him. *Was he being a jerk by making me think he'd pick up the bill, or was that just me failing to understand people, as usual?* She couldn't decide. "Uh, not tonight."

"Okay." Sam shoved his hands into the pockets of his nice suit and shifted his weight. "Well, are you free on Friday?"

"Actually..." Julie sighed. "I had fun and everything, but I don't think there will be a second date."

He flinched, then shrugged. "Okay. Thanks anyway."

"Thanks," Julie managed and watched him stride toward his car without offering her a ride home. *Another tick in the "jerk" column, I guess.*

She pulled out her phone and opened her navigation app. She was seven blocks from home. She didn't have the budget left for an Uber after The Dancing Rose had taken its pound of flesh. Nothing like a long, lonely walk home through Brooklyn in the dark after a disastrous date.

Stuffing her hands into her coat pockets against the early-spring chill, Julie hunched her shoulders and headed downtown, the heels of her boots ringing on the pavement.

Why do I have to be so bad at people? Things would be so much easier if she could read them better.

The knots in Julie's shoulders unraveled a little as she traipsed past the restaurants, car showrooms, and upmarket malls that gave way to seedy tenement buildings and smoky little bodegas. Graffiti splashed the walls, loud and colorful and profane, making her feel at home.

Still, she glanced into dark doorways as she passed them and tugged at the short skirt of her one and only decent dress to cover a little more skin.

That didn't stop a scruffy figure leaning against the wall outside a gas station from wolf-whistling as she passed. She ignored him and continued briskly to the overpass ahead that marked the corner of her home block, but she slipped one hand into the inside pocket of her coat and closed it over the little bottle she'd hidden there.

"Hey, sexy!" the man called again from behind her. "Where you goin' in such a hurry?"

Julie forced herself not to quicken her step, but she quietly uncapped the bottle in her pocket.

"Hold up a minute." The man's footsteps were loud behind her. "I just wanna talk to you."

She was just a few yards from the overpass, and a huge figure detached from the bottom of the bridge and stepped out in front of her.

"Hey," growled the massive man. "My friend here wants to talk to you."

Julie stopped. *Well, crap.* She swallowed. "I'm not in the mood for talking."

"I can think of something else we could do," said the person behind her.

Julie turned. The scruffy man wore a loose-lipped leer. There was a fruity stench to his breath, and as he stared at her, he scratched at one scabby arm.

"You don't want to do this." She tried to keep the quaver from her voice.

"Oh, I think he does." The big man behind her chuckled. "I think I want to, too."

"You'll regret it," Julie snapped. She clenched her fist over the bottle. "Lay a finger on me, and you'll both be sorry."

"Oooh, I'm scared!" mocked the disheveled man, holding up both hands. "Don't hurt me!"

The big man laughed and stepped nearer and Julie whipped around, ripping the bottle from her pocket. "Don't make me use this!" she screamed.

He stopped, blinking at the bottle in the faint glow of a grubby streetlight. "Uh, Scents of Paradise Room Spray, with notes of orchid and macadamia?"

Julie rolled her eyes. "It's the only bottle I had, okay? But that's not what's in it." She stepped closer and jabbed him. "This bottle contains alcohol, vegetable oil, and powdered Carolina Reaper, the hottest pepper in the world." She rested a finger on the trigger. "One spritz of this will make police tear gas seem like a spa day."

The man's eyes widened, and he stepped back. "You think I haven't been pepper-sprayed before?"

"Get it together, Pete," barked the ratty man. Julie heard feet shuffling behind her and spun. She backed away in time to avoid being grabbed. The scruffy man sneered. "In case you hadn't noticed, sweetheart, I ain't had many spa days recently. I think I can handle your little concoction."

"Wanna bet?" Julie growled.

"Leave her, Greg," Pete hissed. "She's gonna fight. We'll grab another."

Greg stepped nearer, hands fisted. Julie held up the spray.

"Seriously. She's gonna get us into trouble," yelped Pete.

"You bet I am!" Julie snapped.

Greg glanced from the bottle to her and back. Then he stepped away, laughing. "I'm just messin' with ya. Go on, then."

Julie gave him a last glare and backed away, keeping the spray bottle in her hand. Pete watched with apprehension.

"Run along home, scared little rabbit!" Greg called.

Julie spun on her heel, resisting the urge to run with all the willpower she could muster, and strode away. She waited until she was safely around the corner and out of sight, then she carefully replaced the cap on the bottle, returned it to her pocket, leaned against a wall, covered her face with her hands, and allowed herself thirty seconds of freaking out.

"Crap, that was close," she breathed, her heart hammering. Her hands shook against her face. "That was so freaking close."

She tipped her head against the wall and stared at the skyline, its bright windows glimmering in the place of stars veiled by smog or clouds. *What a night.*

It was a good thing those two goons hadn't made her use the spray. They had no idea she hadn't figured out how to get more of the spray onto her target than herself.

She pushed off the wall and walked home, keeping one hand on the little bottle in her pocket.

The garage smelled like old oil and stagnant gasoline. When Julie slammed the door behind her, she let out a long sigh and felt the tightness in her neck and shoulders release. As she shuffled past the clutter to the wooden stairs in the back corner, she paused to pop her head around the back door. A greasy woman in a floral housecoat sat on the sofa, smoking and watching *Judge Judy* reruns.

"It's me, Lillie."

Lillie Griswall glanced at her. "Oh, hey, Julie. Good date?"

"Not really."

"Men are pigs." Lillie gestured with the cigarette. "G'night."

"You left this door unlocked again, Lillie. You've got to be more careful. There are creeps out there." Julie knew that was true. "They might take your car."

Lillie shook her head. "Doubt it."

Julie had no idea what that meant. Lillie's car, or at least Julie presumed it was her car, was just a few feet away from the back door. Julie had no idea what it was since it was kept under a dust cover, but people around here would steal anything with wheels. "Please, Lillie? We should be careful."

"Okay. Go on to bed, sweetie. I'll take care of it."

Julie shut the door, shaking her head, and climbed the rickety staircase to the little apartment over the garage. The smell of fuel came up through the gaps in the floorboards. The single, grimy window overlooked the street, and she had had to prop a sheet of cardboard in it for the first few nights to block out the streetlight outside. A little bathroom nestled in one corner, her single bed in the other. She also had a floor-to-ceiling bookshelf that was thoroughly stocked and a tiny kitchenette. It wasn't much, but it was hers.

Julie peeled off the coat and the little black number, hung them up, splashed some water on her face, and fell on the bed with a groan.

At least you got a taste of lobster thermidor, Julie. Better than a kick in the teeth, I guess.

Buzzzz! Buzzzz!

Julie rolled over with a moan and slapped at her rickety nightstand. Her phone slid off and hit the floor facedown with an appalling sound.

"No, no, no!" Julie scrambled to the edge of the bed, now awake, and groped around the floor. Daylight stabbed her eyes through the threadbare curtains. She finally found the smooth, cold surface of the phone and rolled onto her back, breathless, staring at the screen. Her caller ID read **Mom**.

The screen had a small new crack in one corner.

"Ugh." Julie let her head flop against the pillow. "Not you."

She silenced the call, shoved the phone under the pillow, rolled onto her belly, and closed her eyes tight. Seconds later, the phone buzzed again.

Julie groaned. After fishing the phone out, she swiped angrily at the screen, then put it on her pillow and buried her face in it. Her ear landed against the cold surface. "Hnnnghh," she growled.

"Happy birthday to youuuuu!" shrilled a piercing voice. The shriek sliced through Julie's aching head. "Happy birthday to you!"

Julie moaned again. "Seriously, Mom?"

"Happy birthday, dear Juliaaaaaaa!" Rosa Hernandez screeched. "Happy birthday to you!"

"Nobody calls me Julia anymore."

"Aw, my sweet baby. It's so nice to hear your voice. I can't believe you're nineteen already! It seems like just yesterday you were born, all small and slimy with your little face purple and screwed up as you yelled."

"Wow, Mom. Thanks."

Rosa's warm chuckle washed over Julie. "I'm just kidding. You were the most beautiful baby I'd seen in my life. When are you coming to see me again? I thought we could have a nice little barbecue or something to celebrate."

"I don't know, Mom. Maybe this weekend."

"You've been saying that for the past two months. 'Maybe this weekend.'" Rosa scoffed. "I'm not buying it, sweetheart. You've got to set a date."

"I can't, Mom. I'm busy here."

"Oh?" Rosa's voice rose, and Julie immediately regretted using the word "busy." "You've got a job, then?"

"Well, sorta."

"Julie, don't tell me you're still working at that seedy little bodega. Aren't you worried you will get held up at gunpoint or something?"

"You've got to relax, Mom." Julie sighed. "I've sent in over a hundred applications, and I'll have a real job soon."

Rosa snorted. "Well, honey, if I had your body, I'd gladly twirl a pole, take the easy money, and have no shame."

Julie groaned. "Mom!"

"Women are free to be anything we want, you know." Rosa was dead serious.

"Well, I'm also free *not* to be anything I don't want to be," Julie snapped. "While I'm sure I *could* shake my ass on a pole, I'm fine not being an artificial fantasy in white lace, thanks."

"If you say so, sweetie. I'm just saying sometimes a girl's gotta do what a girl's gotta do. I should know."

"Is this going to be another one of your rants about how hard it was being a single mom?"

"There's no reason to get uppity. You're being moody again, Julie. Are you drinking that aloe vera juice I gave you?"

Julie opened one eye to peer at the bottle of disgusting juice sitting near the top of her bookshelf. It was covered with a thin film of dust, unlike the spines of her books.

"Uh-huh," she grumbled.

"Maybe you should raise the dose. It'll clear your skin too, you know. It's good for your eyes. Not to mention you'll be much less constipated."

Julie closed her eyes and allowed her mother to prattle on. No use in trying to stop her. Moving out had been easier than listening to her rave about the latest elixir of life she'd discovered.

"So, aloe vera juice does everything the cinnamon pills were supposed to do last year?" Julie suggested when the chattering slowed.

Rosa sniffed. "Don't be snippy, young lady. I'm just trying to help you."

"I know, I know." Julie sighed. "Hey, at least I went on a date last night."

"Oh!" Rosa crowed. "Tell me everything! Are you at his place right now?"

"Mom! No! I'm not. I'm at home. I didn't even get a kiss."

Rosa drew a deep breath, preparing to lecture. "Julie, honey, I'm all for valuing yourself. It's just you're a little hard up right now to be turning men away, don't you think?"

"I'm not hard up, Mom. I'm being easy. Just very selective." Julie sighed inwardly. "There were no good selections on the menu last night. Assholes are summarily rejected, Mom."

"Listen to you. You're a walking dictionary." Rosa sighed. "Stop reading and go play with people. Too much knowledge is going to kill your future!"

"Unless it's knowledge of the magical benefits of aloe vera?" Julie sniped.

"You know what I mean, young lady."

"Yeah, okay. Anyway, Mom, I gotta go," Julie lied. "I've got applications to send out."

"You do that, honey. Come over this weekend, okay? I love you."

"Love you," Julie muttered.

She hung up, grabbed her pillow, and pulled it over her face. *Oh, Mom, why do you always remind me how sucky my situation is?* Maybe she was desperate enough to try the aloe vera juice.

Julie tipped the last of the mixture into the muffin pan. After shoving it into the oven, she ran a finger around the inside of the bowl and stuck it in her mouth, moaning. Why was the batter always nicer than the cooked product? Maybe raw eggs were the secret. It was worth the salmonella or whatever it was you were supposed to get from raw eggs.

"Cupcakes for breakfast," she muttered, flopping down in one of the rickety chairs in her kitchenette. "Well, it's my birthday." She cracked open her well-worn copy of *Anna Karenina* and set a timer on her phone.

The cupcakes came out of the oven as the mailman arrived, heralded as usual by mad barking from Lillie's horrible little dog. Julie listened to the woman yelling at the mutt while she made ganache from a mix and poured it over the cupcakes. There were even sprinkles in the cabinet.

"Glitter sprinkles!" she muttered, tossing them over the cupcakes with abandon. "Whee!"

"Pookie! *Pookie*! Sit!" yelled Lillie downstairs. The mail van rattled off, and the dog finally fell silent.

Leaving the ganache to set, Julie clattered down the steps and out of the garage. Her mailbox, an old metal pail screwed onto the wooden wall with a rubber lid to protect it from the rain, looked as dismal as ever. She opened it and scooped out a fistful of envelopes. She shuffled through them as she climbed the stairs to her apartment.

"Bill, bill, bill." She tossed the bills on the kitchen counter, where others lay unopened. "'Come to our free dinner and discuss investment opportunities!' Sure, why not? Wait, *who pays?*"

Throwing the envelope angrily into the bin, Julie started the electric kettle and retrieved an instant coffee sachet from her stash, which she kept in an old baked beans can on the counter. They were free at job fairs, which was the only reason she went.

Mug in hand, Julie flung herself onto the chair and grabbed a cupcake from the tray, then bit into it. It didn't solve anything, but it was sweet, rich, delicious, and represented the last of her ingredients. She drank some of the coffee. It tasted like asphalt, and she was out of sugar.

"Let there be something on the job board!" she moaned. Grabbing her Chromebook, she flipped it open and tried to keep the cupcake crumbs off it as she clicked on the job website.

CHAPTER TWO

You have three new matches!

Julie blinked at the screen. "Yes!" she hissed, permitting herself a fist pump. "A birthday gift from the universe, maybe." *Julie, you've got to stop talking to yourself.*
    She clicked on the message, and the three jobs appeared.

Packer for large grocery store

"Ugh." Julie scrolled through the posting. Bagging groceries for eight hours a shift, spending the whole time on her feet? She clicked the next posting.

Office cleaner wanted. Must be quiet and unobtrusive.

Julie tried to picture herself mopping an endless hallway, pretending to be invisible each time a stuck-up corporate ladder-climber passed. She'd throw herself out the window before the first day was over. Well, the last posting would just have to be the best one.

Entry-level position at a customer call center for a tech firm!

Closing her eyes, Julie sipped her bitter, cooling coffee, grimaced, and followed it with a bite of birthday cupcake. Customer call center? She'd sit in a tiny cubicle, staring at a wall all day, wearing an itchy headset. She imagined the calls that would come in. *"Hello? Hello? Is anyone there? Is this a computer?"*

"No, ma'am, I'm not a computer."

"Finally. I've been holding on for ten minutes. Ten minutes, I tell you! How is that reasonable?"

"I'm sorry, ma'am. How can I help you?"

"You can help me by fixing your phone lines. Ten minutes! How can you expect me to hold on for ten minutes?"

"I'm very sorry to hear that. What seems to be the matter?"

"Well, I don't have any new emails from Joe."

"I see. Is your computer connected to the internet?"

"How am I supposed to know that?"

"Well, have you gotten any emails from anyone other than Joe?"

"Of course. Plenty! Just none from Joe."

A deep breath. *"Ma'am, did Joe say he would email you?"*

"No. He usually calls."

Julie imagined hunting down and murdering her imaginary customer slowly and painfully. She'd end up in jail, talking to her mom tearfully through bulletproof glass. She imagined Rosa smuggling aloe vera juice past the guards.

Yeah, no. None of these jobs were going to fly. Frustrated, she slammed the Chromebook shut and put it on the table, then got up to go over to the window and stare moodily at the street outside.

She needed another cupcake, plus more coffee. *Real* coffee this time, not that dried stuff. To buy coffee, she needed a job.

A bell jangled by the apartment's door, making her jump. She frowned at it. It was a simple device: a little metal bell hanging from a nail by the door, attached to a string that ran through a tiny hole in the wall and ended at the foot of the stairs.

The bell rang again, its jangle setting Pookie off barking. The noise rasped over Julie's frayed nerves. She gritted her teeth, put down her coffee, and stomped down the stairs. "I'm coming, I'm coming!"

"Miss Julie Meadows?" inquired the man at the bottom of the stairs. He was wearing a USPS uniform. Weird. Hadn't he just been here?

"Yeah?" Julie growled, hovering on the last step. She wished she'd brought her pepper spray bottle.

"I need you to sign here, please." The mailman held out a large manila envelope and a clipboard with a cheap pen attached to it by a length of dirty string.

Julie sighed. *Must be a bill from someone irate*. "Okay." She scribbled her name. "That all?"

"Yes." The mailman touched his cap with a weird half-bow. "Thank you for your time."

"Whatever, dude," Julie muttered after him as he strode away. She trudged up the stairs, locked her door, tossed the envelope on the table, and made another cup of coffee. She had a feeling she was going to need it to confront whatever was in that envelope. Grabbing another cupcake—her third of the morning, but who was counting?—she tore it open. *Please don't let it be the phone company. I can't go without my phone.*

She scanned the first couple of lines. It was generic—her name, address, birth date, and…

We at the Official Para-Military Agency are happy to announce that you have been drafted into our services, and you must…

Wait. What?

She read it again, and the word leaped out at her. *Drafted*.

This was a sick joke, right? Or a mistake. Or a weird scam. She scrambled to the Chromebook while tossing the paper onto the table and flipped it open, then Googled frantically.

Is there a mandatory draft in the USA?

The United States military has been all-volunteer since 1973.

"Thanks, Google," Julie muttered. Admittedly, it had been a wild moment to doubt something as important as that, but she didn't understand. What scam artist would go so far as to get her to sign for this weird piece of junk mail? What was the Para-Military Agency?

Grabbing the letter, she read it again. It didn't provide any illumination. It said she had to report to an address in one of the swankiest parts of town for a meeting tomorrow morning. It also strategically said that there would be breakfast.

She eyed the remaining cupcakes and shrugged. Maybe "drafted" was a typo. Maybe there wouldn't be any building at that address. Maybe it would be an abandoned warehouse, and she would be kidnapped and sold into sex slavery in Indonesia or something. Still, she wasn't in the position to turn down free food and a possible job opportunity, was she?

It would get her out of the apartment, at least. Her mom's words from earlier that morning echoed through her mind. *Stop reading and go play with people!*

"I hope this qualifies, Mom," Julie said out loud. Then she ate the last three cupcakes for good measure.

Julie gave another yawn, tucked her hands deeper into the pockets of her hoodie, and leaned her head against the bus window. She'd caught the first bus at six AM. The city was filled with pale, watery sunlight.

She began to think she'd wasted good money catching several buses to Staten Island and this Para-Military Agency. Whatever it was.

Rubbing her eyes, she checked her phone. 7:39. Breakfast started at eight. She sat up straighter and used selfie mode to check that she didn't look grotesque.

As usual, she looked fine. Her dark pixie-cut hair was under control, and her eyes were bright and well-defined, even without makeup. She had that going for her, at least—low-maintenance looks. Maybe she should put that on her next résumé, assuming she wasn't sold into sex slavery.

When the bus halted and the driver announced her stop, Julie looked out the window, and her heart stumbled in her chest. She'd been in a lot of places where kidnapping was high on her list of expectations. This was not one of them.

Hitching her backpack onto her shoulder, she stepped off the bus, gaping at the building in front of her. It towered behind stately wrought-iron gates. There was no sign on them. When she peered through the bars, she saw an expansive campus, all green lawns, pine trees, and fountains. Beyond, a blocky building —she counted five stories—loomed over it all.

A small gatehouse stood by the entry. When she approached, its door opened, and a short man with shaggy red hair stepped in front of her.

"I think you're in the wrong place, missy," he began.

Julie fished for the letter in her backpack, her heart dropping. *Have I just spent a fortune in bus fares on a crazy scam?* She found the letter and held it out to him. "I got this letter. I've been, uh, drafted."

The man raised his eyebrows and skimmed it. "Oh. Fine."

Julie had hoped for an explanation, but the man just gave the letter back and hit a button on the wall beside him. The gates swung open.

When she stepped through them, she was distracted by the smell of bacon emanating from the first floor of the huge building.

People dotted the campus, chatting in little knots or hurrying to and fro. Many wore uniforms in bold colors: forest green, royal blue, and scarlet. Others were in scrubs. What kind of agency was this supposed to be? Julie had been expecting black suits and sunglasses. Or military uniforms in camouflage and khaki.

One of the red-uniform people gave her a wide grin as she headed toward the bacon smell. "Newly drafted, are you?"

Julie blinked. Drafted. So, it hadn't been a typo. "Uh, yeah," she managed. "I was wondering—"

"Through those doors," he interrupted. "Take your first left, and you'll be in the cafeteria. We've got to feed you before we break the news, right?"

Julie bit her lip. "Um, right."

Before she could ask more, the man had turned to another person in normal clothes who was wandering toward them. Julie didn't know what else to do, so she trailed over to the towering double doors. If she hadn't known better, she would have thought they were gilded. They led into a vast hallway where her footsteps echoed through the empty space.

The first door to the left led her into a huge cafeteria. She'd been expecting a room like the one in her high school, with gross linoleum and plastic chairs. Instead, three long tables ran the length of a wood-paneled room, covered with scarlet tablecloths and gold runners. Serving staff in elegant suits waited beside a long buffet covered in enormous silver dishes.

She hoped there was coffee. Was the military usually this nice?

Too hungry to ask questions, Julie drifted to the buffet and helped herself to a plate after joining the queue. Some wore ordinary clothes like her. Others wore uniforms or scrubs. A few sported white lab coats.

What am I getting myself into?

The servers gave her heaping helpings of bacon, French toast, fried mushrooms, and fruit. Her plate groaned. She hadn't had a meal this size for weeks, especially not that overpriced lobster thermidor with Sam the Loser. She left the buffet and wandered around, looking for a place to sit. One of the tables was largely empty. She chose an unobtrusive seat halfway down and parked herself, staring at the plate. Could she just start eating? It smelled ridiculously good, better than anything she'd ever smelled. She supposed she was just hungry from getting up so early.

"Hey," someone said from her left. "Mind if I sit?"

Julie looked up. A tall, willowy young man stood beside her, and if his limpid chocolate-brown eyes had a vacant look, the smooth lines of his high cheekbones and sharp jaw more than made up for it. His broad shoulders strained against his green uniform, which was tight enough to suggest the stern curves of his sculpted pecs.

She dropped her eyes, annoyance rising. Great. Another good-looking hunk of meat with a shallow personality and eyelashes longer than hers.

"Miss?" he prompted. When she looked up, he smiled, and his eyes crinkled.

Julie's smile came of its own accord. "Uh, sure."

"Thanks." The young man set his plate down next to hers and took a chair. "These things can be so overwhelming. I don't blame you for looking shell-shocked."

"I'm not shell-shocked!" Julie protested.

He fixed her with that crinkly-eye smile again.

"Okay, maybe a little," she admitted. "It's just, *drafted*? What's *that* mean?"

He chuckled. "You should be flattered. The IRSA 4000 only chooses the best."

"The what now?"

"You know. The system that chose you." He picked up his fork. "So, where are you from?"

"Downtown. Well, the 'burbs, originally." Julie cleared her throat. "How about you?"

"Oh, I'm a prince of the Aether."

She stared at him, trying to figure out if she was supposed to laugh. Or worse, if she should know what that was.

He busily cut a generous wedge of pancake. Julie drew a deep breath and looked down at her plate, remembering why she was here. She grabbed her fork and scooped up some fried mushrooms. They smelled herbal, woodsy, and wonderful. When they hit her tongue, her world exploded with taste. She froze, taking in the complex earthy, salty flavor.

The young man was munching his pancake as though it were ordinary. "So, what are you?"

Julie looked up at him. What was she? A recruit? She didn't know. She chewed, swallowed, and tried to speak, but her mouth felt dull and stupid. Her tongue wouldn't form the words, and when she opened her mouth, her lips were numb.

The young man peered at her intently. "Are you okay?"

She wasn't. It felt as if her chair were tipping underneath her. She clutched the edge of the table, and the room swam. Everything was spinning. *She* was spinning. Nausea lurched in her stomach.

"Hey, are you all right? You're pale." The young man touched her shoulder.

She opened her eyes. She'd been drugged. She must have been. The young man looked different. He didn't look human. His features were sharper, and his eyes slanted. His tight black curls seemed glossier and darker than before. His ears tapered into elegant points on either side of his head.

So, this is a kidnapping, Julie mused as darkness clouded the edges of her vision.

The young man, hallucination or whatever he was, had grabbed her shoulders and was shouting, but she couldn't hear him. The world drifted away, and Julie tumbled head over heels into black oblivion.

Taylor Woodskin dived off his chair and threw an arm around the girl's thin shoulders as she slid out of her seat. He tried to lower her to the floor gently, but her head still thudded on the carpet.

"Hey. Hey!" He shook her shoulders. "Wake up!"

The girl's long lashes fluttered against her cheek. He patted it lightly. "Come on. You're okay."

She didn't move. He couldn't tell if her skin was ashen or if it always looked that way. What should he do, feel her pulse? Where was her pulse? Could she be allergic to the food? It would depend on whether she was Sylthana or a Were or Nox. He wasn't sure if he'd seen fangs.

You're hopeless in emergencies, Taylor. His mother's chiding voice came back to him, as unwelcome as ever.

He straightened. "Healer!" he yelled. "I need a healer!"

"Yes, yes, I'm coming." A stout copper dwarf hustled down the length of the table toward him. She tossed a fox-red braid over her shoulder and crouched beside the unconscious girl. "What is she?"

"I don't know."

"What happened?"

"I don't know that either."

"What *do* you know?" barked the dwarf.

Taylor squirmed. "We sat down. Then we talked, and she got all pale and started to slide out of her chair. Now she's asleep."

The dwarf scoffed and bent over the girl. She rolled her quickly and gently onto her side. "Her pulse is strong."

"What's going on over here?"

Taylor cringed, then plastered on his most winning smile and turned around. Captain Jack Kaplan's bushy black eyebrows were drawn close together like bulls locking horns. The big man glared from Taylor to the girl on the floor and back.

"Speak up, Woodskin," he snapped.

Taylor saluted. "Yes, sir. Sorry, sir. Uh, I don't know, sir."

"She fainted." The dwarf straightened and met the captain's eyes. "I think she will be out of it for a while, but she'll be okay."

"Well, she can't lie here." Kaplan made a slicing gesture with one hand. "Take her to the infirmary, Woodskin."

"Yes, sir."

Kaplan grunted. "Hurry up. I don't have time for this 'laying down on the job' bullshit. We have quotas!"

"Yes, sir!" Taylor crouched and scooped the girl into his arms. She was even lighter than she looked.

"Captain, there's something else you should know." The dwarf approached Kaplan. When he bent down, she spoke quietly into his ear.

Taylor turned to go.

"Woodskin, wait." Kaplan straightened, then glanced at the dwarf. "Are you *sure?*"

She nodded.

Kaplan squared his massive shoulders. "Take her to my office."

Taylor raised his eyebrows. "Your office, sir?"

"Yes, and don't be long about it." Kaplan stomped away.

Taylor carried the girl out of the room, sighing. Whatever was going on, he was sure he was about to get into trouble for it.

CHAPTER THREE

Sharp pain throbbed behind Julie's temples. She wrinkled her nose and reached up to massage it away. What had she drunk last night? Wait, hadn't she been home last night, getting her clothes ready for a meeting?

The meeting! Julie's eyes snapped open. She was lying in a spacious office with a floor-to-ceiling window that looked out over the manicured campus. People milled around on the lawn, and the more she stared at them, the less her world made sense. They all looked like they'd stepped out of *Lord of the* Rings. Dwarves with brawny arms and shaggy hair, wispy elves with pointed ears, a lumbering creature head and shoulders taller than anyone else who looked orc-like. She swore she saw fangs in one smile.

This had to be another hallucination. She stared around the office, which held a vast desk, an equestrian portrait of a huge man with bushy eyebrows, and a cluster of bookshelves. There were two chairs in front of the desk and an armchair tucked in one corner, where the young man from breakfast sat motionless. Well, man-ish. He still had pointy ears.

He'd roofied her and brought her here. Then what?

She stirred, and he looked up. "Oh!" His eyes widened. "You're awake."

Julie struggled to sit up, then sagged against the soft leather of the couch. "Don't touch me!" she snarled, balling her hands.

"Trust me." The young man gave an uneasy bark of laughter. "I'm not planning on it."

A door creaked and slammed, and the huge, hairy man depicted on the painting over the desk entered. He was seven feet tall, and his biceps bulged against the sleeves of his blue uniform like someone had shoved boulders in there. She expected his feet to thunder on the hardwood floor, but he was almost silent as he stopped to contemplate her with glowing amber eyes.

The young man—or elf or whatever he was—jumped to his feet and saluted. "Captain Kaplan, sir!"

"At ease, Woodskin," growled the big man.

This was her boss if she really had been drafted. Julie thought about commenting on being on the casting couch but swallowed it when their eyes met again. This was not a man to whom one mouthed off if one wanted to live.

"Interesting," Kaplan murmured. He strolled over to his desk and sat, then pointed at the chairs in front of him. "Sit."

The elf guy practically levitated into his chair, trembling with the willingness to please and not be in trouble, Julie guessed. She tested her limbs, and they were happy to carry her the short distance to the other chair.

Kaplan interlaced sausage-sized fingers on the desk and stared at her with those amber eyes. "You *are* human."

"Um." Julie shot another glance at the elf guy. "Aren't we all?"

"No. We are not." Kaplan sighed. "That's the problem."

Silence stretched between them. The elf tried to make himself invisible.

Kaplan shook his head. "Of all the humans who could have wandered into the PMA, it *had* to be one who could see us."

"See you?" Julie echoed.

"Yes. If you had just been any ordinary run-of-the-mill idiot human, you would have wandered in here, enjoyed a spectacular breakfast, and found yourself back outside." Kaplan's voice rose. "But no. No, *you* had to have a super-rare genetic mutation, so rare I've never seen it.

"*You* had to be the one human who would be affected by our food so you could see us in our true forms." He slammed a massive fist on the table so hard the wood creaked. "You had to come in here and complicate everything!" His shout made the portrait on the wall rattle.

Julie shrank into her chair. Beside her, the elf did the same thing.

Kaplan's glare was steady, and he kept both enormous fists bunched on the table. Each was the size of Julie's head.

She realized this might be her one chance to defend herself. "Sir," she squeaked, "I, uh, I would never have come here, but I got this letter..."

"Yes. The draft notice." Kaplan sat back in his chair, folding his arms. "A regrettable flaw in the new system. Heads will roll for that."

His tone was so flat and final that Julie gulped. Her usual sass had abandoned her. The elf kept his mouth shut. Kaplan regarded her for an eternity before he finally spoke again.

"Well, we're in this situation now, and we'll have to do something about it." Kaplan shrugged. "I can't just let you go. You already know far too much about paranormals."

Julie's heart fluttered madly. "Sir, I–"

"You have two options." Kaplan spread his hands. "First, you could be mind-wiped."

Her throat was too dry to swallow. "'Mind-wiped?'"

"Yes. My preferred method for mind-wiping humans is decapitation." He gave her a wide smile that didn't touch his eyes and showed off an unreasonable number of teeth. The elf looked at her sharply.

Julie's muscles didn't want to work. "D-decapitation?"

Kaplan's glare was steady. "I can't just let you go. Humans aren't allowed to know about the paranormal world. You can't unsee what you've already seen except by mind-wipe." His grin widened.

"What's…what's my other option?" Julie managed to get out.

Kaplan shrugged. "You could take the job."

"Job?"

"Yes. The job you were drafted for." He raised one of his bushy eyebrows. "You would work in the Military Liaison for Acquisition of Soldiers, or MLAS, as a recruiting officer."

Julie's breaths came fast and hard. "Or die? That's my option? I become an unwilling slave to acquire new recruits, or you kill me?"

"Don't be so dramatic." The captain eyed her. "We aren't politicians."

"So, you won't kill me?" She stopped hyperventilating.

"Oh, no, we will terminate your memory if you quit." The pause was just pregnant enough to contain "decapitation." "This isn't slavery. If you hit your recruitment goals, we offer a nice salary and an excellent benefits package." Kaplan smirked.

"What if I fail to hit my goals?" Julie quivered. She didn't like the gleam in his eyes.

This time, the smile reached Kaplan's eyes. "Then we terminate you." He added, lest there was any confusion about what that meant, "It's not like we can just fire you, right? You know too much."

Julie's world imploded. Her mom's incessant harping filled her mind. "Stop reading and go play with people. Too much knowledge will kill your future!"

Wow, way to go on being right, Mom.

Through the fear making her breaths catch, she felt something hot and familiar. It made her curl her hands into fists and look Kaplan directly in the eye.

"Fine, but I want a sign-on bonus," she stated.

Kaplan blinked, and his smile disappeared. She froze. Had she pushed it too far? No. A little smirk tugged at the corner of his lip before it disappeared.

"A sign-on bonus?" squawked the elf.

She shot him a furious look. He'd seemed nice, but she couldn't forgive him for drugging her or whatever had happened back there. Did she buy the genetic mutation thing? Then again, what other explanation was there for his sharp features and pointed ears?

"Quiet, Woodskin," Kaplan barked. He returned his attention to her. "You do realize what I just threatened you with?"

"Death. I know. However, if I'm going to be forced into this job under duress, you might as well make it worth my while." Giddy with bravado, Julie raised her chin and met his eyes again. "I'll accept four thousand."

Kaplan laughed. "Four thousand dollars! I don't sign even my best recruits for a penny over two thousand, and you're *human*."

"Your first human. You don't know how much of an asset I might be." Julie jerked her chin up. "Five thousand."

Kaplan's eyes narrowed, burning amber. "I don't think you understand the situation you find yourself in."

"Six thousand."

The elf stared at her wide-eyed, and his skin turned gray.

Kaplan sat back, folding his arms. "Three thousand, and I won't kill you where you stand. Deal?"

She blinked. *He's giving in?* "Deal," she agreed smoothly.

"Fine. And stop wearing so much makeup," Kaplan growled.

Julie bit her tongue to stop herself from saying that she wasn't wearing any. Clearly, the captain was just…captain-y. Dickish, but that was an opinion best kept to herself.

"All that's left is to introduce you to your new partner." Kaplan gestured at the elf. "Taylor Woodskin."

"What? Sir!" Taylor protested.

Kaplan leveled a glare at him, and the elf shrank several inches. "Why did you think you were here?"

Taylor squirmed. "Well, I helped her after she passed out."

"It's high time you were paired with someone motivated." Kaplan gave Julie that toothy grin again. "Get your new partner to orientation, Woodskin, and ensure she hits those targets."

Kaplan turned to a file on his desk, and Taylor got up. Julie couldn't wait to get out of this room. She flew to her feet and scampered out the door.

Taylor was about to follow the human girl from Kaplan's office when the big man got to his feet and cleared his throat.

Quailing, Taylor let the door swing shut behind the girl and turned to the captain, whose arms were folded again. Those forearms were probably bigger than his thighs, Taylor thought idly.

"Woodskin."

"Yes, sir."

Kaplan frowned. "No mention of all of the ways she can lose her memory. Got it? I don't want to have her give up without at least a few months of productivity. You know how far behind we are on our quotas. You *also* know how weak-minded humans are."

"Sir..." Taylor began. This wasn't right.

"That's an order, Woodskin." Kaplan's lip curled. "You do know how to take orders, don't you?"

Taylor swallowed. Not trusting his voice, he nodded, then stepped out to catch up with the human girl.

Whatever Taylor and Kaplan had been whispering about while Julie waited in the communal office outside, it couldn't have been good. The elf's face was unreadable, but he rubbed the palm of his right hand over the back of his left, a nervous gesture, when he joined her in the larger space. He stared at her.

She stared back until it became evident that he wasn't going to break the silence. "Um, hello? Aren't you supposed to be getting me oriented?"

"Right!" Taylor jumped. "Yes. Ahem. Paperwork first."

"Let me guess." Julie followed as he strode into the large office. It was a standard setup with desks and filing cabinets, except that all the desks were occupied by paranormals. "Magic scrolls? Pens that write with my blood?"

"You've been reading too much *Harry Potter*." He laughed, loosening up.

As it turned out, the paperwork was decidedly mundane and human, except that the person sitting behind the desk in a cute pink summer dress had two tiny antlers protruding from her curly hair.

Julie signed a bunch of papers without reading the fine print, which she was sure would include something about death by decapitation. Insurance, potential salary, ID card. It clipped to the front of her blouse without much drama and read "MLAS Recruiter."

"That's it." Taylor nodded. "Now for training."

"Training?" Julie raised her eyebrows. "How long does that take? I'm keen to get to those targets if you get my drift."

"You're also new to this world." He smiled and did that crinkly-eye thing again.

She looked away. "I asked a question. How many weeks?"

"Weeks?" Taylor chortled. "About ten minutes."

"What?"

He led her to an elevator, and they zipped up a floor or two, then stepped out into a quiet hallway with cream carpet. It was more workmanlike than Kaplan's sumptuous office.

"Taylor, what did you mean about ten minutes?" Julie demanded. She had to jog to keep up with him as he strode down the hall.

"Here." Taylor pushed a door open. "Behold the orb!"

She stared from him into the room and back. It was a white room without windows, and light emanated from the walls. A small pedestal stood in the middle, upon which rested a glowing blue sphere a foot in diameter. It was covered in dark indentations.

"The orb?" Julie snorted. "Imaginative."

Taylor deflated. "You're not easily impressed for a human."

"Try me."

He shook his head. "Sit in the chair and put your hands where they fit."

"Where they fit? What's that mean?"

"Just try it."

Julie crossed the floor, her sneakers squeaking loudly on the smooth surface, and sank into the chair. When she looked closer at the sphere, she saw that the indentations were handprints. Well, prints, anyway. Some had three or six fingers. Others had none.

Two looked human, and when she put her left hand in one of those prints, it fit. She glanced at Taylor, who was waiting in the doorway. "Is it going to put me in a trance or something?"

"It's hard to explain. Put both hands on it." Taylor gestured at the orb.

Julie hesitated, but the hand she was resting on the sphere hadn't melted, exploded, or turned black, so she did the same with the other hand. Nothing happened.

"Taylor, is this a joke?" she demanded. "If it is, it's not very—"

Taylor disappeared. The room disappeared. Everything disappeared, and for a terrifying moment, the world was black. Then,

Julie stood before the most immense creature she had ever seen. It towered over her, its scales glowing blue. Twin columns of smoke rose from its nostrils. It moved sinuously, its spiked tail dragging across the stone. Its head was the size of a bus, and its eyes glowed electric blue when it looked at her. It opened a mouth big enough to swallow her apartment, and she saw magma boiling in the back of its throat.

Screaming, Julie threw up her hands to protect herself. She heard music when she expected the crackle of her roasting flesh. When she dared look up, she was surrounded by laughter and dancing figures. One of them looked like Taylor. She reached toward him, forming a question, but he was gone, and she was standing in front of the open maw of a mineshaft as trucks laden with ore rumbled out of it. A copper-haired young man was driving the nearest truck. He didn't look at her as the vehicle rumbled past.

The scenes changed too quickly for her to remember them. Battles, banquets, business deals. A rearing horse, its neigh belling through the air. Faces, events, and names streamed by so fast that she couldn't grasp them.

Silence, then a glowing light. When Julie looked up, the moon hung over her, pouring silver light down on her. She reached toward it, then her eyes snapped open. She sat in the white room with her hands on the orb, panting.

"Still nothing?" Taylor quipped.

Julie glanced at him. He was smirking.

"Okay, I'm not gonna lie. That was cool." Julie allowed her hands to slip into her lap, then frowned. "I saw a lot of things, but I can't remember. I think I saw the moon? How does that help me?"

"The orb uploads data directly to your brain." Taylor tapped the side of his head. "You won't remember what it did to you because it happens too fast. You know things now that you didn't know before."

"Doesn't feel that way."

"I'm not so sure." Taylor grinned. "I bet you can tell me something about the Lords of the Deep."

"Obviously. They're a dragon clan and live for thousands of years. They're not into dynastic rule because they don't see the point in ruling the younger races." She blinked, then stared at the orb in awe. "*Dude.*"

"I know. It's amazing." Taylor chuckled. "Like Wikipedia but instantaneous, and you don't need an internet connection. Plus, there's no way for humans to access this, and... Uh, sorry. No offense meant."

Julie raised an eyebrow. "Only a little offense taken."

"Right." He ran a hand over the back of his neck. "Well, there's no way for humans to read any of it, so it keeps us safer. Luckily, they haven't figured out how to read minds yet."

"Can you?"

"Can I what?"

"Can you read minds?" Julie persisted.

Taylor threw his head back and burst out laughing. She got up, arms akimbo, and stared at him until he wiped the tears away. "Can *I* read minds? You slay me, Julie." He shook his head, still chuckling. "An Aether elf reading minds. What a thought!"

"Well, excuse *me* if my new magical mind index thing isn't working properly yet," Julie snapped.

"Sorry. It takes a little while to kick in." Taylor smiled. "I can't read minds, but I know some paras that can."

"Paras?"

"Paranormals." Taylor shrugged. "I've heard there's one called a Mind Eater. It's a one-sided conversation if you understand what I'm saying. However, I'm told that when it ingests the brain, it learns a lot about whatever it ate for a little while. Eventually, it forgets the knowledge."

"That's..." Julie paused. "Actually, that's cool. Not as cool for the person whose brain is eaten, but imagine if a person dies naturally, and you grab the brain before it expires. You could preserve their knowledge and memories."

"Why? It wouldn't be them."

"No, but imagine if it was a scientist or someone on the edge of a breakthrough." Julie shrugged. "You could help society."

"I suppose." Taylor's face was gray again. It made him look sick.

"Am I grossing you out?" Julie teased.

He folded his arms and leaned against the doorframe. "You're an odd human. Do you know that?"

"Why? It's practical. I'm not suggesting we kill to try it."

"Are you sure you're not half-drow?"

"Drow?" She blinked, information flying through her mind more quickly than she could comprehend. "A reclusive, deadly group of elves known for their craftsmanship but otherwise mysterious. They seldom interact with other races. Whoa! I'm still not used to that."

"At least it's working," Taylor offered.

"They're, like, dark elves."

Taylor flinched. "Yeah, but it's not politically correct to call them that."

"Sorry. I was going to say how it's very D&D of you to call them drow." Julie spread her hands.

"I was just saying you have their sarcastic streak." Taylor grinned.

"Nope," Julie confirmed. "No dark elf blood in me."

He sighed. "Great."

Julie's phone binged. She jumped. She'd assumed it had been taken from her, but Taylor didn't react when she pulled it out of her pocket and glanced at a message from dear old Sam.

Hey, I had a good time the other night. Same again sometime?

"Dickhead," she muttered.

"What?" Taylor straightened.

"Not you." Julie dropped her phone into her pocket. "What's next? Do we get lunch?"

"Well, your orientation is done." Taylor stepped back, holding the door open. "You can go home now. Come back to work at nine tomorrow morning."

"Oh, shit." Julie sighed and stepped out of the room. "I'm going to need a closer place to live."

He snorted. "You know everything around here is super-expensive, right? I'm a prince, and I can't afford half of these places."

Julie eyed him. "Well, I don't know about princes, but I don't have a trust fund, so we have to get recruits so I can make those bonuses Captain Jack Sparrow didn't tell us about." She'd read about them in the paperwork.

"Kaplan!" Taylor hissed, eyes widening. "He will throw a bus if he hears you call him a pirate."

"Fine." They headed back to the elevator. They stepped inside, and Taylor hit the button for the ground floor. "No pissing off the dark and moody boss. Got it."

Taylor shook his head. "Not even a drop of drow blood? I think you have a death wish."

She swallowed, thinking about what might happen if she told any human that paranormals existed. She could only assume, since her mom and Lillie hadn't been drafted, there would be only one option for them. *Termination.* The memory of Kaplan's toothy smile sent a shudder down her spine.

"No death wish." She grinned to cover her nervousness. "I have a snarky streak a mile wide."

"You don't say." Taylor cocked an eyebrow at her.

The elevator doors opened, and they were back in the giant fancy hallway. Taylor opened one of a series of lockboxes in the wall and produced Julie's backpack, which she snatched from him. "Oh, thank you!" she gasped. "I thought my stuff was gone."

"Of course not." Taylor raised his eyebrows. "I'm not a thief."

Her cheeks warmed. "I'll see you tomorrow morning, I guess."

"See you."

Julie took a few steps, then turned to him again. "Earlier, when you said Kaplan would throw a bus. Did you mean, like, a *bus*? A real bus?"

Taylor nodded. He wasn't smiling.

CHAPTER FOUR

Julie splashed her spoon around in her ramen noodles, letting them cool as the scent of artificial chicken flavoring steamed toward her face. Soon she could buy real chicken for lunch. Assuming she survived long enough to collect a paycheck.

"Yes, Mom, it's a real job." She blew softly on the bowl.

"Oh, honey, I'm so happy for you!" Rosa cried. "Does it pay well?"

"Really well." Julie allowed herself a private smirk of satisfaction. "I got a three-thousand-dollar sign-on bonus."

"*What?*" Rosa shrieked. "That's fantastic for a girl with so little experience!"

Julie shook her head. Only her mother could be patronizing at a moment like this. "Whatever you say, Mom."

"So, what's the job?" Rosa bubbled eagerly. "Did you decide on stripping, after all? I bet any nightclub owner would pay that bonus for your bod."

"Mom!" Julie groaned. "I am *not* going to be a stripper. It's...in recruitment." She cleared her throat. "For an insurance company."

"Aw, hun, that's wonderful. Listen, you're going to be very

busy now, so I think you should double your aloe vera dose. It'll boost your mood, energy, and concentration, and..."

"I gotta go, Mom. I've got to talk to Lillie about moving somewhere closer to work."

"It's so good to hear you say that!" Rosa trilled. "It's about time you got out of that dump. Okay then, honey. Have a wonderful first day tomorrow!"

"I doubt it," Julie muttered once she'd safely hung up. She ate her noodles slowly, wondering if she'd done the right thing by telling her mom anything. But she'd have to explain her new routine somehow. This was the best way to keep Rosa from asking questions that could get her into the same trouble as Julie.

She glanced at her phone. Past three in the afternoon, and she still had so much to do. She needed to get onto the seven o'clock bus if she was going to make it to work on time tomorrow morning. Work. Indentured servitude. Paid slavery. Labor under duress. Whatever she was supposed to call it.

She sighed. Her mom was right, this place was a dump, but she'd grown attached to it. Dumping her bowl in the sink, she clattered down the stairs and listened for Lillie's TV in the living room, then knocked on the door. "Ms. Griswall? Are you home?"

"Come on in," Lillie shouted over Judge Judy, who was giving a scathing verdict.

Julie pushed the door open and stepped tentatively into the living room. Lillie had switched out her housecoat for a set of fluffy pajamas. She clutched a cigarette in nicotine-stained fingers. Her eyes were still on the TV, and she absently stroked her fluffy cat with her free hand. It purred and rolled onto its back at the sight of Julie.

"Um, Ms. Griswall, I was hoping we could talk."

Lillie gestured at the free spot on the sofa with her cigarette. "Sit down, dear. What's with calling me Ms. Griswall all of a sudden? I told you, I go by Lillie. Ms. Griswall was my mother."

"Yes, Lillie." Julie slid into the grimy space beside her, trying not to stare too overtly at the clutter around them. The wallpaper was peeling in the corners. Empty pill bottles and fast-food packaging were strewn over the coffee table alongside old magazines and cat food sachets. Lillie's hair hung over her shoulders in an unkempt white shock, and she drew another long drag on her cigarette, eyes still glued to the TV.

"Something wrong?" A cloud of cheap smoke puffed out with the words. "Mice in the ceiling again?"

"Oh, no. Nothing like that. I just..." Julie sighed. "I think I'll have to give notice on my apartment."

Lillie muted the TV. Turning to Julie, she raised her eyebrows. "Sorry to hear that, honey. It's been nice hearing someone else's footsteps around here."

Julie bit her lip. "I'm sorry. I've liked staying here too, but I've got a new job."

Lillie mustered a smile. "That's good news."

"Yeah, but it's far away. It takes me almost two hours to get there by bus. I have to get on a lot of different buses, you see."

"I see." Lillie pulled at her cigarette. "Well, you could always use Genevieve."

"The car?" Julie blinked. "Does it run?"

"I start her up now and then. She runs fine. I just can't drive anymore." Lillie gestured at her thick glasses. "Blind as a bat."

"Well, my new job partner mentioned I'd need to find transport. For work." Julie tried not to think about what lurked under the dust cover in the garage. Some beat-up little hatchback, probably.

"If you'll run some errands for me, we'll say using Genevieve is included in your rent." Lillie grinned. "It'd be good to have someone to take care of her again. She isn't meant to waste away in the garage."

"I like staying here." *Plus, I feel bad leaving you all alone*, Julie added silently, stealing another glance at the chaos around her. "You're being kind. Thanks, Lillie. I'd love that."

Lillie leaned on the sofa, still petting her cat. "It's time for another hellion to bother the cops around here, anyway."

Julie smothered a smile. "I'm not so sure about that."

"I know a hellion when I see one, dear." Lillie cackled. "Just because I can't see far enough ahead of me to count a six-pack, much less drive, doesn't mean I can't see what's right in front of me. If I were younger, I'd take you out and show you." This time, her grin was wide and steady.

Julie couldn't hold back a surprised laugh. "I'm sure you would." She was, too. This was a side of Lillie she'd never seen.

Lillie patted Julie on the shoulder. "There's a mechanic down the street. Why don't you take her out for a spin and see if she needs any work?"

"I'll do that. I have a sign-on bonus coming, so I can have her serviced." Julie grinned. "Thanks, Lillie. You're being great."

"I was young too, once." Lillie's eyes wandered to the wall, resting on a portrait that Julie hadn't noticed. It showed two young women leaning against a bridge railing, laughing. They looked so similar that she couldn't tell which one was Lillie.

Julie didn't know what to say. She squeezed Lillie's arm. "I'm glad I don't have to go."

"Me too, dear." Lillie sighed. "Now go on. The keys are in the ignition."

Julie felt a spark of excitement. She thanked Lillie again and hurried into the garage, carefully locking the back door behind her. The mysterious shape under the dust cover stood where it had been standing for the six months since Julie moved in. Lillie must have started it on the days she wasn't around. At any rate, Julie had never seen the car.

Hellion. She approached it slowly. Suddenly her suspicions about some little hatchback seemed unlikely. She gripped the dust cover with both hands and stepped back, pulling hard.

With a rush of fabric, the cover fell to the floor and kicked up a cloud of dust, and Julie looked at a poem of speed composed in metal.

"Whoa." The gasp escaped her in a rush.

The car was long and low, its color between silver and gold, like fine champagne, shining despite the flecks of dust on the paint. Its lines were aerodynamic, from its flat back to the long hood. It had black detailing on the hood and rear wing, and a black stripe ran down the side.

Genevieve was no hatchback. Julie didn't know much about cars, but she knew that whatever this was, it was old, fast, and beautiful. A muscle car. She went up to it, allowing her fingers to brush along the hood, and peered through the front window. There were bucket seats inside, covered with fine tan leather. The driver and passenger seats looked worn. The steering wheel was adorned with a silver plate engraved with a galloping horse.

"A Mustang." Julie couldn't help laughing as she stepped back and admired the car again. "Genevieve is a *Mustang*."

She tried to picture Lillie driving this thing and failed. Laughing, she opened the garage door and hurried to the driver's side. When she slipped into the seat, it surrounded her like a hug. It took some tinkering to slide the seat back to accommodate her long legs. She turned the key, and for a second, the engine sputtered.

Then it roared like something hungry.

"You beauty," Julie beamed, running her hands over the wheel. "Genevieve, you *beauty*."

Death threats notwithstanding, at least one thing about this day went well.

A piercing memory flashed through her as she put it into reverse. Dad. Sitting beside her, his voice slow and easy. *Let it out real slow, honey. Keep checking your mirrors. That's it. That's it.*

She shook her head to dislodge the memory. She wanted to remember everything Dad had taught her about driving, but this wasn't the time to remember *him*.

Genevieve purred out of the garage, and once Julie had pointed her nose down the street, she gently tapped the accelerator a couple of times. She was rewarded with an intense roar from the engine that thrummed through her entire body.

It was a little intimidating. "Easy now, Genevieve," she told the car. "We're going to be friends, okay?"

Carefully, she eased out of the driveway and rolled down the street.

The mechanic's eyes were the size of saucers. Julie was uncomfortably aware every young guy in the place had stopped whatever he was doing and was staring steadily. She ran a hand over her hair, avoiding their eyes, and gave the mechanic a nervous smile. "So? Will you be able to do an oil change and put on some new tires?"

The mechanic ignored her as though she didn't exist. He walked up to Genevieve instead, practically drooling.

"A 1971 Mach 1 Mustang 429," he almost whimpered. "I've hardly seen one. Where did you get it?"

"She's my landlady's." Julie cleared her throat. "*It's* my landlady's." She shot the nearest guy an angry glance to tell him that his staring was not appreciated and reached for the pepper spray bottle in her pocket.

The guy walked past her and reached into the driver's side, popping the hood. The mechanic opened it, and a collective sigh arose from the surrounding men.

Oh. Julie fought back a smile. They weren't staring at her. They were staring at Genevieve.

As one, the men clustered around the hood to peer at the engine.

"The 429 V8 Cobra jet." The mechanic was grinning. "This

baby's got three hundred seventy-five horses in here. Ford put a bigger engine in the Mustang in '71 because of the EPA regs."

"Pewter." One of the guys ran a hand over the hood. Julie guessed he was referring to the color. "With the trademark stripes."

"She's a beaut, all right." The mechanic remembered Julie existed and turned to her. "What did you want with it?"

Julie shrugged. "I don't know much about cars, but whatever she needs. New tires and a service, I thought?"

Generalized groaning came from the guys. Julie smirked. Genevieve was hers to drive, whether they liked it or not.

"Sure. I can do that for you." The mechanic grinned. "I'll put better tires on, newer ones. They used to think the 429 was slower than its little brother, the 351, but the truth is the tire technology of the time just couldn't keep up to the torque of this engine." He slammed the hood. "I'll do a little tune-up or two. This 429 is going to SING!"

A couple of hours later—which Julie spent shopping at the little grocery store on the corner—the 429 did indeed sing. Clueless though she was, Julie easily heard the difference when she backed Genevieve out of the garage. The car rumbled, deep and furious, and Genevieve roared a battle cry when she gave the accelerator a little tap.

Whoops and whistles rose from the audience that had gathered to watch her leave. Julie was relieved to know that they weren't meant for her. She gave Genevieve another rev for their benefit, and they all cheered as she drove away, feeling the new power surge through the car.

"This has been a weird day, girlfriend," she told Genevieve, patting the steering wheel.

The TV was still on when she got home just after five and

carefully locked the garage behind her. She carried the grocery bags and shoved into Lillie's living room.

"Sorry for not knocking," she called to the figure slumped on the couch.

Lillie looked up with a smirk. "So, what do you think about Genevieve?"

"I think she's the best part of my day." Julie meant it. She dumped the grocery bags on the single scrap of available surface of the kitchen table. "Come on out and see her."

"Thanks for the groceries." Lillie got up stiffly and shuffled to the door. "You didn't have to."

"Of course I did. That was the deal."

Lillie stepped through the door into the garage and clasped a hand over her mouth for a second. Julie thought she might cry, but she was beaming when she lowered her hand.

"Genevieve!" Lillie breathed, hobbling over to the car. "My baby is back."

Julie let out a breath. Lillie raised a hand to her cheek, brushing away a tear, and turned to Julie. "You put new tires on her."

"Are they okay?"

"They're perfect, dear. Take them out of your rent since you paid for them."

Julie watched as Lillie ran her hands over Genevieve, and her smile grew. She wasn't sure she'd ever seen real joy on Lillie's face.

Maybe good things could come from this, after all.

We're sorry. It looks like there are no results for your search. Please try again.

Julie snorted, hardly surprised that there hadn't been any results on this social media site for "Taylor Woodskin." Did he have a human alias? Were there special magical social media sites for paranormals?

Why did she even care?

She tossed her phone under her pillow and rolled onto her belly, staring out the window at nothing. She'd tried to go to bed at nine like a responsible adult, but sleep wasn't coming to her. She doubted it would come. How did you sleep the night before your first day at a job where your options were to perform or die?

"What have you gotten yourself into, Julie?" she groaned, running her hands through her short hair and squeezing.

The faint prickle of pain seemed to clarify her brain. If she wasn't going to sleep, she might as well enjoy the one good thing about this day so far—Genevieve. Lillie had said she could drive it whenever she wanted, so she guessed it would be okay.

She shrugged on some sweatpants and a hoodie. As she tiptoed downstairs, she couldn't hear Lillie's TV and hoped Genevieve's engine wouldn't wake the old lady. Fruitlessly shushing the powerful car as its sound growled through the garage, she backed it out, then locked the garage door behind her.

It would be a good idea to look for a route to work, anyway. She guessed being late to work was decapitation-worthy in Kaplan's world. Sitting in the idling Mustang, she typed the address of the Para-Military Agency into her GPS and propped it up on the dash. The soothing voice told her to take the next left.

Genevieve purred through the streets, which were far from abandoned here at this time of night. Seedy types hung out on street corners. Clubs pounded out deafening music and pulsing light. Teenagers, high on life, staggered over pedestrian crossings in miniskirts and stringy tops, giggling as they stumbled over each other.

The crowds thinned as the GPS guided Julie nearer to the PMA. The streets were almost empty as she crossed the Verrazzano-Narrows bridge, and water spread out in silent darkness around her. It wasn't a long drive now that Julie traveled at Genevieve speed instead of bus speed and could skip waiting around at bus stops. She'd been driving for about half an hour when she glanced at her phone screen and saw that she only had a few minutes left before she reached her new workplace/prison.

Around her, large buildings towered on either side. She was surprised to see that some weren't office buildings but houses.

"Who needs a house that size?" she muttered when the dark figure darted across the road in front of her.

"Crap!" Julie stamped on the brake with all her strength. Genevieve squealed to a halt, and Julie's body slammed against the seatbelt. A dark, shadowy figure loomed in front of the car, and Julie held her breath. The thing wasn't human. It was huge and black and hairy, with a loose lower lip hanging down to reveal jagged yellow fangs rising from its bottom jaw.

Before Julie could grab her pepper spray, the thing bolted across the road and leaped over a wall with effortless power. Slowly, she unpeeled her shaking hands from the steering wheel, looking left and right. Did that thing have friends?

How many paranormal beings had she run into during her life before she'd eaten the magic food that opened her eyes?

The thought chilled her almost more than the encounter. She was about to make a U-turn and get out of here when something stirred to her right. Something—some*one*—was lying on the sidewalk just a few yards ahead of her, dark fluid pooling around them. They tried to get up but only got halfway before crumpling to the ground.

"Oh, shit." Julie pulled over with shaking hands. The headlights fell over a young man, who lay curled on his side, one hand clasped over his left shoulder. Blood oozed between his white fingers.

She left the key in the ignition for a quick getaway and scrambled from the car. "Hello?" she yelled. "Are you okay?"

"Do I look okay?" the young man ground out. He tried to sit up again but sagged to the ground with a soft groan.

Julie trotted over to him, trying to remember anything about the first aid class she'd done in high school. The blood was oozing, not pulsing. That was good, right?

"What happened to you?" she blurted, untying her hoodie from around her waist.

"Mugged," growled the young man.

"Here." Julie wadded her sweater into a ball and pressed it to the young man's shoulder. Pressure. That was the thing for bleeding, wasn't it? "Press on that."

"Thanks."

"I'm calling 911." Julie groped for her phone.

"No. No, you're not." The young man looked up at her, and his eyes were red. Not bloodshot: the irises were scarlet on the outside. They darkened to the deepest crimson and then seamlessly into the pupil's black. "You're not going to call 911." His voice was slow and soothing now, although still taut with pain. "You're going to take my arm and help me up. Then, you're going to guide me to your car."

Julie relaxed. This wasn't so bad. No reason to call 911. She could do what the soft, soothing voice told her. "Okay," she heard herself saying. "I'm going to take your arm and help you up."

"That's right." The young man smiled, and that was when Julie saw the fangs. Small, white, and tasteful, they extended from his upper jaw and ended in razor points that gleamed in Genevieve's headlights.

A brief scream escaped her, jolting the hypnotic voice from her mind. What was she *doing*? She never did as she was told! The realization crashed like a breaking wave, and she slapped him with all her strength.

"Ow!" he shrieked, cringing and raising his free hand to his face. "You *slapped* me!"

Vampire, Julie's training was supplied belatedly. Ancient

species of undead. Capable of using mesmerism to compel others to do their will.

"You stop that!" Julie yelled, waving her finger in his face. "You stop your mind control thingy thing right now! I am *not* interested!"

The vampire's red eyes widened. "How did you know?"

"I know you're a vampire," Julie barked. "I swear to you, if you use that juju on me again, I'll leave you to bleed out and die!"

The vampire gaped. "You smell human."

"I *am* human. I'm a Para-Military recruiter, I'll have you know. You're definitely not getting recruited, young sir!" she spat.

The vampire's lips twisted. He snorted. "A human recruiter? Interesting. Old Kaplan must be desperate."

"I don't like your tone," Julie snapped, "and I've got a good mind to leave you here to drink your own blood or whatever."

"Drink my own blood? I'm a vampire, not a barbarian, you speciesist." The vampire sniffed, struggling to sit up again. This time he almost managed it before pain spread across his pale complexion.

Julie folded her arms. "What happened to you, anyway?"

"I told you. I was mugged. Your precious PMA would do well to do something about the yeti problem."

"They're not..." Julie stopped. "Never mind."

The vampire lay on his back, his chest heaving. "So," he croaked, "what's stopping you from leaving me here, then?"

Julie sighed and approached him, grabbing his arm. "You could have asked. Where do you want me to take you?"

"To my Sire's house." He whimpered as she dragged him to his feet. "It's just a couple of blocks away."

He was lighter than he looked, and Julie supported him to the car with relative ease. She tugged the passenger door open. "Try any funny business, and I'll pepper spray you."

"Trust me." The vampire chuckled weakly. "I don't have it in me right now."

Julie couldn't tell if blood loss was making him pale and sweaty or if that was a vampire thing, so she kept a hand near her pepper spray bottle just in case. "Who is this Sire of yours, anyway? Your dad? Your king?"

"Sort of both." Still pressing her sweater to his shoulder, the vampire leaned his head back and let out a ragged groan. "He'll help, anyway."

"Okay, but I'm warning you, if your dad, or whatever he is, tries any of that mind control stuff on me, I'll slap him, too."

"He won't." The vampire grimaced. "I'll probably be in trouble for trying it on you."

She slipped into the driver's seat and closed the door, locking it just in case of any more yetis. "Good. What's your name, anyway?"

"Malcolm Nox." He dropped the last name like it meant something.

Julie shrugged. "Julie Meadows. Which way am I going?"

It turned out Malcolm's destination really was two blocks away, short work for Genevieve. Julie kept half an eye on her fanged passenger as she drove, but no further juju was forthcoming.

"Here it is," Malcolm croaked.

Julie had been expecting a creepy mansion with red lights in the windows, cobwebs draped from the front porch, and bats swooping around pointed turrets. Instead, she pulled to a halt in front of the highest walls she'd ever seen. They offered only a glimpse of a towering home beyond, all floor-to-ceiling windows that mirrored the streetlights.

She eyed the windows. "Don't vampires fry in the sun?"

"So speciesist." Malcolm gritted his teeth. "Just hit the button on the intercom. You'll get through to the butler."

Julie rolled down the window and pushed the button.

"Nox residence," purred a smooth voice.

"Hey, yeah. I've got Malcolm with me. He's hurt."

"What?" A sharp voice interrupted the first. "*Malcolm?*" Malcolm flinched and raised his voice. "Hello, Sire."

"I'm coming right down there. You better not have done anything stupid!" barked the voice.

The intercom shut off, and Malcolm sighed. "He's not going to be happy about this."

"Seems a little harsh," Julie offered. "I mean, it's not your fault you got mugged, is it?"

"Not that." Malcolm grimaced.

Before Julie could ask, the solid metal gate in front of Genevieve rolled open, and Malcolm gestured for her to drive. Genevieve purred through the gate into a huge courtyard lined with rose bushes. The mansion loomed over them, half-hidden by the courtyard wall and massive old spruce trees.

A tall figure strode toward them, wearing a well-cut suit that accentuated his frame. His eyes were the same as Malcolm's: red on the outside, fading to black. Right now, they were narrowed.

"Malcolm!" he shouted.

Malcolm cracked the door. "I got mugged. By a yeti. He swiped me good." Flinching, he indicated his bleeding shoulder.

"Yeti!" The older vampire glared daggers at him. "What are you talking about?"

Malcolm glanced at Julie. "Don't bother, Sire. She knows about us. She's from the PMA."

"A human!" The older vampire's brows disappeared into his generous black hairline. He regarded her and then turned and called, "Perkins! Get him inside."

"Yes, Sire."

Julie jumped. She hadn't noticed the shadowy form lurking behind one of the spruce trees. He moved forward as smoothly as though he was running on an oiled rail instead of walking like a human being—well, vampire being, she supposed—and took Malcolm's arm to help him from the car.

The older vampire stepped forward and assessed him with a sharp glance in the glow of Genevieve's headlights. His eyes softened, and he reached out to lightly touch the reddening bruise on Malcolm's cheek. "An insult?" He growled.

"Uh, no." Malcolm cleared his throat. "That was her, actually." He jerked his head in Julie's direction.

The older vampire spun to face her.

"Hey!" Julie threw up both hands. "Don't be mad at *me*. He tried to use some freaky mental juju on me."

"Malcolm!" The older vampire stared at his son. "You tried to mesmerize and compel her when she was helping you?"

"I was scared!" Malcolm protested.

The older vampire snorted. "You will do well to remember your manners."

"Yes, Sire."

The butler moved off with Malcolm, and the older vampire turned to Julie with an elegant bow. "We are in your debt, madam. I apologize for my son's lack of decorum."

"Uh, thanks," Julie managed. She rubbed away goosebumps on her arms, backing toward the car. Part of her almost expected him to stop her, but he stood motionless as she got into Genevieve and reversed from the mansion. He was still standing there when she ground the gears and drove away.

It was well past midnight when Julie got home and stumbled up the rickety stairs to bed. When she crawled beneath the covers, sleep held her in its warm embrace until her alarm buzzed early the following morning.

CHAPTER FIVE

Julie's eyelids felt leaden. She yawned as she poured hot water into her mop bucket and added a generous dollop of soap.

"Look on the bright side," she told herself. "It might be seven in the morning, and Lillie might kill you if you leave a stain on Genevieve's passenger seat, but at least you're a girl. You can get blood out of *anything*."

She clomped down the stairs, lugging the bucket and some rags and wishing she'd had the energy to clean up Malcolm's blood when she got home last night. But it had been a long day, and it had already dried when she got home.

"Morning, Genevieve."

She had no need to switch on the garage lights. The large window in the east wall let in a generous shaft of sunlight. Julie put down the bucket and looked through the passenger window at the nasty dried stain over one side of the passenger seat.

"Ugh." She opened the door. "Maybe I should recruit Malc–"

She stuttered to a halt. Sunshine poured into the car when she opened the door, and the blood changed as soon as the golden rays hit it. It turned brown, then gray. Flaking off from the leather, it floated quietly to the bottom of the seat.

"Shut the front door." Julie reached out and gave the substance on the seat a gentle poke. The blood had turned into dust. She stared at it, waiting to be weirded out. *Honestly, this is not high on the list of weird things that happened to me in the past twenty-four hours.*

At least that made cleanup easy. She went to get the vacuum cleaner.

The fact that vampire blood turned to dust in sunlight was vaguely creepy, but at least it meant Julie had time to swing through a Starbucks drive-through and treat herself to coffee and a bagel on her way to work.

She sipped the coffee slowly as Genevieve crawled over the Verrazzano-Narrows bridge, clogged like a sickly artery with traffic, but she hardly cared about that. It was so incredible to taste real, hot, fresh coffee. She closed her eyes for a second as another sip slid down her throat. So maybe this new job was going to get her killed. At least she'd die full of real coffee.

When Genevieve rumbled to a halt outside the wrought-iron gates of the Para-Military Agency, Julie was wholly unsurprised to see that yesterday's short redhead guy now turned out to be a dwarf. He shambled up to the window, his red beard hanging almost to his belly button in a fat braid.

"Come back, did you?" he asked.

"Yep." Julie scrabbled in the glove compartment for the ID that Taylor had given her yesterday. "I'm officially a Para-Military recruiter."

The dwarf scanned her ID impassively, just as he'd done with her letter yesterday. "You need a vehicle pass."

She flipped a finger at him when he turned to enter the gatehouse, feeling vaguely better for it. He could have told her to run yesterday. She wouldn't have been in this mess if he had.

He returned with a pass that she stuck on the inside of Genevieve's windscreen. It bore the PMA's complex symbol, all wings and swords and claws. "Looks like an insurance company logo to humans," the dwarf explained. "Well, most humans."

At 8:59, Julie parked Genevieve and headed into the grand entrance hall. Taylor was waiting for her. He leaned against the wall, arms folded, and his eyes widened when she came in. "You came."

"No shit." Julie raised her eyebrows. "It's perform or die, remember?"

"Oh, yeah." Taylor rubbed the back of his neck. "I remember."

They got into the elevator, and Taylor hit the button for floor number three. She noticed for the first time the buttons made little sense. There seemed to be several symbols from the Greek alphabet, numbers minus one through minus twelve, one with a rearing horse on it, and one labeled "Switzerland."

Before Julie could ask about "Switzerland," the elevator stopped, and she and Taylor stepped out into the roomy communal office. He led her to a corner opposite the elevator near Kaplan's office. Two desks were pushed up against each other, each with its own filing cabinet.

"Filing cabinets?" Julie dumped her backpack on the bare desk. Taylor's was covered in the chaos of papers and a couple of action figures. Very human-looking action figures. "What is this, 1995?"

"No computer records that humans can read, remember?" Taylor told her. "Oh, and here are your uniforms." He dumped them on her desk, wrapped in plastic. They were both green, like his. "This one's your dress uniform for special occasions, and this one is for every day."

"Should I change?" Julie picked up the everyday uniform.

"Not if you want to go out in the field and get recruits today." Taylor shrugged. "There's no dress code rules for actual work.

The prerogative is to get recruits, no matter how you have to do it. The only rule is don't cause trouble!"

"Also, don't get decapitated?" Julie suggested.

"I guess." Taylor chortled awkwardly.

Julie smoothed down the front of her black shirt, which she'd matched with a muted gray sweater and jeans. Chic but competent. *In the human world, anyway. Maybe I'm dressed like a clown in this one.*

"Come on." Taylor turned away. "Let's go speak to Kaplan."

"Do we have to?" Julie hissed, following.

He grimaced. "Captain's orders."

As they stepped into Kaplan's office, Julie wondered what he was supposed to be. She made a wry mental comparison between his powerful bulk and last night's yeti, then dismissed it. He was hairy, but he wasn't *that* hairy. Plus, that smile… It was almost carnivorous—not predatory, exactly—as he watched her come in.

Is there such a thing as werewolves? In Malcolm's words, she wasn't sure if it would be "speciesist" to ask. She wasn't about to risk it.

"Woodskin. Meadows." Kaplan nodded at them, and they stood in front of the desk. Julie resisted the urge to put her hands on her hips. She glanced at the warlike portrait hanging behind the desk.

"Good morning, sir." Taylor stood smartly at attention.

"Morning, sir." Julie failed to erase the sarcasm from her voice.

Kaplan ran her through with a look, then glanced down at the papers on his desk. "You received your training yesterday."

Julie nodded. When Kaplan looked at her, she added, "Yes, sir."

"Fine." He cleared his throat. "Well, go and show me what you're made of. You don't have any authority, so you can promise whatever you want. We don't have to provide anything."

"That's a low blow. Promise and no delivery."

Taylor cringed.

"Sir," Julie added.

"I can't help what you tell them, but they don't get signed off on." Kaplan's grin reappeared. "That's called a life lesson. Eventually, they might come to appreciate the lesson."

"Yes, sir," Taylor spoke before Julie opened her mouth.

"Dismissed." Kaplan waved a hand at them.

"Great," Julie muttered as they turned. "I'm twirling a pole, just with clothes on." She thought she saw him smirk out of the corner of her eye, but that was impossible. He couldn't have heard her. Right?

Werewolves. She shuddered.

Like wolves, werewolves can hear sounds with a frequency of as much as eighty kilohertz, her training supplied helpfully.

"Crap," Julie mumbled.

"What was that?" Taylor looked down at her.

"What? Nothing." Julie sank down into the chair by her desk. "Okay, so I've got two questions, Mr. Partner."

"Shoot." Taylor sat back and swung his chair gently.

"First, why was I drafted in the first place? I'm not supposed to be, am I?"

Taylor shrugged. "Computer glitch."

She stared. "My life is hanging by a thread because of a *computer glitch?*"

He waved a hand. "I'll take you down to IT later. Besides, your life isn't hanging by a thread. You just need a recruit, that's all. There's a nice signing bonus for getting one."

"Well, yeah, like not getting killed?" Julie sassed.

"Like a few thousand dollars." Taylor raised his eyebrows. "Still sound good to you?"

Julie sighed. "It's not like hunger will be a problem if I fail, but you've got a point. Money in the bank would be nice. Anyway, that brings me to my next question." She opened a desk drawer and fished out a notepad and pen. "Do you have, like, a top ten wanted list like the US military? Looking for certain people who suit certain positions?"

Taylor laughed. "Ambitious, are you?"

"Ambitious or dead."

"Fine." Taylor glanced at her notepad. "We recruit by para-type here."

"Para-type?"

"Species," he translated. "Weres, witches, elves, dwarves, warlocks, vampires, drow… it's a long list."

"Yeah, I got that." Julie tried not to feel overwhelmed by the surge of information running through her mind. "What's the best one to get? I guess some are more difficult than others?"

"Yes, but you don't need to worry about that. Just go for something doable to start with."

Julie slammed a hand down on the table. "Dammit, Taylor, you keep forgetting that if I don't perform, I die!" she yelled. "I don't need doable. I need the *best!*"

He leaned back, blinking. "Okay, okay. I'm trying to help you here."

"No, you're not. You're patronizing me, and it's not gonna fly."

He held up both hands. "Sorry."

She relaxed, letting her hands slide into her lap. "Now, are you gonna answer my question or what?"

"Sure." Taylor hesitated. "The top three signing bonuses are drow, warlocks, and vampires."

Her thoughts flashed to Malcolm. *At least I know I can handle those.* "Great." She cracked her knuckles. "Now, where do I get a list of specific people to recruit?"

Taylor grinned. "Time to go visit IT. I think you've got a bone to pick with those trolls. They're on the fourth floor."

Julie rose and headed for the elevator. She was halfway across the office when she stopped to turn back. "Wait, did you say *trolls?*"

Trolls.

Julie tried to quit staring, but the young...woman? Female? Whatever it was standing in front of her, it was difficult not to stare. Her figure was lean and slender under her white coat, and she was six feet tall. She wore her straight blonde hair pulled into a ponytail, striking against her greenish skin, and squinted down at Julie through rectangular glasses.

"...still working out a few kinks after the switch from the old system," the troll said. "This new system is incredible. You'll soon see. It's going to boost efficiency by up to a hundred and fifty percent." Her eyes gleamed behind the glasses.

"I'm sorry." Julie held up a hand. "Are you really a troll?"

The troll blinked. "Yes."

"You do *know* what an internet troll is, right?"

The troll sighed and looked over her shoulder at a male colleague sitting at one of the desks in this humming server room. "You were right, Gnerk," she called. "The human *does* know the stereotypes."

"Told ya." Gnerk helped himself to a mint from a bottle on his desk. His white coat had "IT" in a circle on the back.

"Look." Julie squinted to read the female troll's name on the front of her calf-length lab coat like she was a Medical Doctor for Computers. "Look, Qtana, I'm sorry." Julie spread her hands. "I just...well, two days ago, I had no idea trolls even existed."

"It's pronounced 'Kitana.'" The troll softened.

"Okay." Julie tried a disarming smile. "So, you were telling me about this new system of yours?"

"Oh, yes! It's amazing." Qtana's sparkling-eyed grin returned. "Do you have any idea how extensive the firewall had to be to keep the humans out? That system is the result of years of programming. It's a triumph of information technology."

"So, one or two little glitches are par for the course?" Julie guessed.

"Pretty much." Qtana deflated. "See, Kaplan wanted us to try drafting recruiters since we're desperate. We guessed that the most desperate paras out there would be the ones searching for human jobs. So, we had the system search for people who had spent money trying to blanket the city with job applications."

Julie groaned. "I paid $29.99 for that crap."

"This is where it got you." Qtana spread her hands. "It was supposed to filter out the humans and send the draft notices only to paras, but we got our recruitment database and human databases crossed."

"Good thing you caught it in time," Gnerk smirked, "or humans would be dying left and right!"

Still a possibility, for this human, at least. Julie decided against saying it out loud.

"The IRSA 4000 is going to revolutionize programming." Qtana beamed.

"Wait. IRSA 4000?" Julie raised an eyebrow.

"Internal Resource Soldier Acquisition," Qtana clarified.

"I was wondering more about the 4000. Didn't you say it was a new system?"

"Well, yeah. We had to replace the old one. It was getting senile. Not to mention cranky." Qtana grinned. "We just gave it the '4000' so that it sounded more...developed."

"Okay, then." Julie sighed, passing a hand over her eyes. "My partner told me you could help me with a list of specific individuals for recruitment."

Qtana nodded. "Sure, we can do that. It's just going to take a while."

"A while?" Julie stared at her.

"Yeah. You'll have it by tomorrow." Qtana gave a wide, placating grin.

Julie groaned inwardly. *I don't have that long.* Then again, she didn't know how long she had. It wasn't like Kaplan had given her a specific target. "Can't you do it any quicker?"

"Hey." Qtana folded her arms. "The old system would have taken almost a week."

Julie shrugged her off and turned to go, then paused. "You said there was an old system, and it was, well, *senile?*"

Qtana groaned. "So senile. Don't forget cranky."

Senile and cranky. Julie headed for the elevator. Maybe just a little more helpful than the IRSA.

CHAPTER SIX

Taylor squinted at the computer, his mind racing. Which one? He moved the cursor left, then right. One of these squares hid victory. The other hid disaster.

"Actual trolls run IT!" Julie crowed. "I can't get over it."

"Shit!" Taylor jumped, clicking at random, and the screen turned red. His cheeks flushed gray as he looked up. "Meadows!"

"Scared you, did I?" Julie grinned at him. The dimple on the left was just a tiny deeper than the one on the right.

"I was busy," spat Taylor.

She leaned over his desk. "Yeah, busy playing Minesweeper."

His cheeks warmed all the more, and he hastily closed the window. "What do you want?"

"What do I want? I want my experienced partner to help me out here. That's what I want. Your magical IRSA can't get me a recruitment list until tomorrow." Julie frowned.

Taylor sat back in his chair, folding his arms. "Experienced partner? Is that what Kaplan called me?"

"Well, sort of." Julie narrowed her eyes. "Aren't you?"

Taylor sighed. "Okay. I can see that there's something I need to explain."

She sat back with a huff. "I can tell I'm not going to like this."

"I'm not just a recruiter." Taylor gestured at the office around him with a languid hand. "I'm an Aether Elf prince."

"So, you said." She shrugged. "So what?"

Aren't humans supposed to be a little easier to impress? Taylor pushed the thought aside. "So, I'm not here to break any records or save any worlds. I'm just here not to mess it up."

She laughed. "Seems like a weird place for a prince to be."

"Fine. You want the truth. Here's the truth." Taylor raised his hands, palm up. "I'm sixth in line to the throne. I'm not particularly useful to the royal family or anyone else. After a few…mishaps, I was sent here to stay out of the way and avoid bringing disgrace upon the family. So that's what I'm doing. *Staying out of the way.* That's my one great goal."

Taylor expected Julie to be mad, but instead, she gave him a long, slow, assessing look. He tried not to like it too much.

"Here's what I think." She sat up. "You're rising to low expectations. You could do better, but you don't because no one's ever expected better from you."

"Oh, so now you're a shrink, too?" Taylor spat.

"Don't get defensive on me. Taylor, listen, you might be here just to avoid messing things up, but I'm here to *survive.*" She rested a clenched fist on the table. "You've got to help me."

He stared at her. She looked at him like he was her last hope, and no one had ever done that.

"Don't expect miracles." He dropped his eyes.

"Well, you can start by telling me about Malcolm Nox."

"Nox?" Taylor looked up sharply. "How do you know about the Nox?"

"You say it like they're important or something." Julie's tone was maddeningly casual.

"Important! They're Vampire Royalty, Meadows. You don't want to screw with them."

"I didn't screw anyone. I slapped him."

Taylor's stomach swooped. "You...*slapped* a vampire?"

"He was trying to put his hoodoo voodoo juju cooties on me."

"You *slapped* him?" Taylor squeaked.

Julie threw up her hands. "What part of hoodoo voodoo did you not understand?"

Taylor passed a hand over his eyes. "It's called mesmerism. What did you do to make him do that?"

"Nothing." Julie tipped up her chin. "I was helping him. He got mugged by a yeti, and I stopped to help him out. He was hurt, and his dad didn't seem happy."

"His *dad*? You mean his Sire?" Taylor squawked.

"Yeah, whatever."

Taylor groaned. "Well, it's considered rude, especially since you were helping him. Julie, Malcolm Nox is royalty. You *slapped* him."

"If you don't stop saying 'slapped' like it's the end of the world, I'm going to slap *you*." Julie narrowed her eyes.

Taylor smirked. "You wish."

She moved fast for a human, he had to give her that. Still, he saw the slap coming in her eyes long before it reached her arm and sent her hand flying toward him in a smooth arc. Her forearm struck his palm with a soft slap, and he closed his fingers around her wrist.

"Oh!" Her eyes snapped open. "You're quick!"

Taylor allowed himself a moment to bask in her surprise.

It dissolved into a frown. She eyed his hand, a few inches from his face. "How did you move so fast?"

"I'm an elf, and even if I'm sixth in line for the throne, I've been trained in combat my entire life." He let her arm go.

It hovered in the air for a moment, and her eyes darted to his cheek, but she thought better of it and let her arm sink to the desk. "Can you train someone?"

"You?"

"Well, there's no one else here," she deadpanned.

"You always this snarky?"

"Only when I'm stressed." She paused. "Which will probably be until I have the points I need to not die."

"Oh." Taylor sighed. "Fantastic."

Julie sat back. "Seems like that's going to take a while. I can't wait for the IRSA to spit out its list, Taylor. What else takes forever? Finding people's addresses?"

"The trolls in IT are still working out the glitches."

"Everyone keeps saying that, but I don't want to die." Julie folded her arms. "I need a different system."

"There isn't one."

"I know that's not true." She leveled her glare at him. "We had a system before the IRSA."

"Oh, you mean old DumbleDork?"

She quirked an eyebrow. "Like the guy in *Harry Potter*?"

"Yeah. The trolls in IT didn't like the movie, so they changed the name of the old system, and it stuck."

She bit her lip. "Can you show it to me?"

"Why?" Taylor raised his eyebrows. "You're not thinking of using *that*, are you?"

"If I want to hit my quota, I will need help. If this old system is still active, I think it might be our best chance."

"*Our?*"

"Hey." She smiled. "We're a team. If I get a person on board, we both get a bonus cut, right?"

Taylor studied her, trying not to laugh. "I have a 'trust fund,' as you'd put it."

"Right." She grinned. "Do they know what you're spending your money on?"

"Obviously." Taylor shrugged. "It's all on a credit card. We have no problem spending human cash."

"Well..." Her grin widened. "Let's get someone on board, and we'll open you a new account so that no one knows what you buy." Julie winked.

Taylor tried to ignore the fluttering sensation down his lower back, considering her words. Money of his *own*. The idea had never occurred to him, but it was alluring, even if he was sure he was being manipulated.

"Okay, then." Taylor sighed and got up like it was a chore. "Let's take you to see DumbleDork."

Julie permitted a small breath of relief as she got into the elevator. Even if she had to bribe him to do it, at least he would help her.

He hit the button marked minus twelve, and the elevator started moving with a jolt.

"You've got your ID, right?" Taylor asked.

"Yep. Why?" Julie patted the card dangling from her shirt.

"We have to go through security when we get to the Warehouse."

"The what?"

"Well, technically, the Shrine for Previous Technology and Magic, but we call it the Warehouse."

The elevator shuddered to a halt, and the doors opened. A breathtakingly cold wind swirled inside, yanking Julie's clothes and snatching at her hair. Snowflakes scattered against her face, and she staggered back with a yelp, struggling to comprehend what she saw. Snow. Blue sky. A mountaintop, with a few muffled figures in thick clothing, crouching nearby.

"What the!" Julie squawked.

Taylor calmly pushed button twelve again, and the doors closed, leaving just a few snowflakes scattered on the floors. "Sorry about that. Sometimes things get scrambled because of the magical confluence of spatial dimensions."

"Because of the *what*?" Julie stared at him. "Where was that?"

"Switzerland."

Julie glanced at the button labeled with the same name. "Why?" she croaked.

"Oh, the scientists are studying yeti movements there. Might be related to yeti gang activity here in New York."

Julie tried to smooth down her hair. "Well, crap."

This time, to her intense relief, the elevator doors opened onto a small, bare room. Two sturdy elves stood in front of a vast metal sliding door with their hands folded. Each had a leather scabbard at his side. Julie couldn't guess what they held, but she was sure blades and projectiles would be involved.

Taylor led her up to the two elves and jerked a thumb at her over his shoulder. "Just showing the rookie some artifacts."

The taller elf flashed a glance at her. "So there really is a human in the PMA now?"

The other elf chided his colleague sharply, then turned to Julie. "Are you taking anything in?"

She slid a hand up and down her body. "Only what you see here."

Taylor averted his eyes. The taller elf's lips twitched. The shorter one eyed her. "So, not much."

Before she could think of a retort, the elf hit a button, and the doors buzzed and slid open. Taylor and Julie stepped into a warehouse of such enormous proportions that Julie's mind stuttered as she tried to comprehend it. The warehouse alone must have been bigger than the entire PMA building had seemed from the outside. Low, yellow lights barely illuminated silhouettes of boxes and shelves and of other gnarled, twisted figures that made goosebumps rise on Julie's skin.

"Spooked?" Taylor smirked.

"No." Julie folded her arms.

Then something called from deeper inside the Warehouse, a voice that cracked and rattled like a dry leaf in the wind: "Come...closer...children!"

Julie tried not to jump too obviously, but Taylor still chuckled. "Come on. It's this way."

He led them into a narrow passage among the dusty boxes, and Julie stuck close, looking around as they walked. The yellow light caught on something scarlet, which shimmered. When Julie peered closer, it was a flat, hard object about the size of her outspread hand. The light made its surface dance like fire.

"What's this?" she asked, poking it.

"It's a dragon scale." Taylor frowned. "Don't poke it."

"How about this?" Julie picked up a cast of an enormous pawprint.

"That's the signature of the werewolf who raised Romulus and Remus."

"Children..." the creepy voice wheezed. "Come to me."

"What?" Julie squealed. "You mean it's true? A wolf raised the founders of Rome?" She gaped at the cast. "This must be really old."

"*Were*wolf, actually. It's over twelve centuries old. Put it back."

Julie did so, but only so she could jog after Taylor and gape at a glass case containing a shining length of something that looked like ice but glittered like a diamond. When she read the plaque at the bottom of the case, she gasped. "What? There was a Merlin, and this is his wand?"

Taylor stopped, glancing at it. "Well, if I remember correctly, that's his third wand. The first two blew up—he didn't have the moonlight and water crystal balance quite right—and this is his third. He decided to stop casting magic and become a fish after Camelot fell."

"A fish?" Julie blinked.

Taylor shrugged. "Must have seemed more peaceful after all that Lancelot and Guinevere drama. Last I heard, they think he got caught and eaten."

"Eaten." Julie's face blanched. She could only hope Merlin hadn't become a lobster.

"Hey!" The voice suddenly seemed far less dry. "Quit looking at all that pointless old stuff. Get your asses over here and talk to *me*!"

Julie raised her eyebrows. "The IT trolls did say the old system was...cranky."

"That's one way of putting it." Taylor led her around a turn and gestured. "Behold." Sarcasm dripped from his tone. "DumbleDork."

Julie gasped despite herself. A gigantic pointy hat was sitting on a pile of boxes with a yellow lamp glowing upon it. It was royal blue, covered in swirling insignias of gold and silver.

"Whoa," she murmured. "Is that Merlin's hat?"

A faint *poof* sounded, and Merlin's hat disappeared. In its place was a chic black fedora. The voice emanated from, to all appearances, the hat, which bounced up and down. "I'm not associated with that self-important, stuck-up pontificating pig!"

Julie stared at it. "So, DumbleDork?"

"I am the Drafting for Undergraduate Magical Bachelors...um..."

"So," Julie quipped, "DUMB?"

"I didn't give myself a name." The hat stopped bouncing.

"Sexist much?" Julie added.

"What?" The hat sounded rattled.

Julie guessed it wasn't expecting wit after being stuck down here for however long. "Bachelors. Men," she clarified. "What about women?"

"Bachelorettes?" the hat quipped. "How about I just say B stands for Braindead and leave it at that?"

"How about I stick you in that Iron Maiden over there and close the door?" Julie suggested. "Technically, you'd still be here, and I wouldn't get in trouble."

The fedora turned to Taylor. "So, elf, why are you here with this sadistic witch?"

Taylor burst out laughing.

"Excuse me. I'm the one who came down here looking for you." Julie planted her hands on her hips. "I'm here to make you an offer."

"An offer?" The hat turned to her. "What could *you*, a pathetic little creature, offer a millennia-old magical artifact?"

Julie smirked. "Freedom."

The hat was very still. "I'm listening."

"I need some help. I'm a recruiter for the PMA, I need recruits fast, and the new system is… not forthcoming with the information I need."

The hat cackled. "Oh, so their precious IRSA isn't everything it's cracked up to be, is it?"

"Not exactly." Julie sighed. "So, I need you."

"You'll take me from this Warehouse and allow me to use my massive number of skills and intellect?" the hat wheedled. "

"Humble, aren't you?" Julie raised her eyebrows.

"If one is telling the truth, it isn't bragging, and there's no need for becoming falsely humble," the hat retorted.

"Well, I can't call you Dumb." Julie sighed. "I could call you Dick."

"Scandalizing."

"It's short for Richard, you know. A king."

"Are we back on *Sword and the Stone* concepts?" The hat snorted. "I can switch to a sword, but I was told it wasn't couth to carry a sword more than a hundred years ago."

"No." Julie smiled.

Taylor checked his watch. "Are you going to exchange banter all day, or will we get some work done?"

"Fine." The hat paused. "I accept. How are you going to get me out of here?"

"That depends." Julie studied the hat. "How many different styles can you turn into?"

"Why?" The hat leaned back. "Do you have a large wardrobe?

Because of everything wrong with you, your fashion sense isn't too bad."

"Something like that." Julie grinned. "I'll be back tomorrow."

In daylight, the Nox mansion's curtains were all drawn. Julie looked at them with interest as she stopped Genevieve in front of the solid metal gate and hit the button on the intercom.

She had to push it twice more before the butler spoke. "Nox residence." His voice was hoarse.

Must be morning for vampires. "Hi, Mr. Butler. It's me, Julie. I brought Malcolm here last night. I just wanted to check how he is."

"Young Master Nox will be all right. I will be sure to pass on your concerns." The butler's voice disappeared with a click.

Dismissed. Julie glanced up at the mansion again, then shrugged and backed Genevieve into the street.

Lillie readily agreed to go out for burgers when Julie got home, to her surprise. Julie returned downstairs after taking a shower and changing into a comfortable pair of leggings and her favorite floral shirt. Lillie waited by the back door, a little red purse hanging from her arm. She'd squished her hair into a bun and put on lipstick, and it felt good to see her like this.

Lillie slipped easily into Genevieve's passenger seat. When Julie started the engine, the old lady leaned forward and ran a hand over the car's dashboard. A smile tugged at her lips, and her milky eyes filled with tears.

"Lillie?" Julie spoke quietly. "Are you okay?"

"I'm fine." Lillie sat back. "Burger time."

Julie drove carefully, heading for her favorite burger joint a few blocks away. When she stepped on the accelerator, Genevieve responded with a guttural roar. Lillie let out a little whoop, giving the car's dash a companionable slap. "Still got it, old girl!"

Julie laughed, staring at Lillie. She didn't know her landlady as well as she thought.

They stopped at a red light. Beside them, a sleek silver BMW roared its engine, and Julie glanced at the driver, surprised. He grinned at them, and the engine revved again.

"They want to race, dear," Lillie informed her.

"Race?" Julie squawked. "In town? Are they *nuts*?"

"No, just full of testosterone." Lillie smirked. "In my day, I woulda smoked 'em!"

Julie shook her head. The light turned green, and Lillie flipped a middle finger at the BMW driver, who pulled away with a squeal of tires.

"Lillie!" Julie squeaked.

"What?" Lillie cackled. "I was young too, once."

Julie laughed. She put her foot down and Genevieve surged forward with an intoxicating roar of power. She was starting to get why Lillie got so excited about the car.

Straggles of gray hair had come loose from Lillie's bun, but when they pulled into the garage later that night, the old lady's eyes were brighter than Julie had ever seen. She'd polished off two burgers and a stack of fries like she hadn't eaten in weeks.

"Thank you, dear." Lillie smiled up at her as Julie opened the passenger door for her.

"Anytime." Julie held out a hand to help her out of Genevieve. "It's the least I can do, given that you're letting me use Genevieve."

Lillie's face was still as she turned to the car and rested a hand on the roof. "It's good to see my baby up and running again. We had such good times together until..." She swallowed.

Julie squeezed her hand. "Are you okay?"

"What? Oh, I'm fine, dear." Lillie's smile eased into place. "Thank you for this evening. It was lovely."

"I enjoyed it, too." Julie walked Lillie up to her back door.

"Hey, Lillie?"

"Yes, dear?"

"You'll call if you need anything, won't you?"

Lillie smiled. "Thank you, dear."

Julie shut the door softly behind her landlady and clambered up the steps to bed. She lay there for a long time, gazing at the ceiling, as her plan built in the back of her mind.

Julie rubbed itchy eyes as she stepped out of the shower the next morning, wrapped in a towel. Sleep had come slowly for her, and it had felt like she'd only napped for a few minutes when her alarm had woken her.

"Come on, Julie," she mumbled, stumbling to her closet. "Pull yourself together."

She rifled through her drawers, then chose her confidence-boost outfit: high-heeled black boots, studded jeans, black shirt, and leather jacket. Slipping the jacket over her shoulder, she shook her damp hair and looked up at the handful of hats hanging on the back of the closet. She needed something memorable. Something that would stand out. Reaching up, she gripped the hat in the middle, put it on, and turned to the mirror.

Julie hadn't worn the cocky little fedora often. With its blood-red band, it made a bold statement. She grinned, gripping the brim and putting it slightly off-center in a rebellious way.

This hat was unforgettable. She was counting on it.

Time to get some recruits.

CHAPTER SEVEN

The guard shuffled from his gatehouse as Genevieve purred to a halt before nine. Julie rolled down the window as he approached. "Morning, Fred!"

The dwarf's hairy eyebrows disappeared into his low, ginger hairline. "Ain't you a quick one," he grumbled, hiding a smile beneath his beard.

"So I'm told." Julie grinned, touching the brim of her extravagant hat. "See ya."

Fred squinted at her vehicle pass, shrugged, and hit the button for the gate. Julie drove through and waved cheerily. Taylor had taken a minute to remember the guard's name when she'd asked him yesterday. Julie had had to explain she felt bad for giving him the finger behind his back. Maybe the poor guy was in the same boat as her. Performance or death.

Performance, she told herself, clenching the steering wheel as she maneuvered Genevieve toward the large indoor parking area. *I choose performance.*

The lot was shadowy, and Julie tried to focus on the road rather than the modes of transport parked here and there. She passed a hearse. A carriage stood in one corner, unhitched, but the harness hanging beside it was obscenely large. A pack of husky-like creatures lay in a heap around a dogsled, napping. Beside them, a row of broomsticks was propped up against the wall.

Julie parked between a normal-looking VW Beetle and a hitching post holding an enormous gray horse with eight legs and flaming red eyes.

Sleipnir, her training informed her, her voice speaking with mechanical calm. *Eight-legged mount of Asgardian royalty.*

"Hey, Sleipnir." Julie reached out a hand. "Are you friendly?"

The horse pinned its ears back. Julie decided to avoid losing her fingers and gave the stallion a wide berth.

Taylor waited for her in the big entrance hall, fidgeting. The moment he saw her, his eyes darted to the fedora.

"Are you serious?" he hissed, glancing around the hall with furtiveness.

"Taylor!" Julie grabbed him by the elbow and towed him to the nearest elevator. She hit button number three, carefully avoiding the one marked "Switzerland." "Can you be any more obvious? Why don't you just yell out we're going to do something wrong?"

"So, you *are* planning something." Taylor's eyes narrowed as the elevator shot upward.

"I told you I've got to do something. The IRSA 4000 isn't working fast enough." Her palms began to sweat. "It's day two, and I don't even have a name to run down."

"Julie, I don't think you understand." Taylor ran a hand through his hair. "You're talking about stealing a magical artifact thousands of years old. I don't think you can measure Dumble-Dork's value in human currency. It's just...." Lost for words, he threw his hands into the air.

The elevator chirped, and the doors slid open. Julie hurried across the communal office, lowering her voice. "What else would you have me do?"

"I don't know. Something that won't get you killed?"

"That would be *getting recruits*," Julie snarled. She dumped her bag on her desk and fell into her chair. "My life is on the line here, remember?"

"I don't think you understand." Taylor sat opposite her and leaned over the desk. "If you go through with this crazy scheme of yours, Kaplan *will* mind-wipe you."

"Mind-wipe." Julie sat back in her seat with a huff. "Let me guess. Another euphemism for me dying horribly, right?"

Taylor gritted his teeth. "You can't do this."

"I have to do this. If I do, I might get killed. If I don't, I won't get recruits and *will* get killed." Julie pushed back her chair and straightened her hat.

Taylor ran a hand over his face. "Julie, if you do this, the termination will be the least of your worries."

"What else am I supposed to do, huh?" Julie spat.

Taylor stared. "I don't know."

"Then it looks like we're going with my plan. It's the only one there is." Julie got up and realized her hands were shaking. She folded her arms to hide it. The captain's door caught her eye, and her fear turned into anger. She stormed toward it, vaguely aware of Taylor trailing after her, protesting.

"Captain Kaplan!" Julie hammered on the door.

"Julie!" Taylor hissed.

"Enter," Kaplan snarled. The timbre of his voice had a depth to it that made Julie's hands tremble more. She ignored them, pushed the door open, and strode up to the desk, where Kaplan peered at a computer screen as old as Taylor's. Julie guessed it didn't even have any connectivity.

Kaplan glanced at her, then at the screen. "I'm not interested in any excuses, Meadows. I'm well aware you haven't brought me a recruit yet. Have you forgotten about our…deal?"

"I'm not here to make excuses." Julie tipped up her chin.

Kaplan sat back and looked at her, narrowing his eyes. They

were so amber and piercing that Julie's gaze wandered, only to rest on a tiny model of a guillotine on the desk. The morning light illuminated its edges, which suggested it was serviceable for its size. She swallowed.

"Well?" Kaplan snapped.

She glanced at Taylor, who clammed up. His eyes were round and wide with fear. *Fat lot of good you are, Woodskin.* Returning her gaze to Kaplan, she blurted, "I want to know what I *can't* do to get recruits."

He frowned. "You've been through the training."

"Yeah, I know, but I want to know if there are rules we can break to get recruits." Julie smirked. "I hear from the trolls you're a little desperate."

Kaplan made a deep, rumbling in his throat at the word "desperate" but sat back in his chair in unnerving silence.

Julie's mouth tasted like sandpaper. "I can dress like I want, right? Are there other things I can do? Can I use vampire mind juju? Can I draft people like you drafted me? Can I—"

Kaplan held up a massive hand. "Breathing."

She blinked. "What?"

"I want breathing paranormals." Kaplan quirked an eyebrow. "Prove that you can get a breathing paranormal to join by Friday..."

Julie's heart stuttered. *"Friday?"* She paused. "You mean the last Friday of the month, right?" She cleared her bone-dry throat. "The Friday after this week?"

"No." Kaplan eyed her. *"This* Friday. By five o'clock."

Julie's blood pounded in her ears. This was why she hadn't asked about her deadline. *Deadline.* The word echoed hollowly in her mind, emphasizing *dead*.

Kaplan's smile was wide and toothy, not touching his eyes. Julie clenched her hands into fists. She wasn't going to give him the satisfaction of seeing her fear. Somehow, her voice was calm when she spoke. "Fine. What *can't* I do to make that happen?"

"Stab someone?" Kaplan shrugged. "They have to sign of their own volition. No magic, no mesmerization. Other than that, I don't care, recruiter." His smile vanished. "Now get out there and get me a recruit!"

His voice wasn't loud, but his hand slamming down onto the table rattled Julie's bones. She ducked out of the office, aware of Taylor's footsteps right behind her, and strode toward the elevator. Her hand went to her hat, and she cocked it to one side at a bold, careless angle.

Taylor was panting when he caught up to her at the elevator. "Well, shit, Julie." He gasped. "How are we going to get you someone by Friday?"

Julie drew a few deep breaths, hitting the button for Floor Twelve. Taylor's hands shook. Slowly, her heart stopped hammering so loudly.

"It's Wednesday now. Wednesday!" Taylor freaked. "What are we going to *do?*"

Julie turned, smirking. "You heard Kaplan."

"Yeah. I heard him screw you." His brow furrowed, and he huffed. "I know he can be an ass, but this is usually beyond him."

"No. Not that." Julie grinned. "He said I could do *anything* except stabbing or mesmerization." She touched her hat. "That 'anything' includes using the older system to help me recruit if the IRSA 4000 isn't working, don't you think?"

Taylor's jaw dropped and the frown disappeared, replaced by wide eyes. "That's why you went into the office first?"

Julie shrugged, not hiding her grin.

"That's...devious." Taylor blinked.

"Yes, I know. Very drow of me." Julie sniggered. "We're still not telling anyone."

The elevator doors opened, and the same guards as the day before stood outside the Warehouse doors. The taller one scribbled on a clipboard while he glanced at her ID.

"Anything to declare?" grunted the shorter one.

Julie gestured to her body again. "Just this."

The shorter one's face burst into a wide grin. "Still nothing!"

This time, both elves chuckled, and Julie shook her head to hide her relief as she followed Taylor into the Warehouse. It was tempting to stare at the artifacts surrounding them, but Kaplan's deadline nipped at Julie's heels like a hunting dog, and she hurried straight to the spot where they'd last seen DumbleDork.

The hat, once again a wizard's cap covered in insignias, was sitting right where they had left it. Its point drooped sadly, and it looked like any dusty old hat.

"Um, DumbleDork?" Julie whispered.

The point straightened immediately. "Julie!" the hat chirped. "So you *did* come back."

"Of course I did." Julie swallowed the rest of her sentence. *I need you.*

"You, too, elf." The hat turned to him.

"It's Taylor." Taylor glanced around, shifting his weight from foot to foot.

"I know that, you idiot. What use would I be if I didn't know the name of a young elf prince standing right in front of me?"

"We don't have much time." Julie stepped forward. "I have a plan to get you out of here, but first, I need to know if you can help me get recruits. Quickly." She paused. "I need to sign someone by the end of Friday, or I'm literally dead meat."

The hat drew back. "I told you recruiting was my job before I got thrown into this dusty Warehouse."

"So, you'll still help me?" Julie asked.

A moment of silence followed. "Friday, you said?"

"Yes. *This* Friday," Taylor stressed.

"It's not a long time, is it?" The hat crumpled in on itself. "I want to see the outside world again, but not just for two days."

"Two days is better than nothing." Julie put her hands on her hips. "It's better than letting me *die*, isn't it?"

The hat straightened. "Fine, Julia."

"Julie. Only my mom calls me Julia." Julie stepped forward. "You'll help, then?"

"I suppose I will. Heaven forbid the world to be robbed of one more ordinary little human, right?"

Julie scoffed to hide the tide of relief rushing through her. She took off the fedora and held it out, turning it this and that. "Can you turn into this?"

The hat immediately transformed, with a faint *poof*, into a replica of the fedora. "Can you turn into this?" it mocked her in her voice.

Julie grinned, looking at Taylor, who was wide-eyed. He glanced at the doors, but they were still soundly closed.

"Let's go, then." Julie set down her fedora, reached out, and picked up DumbleDork. It was faintly heavier than her hat, and a tiny crackle of warmth nibbled at her fingertips when she touched it. Or maybe that was just her imagination.

She lowered the hat onto her head, and this time she felt a brisk tingling through her hair that lasted for a few seconds. "What was *that*?" she asked.

Just me connecting directly to your neurons.

"Crap!" Julie jumped, ripped off the hat, and scrubbed her fingers through her hair. It felt as though someone was talking inside her head. Taylor threw back his head and laughed, a musical sound that did nothing for Julie's rising embarrassment.

She held the hat in front of her, staring at it. "What was *that*?"

The hat twitched. "I'm not going to be able to speak out loud to you all the time if you want this trick of yours to work. How did you think we were going to communicate?"

Julie felt her cheeks warming as Taylor kept laughing. She forced a smile. "Well, you could just text me."

The hat contemplated her. "Text you? Don't you know that paranormals are secret? I don't connect to *human* devices." It sniffed.

"Sure, sure." Julie raised the hat gingerly onto her head. This time, the prickling feeling didn't seem as bad, and when the hat spoke into her mind, it was with unexpected gentleness. *Here I am. Try not to freak out this time.*

"Okay." Julie laughed. "I can get used to that."

Don't talk out loud, the hat instructed. *Talk to me in your head.*

Well, that's awkward, Julie thought back. *Can you see everything in my head?*

Everything. The hat's tone dripped with smugness. *Especially how much you like the way Taylor's eyes crinkle when he smiles.*

Shut up! Julie squealed inwardly.

Taylor was staring at her, nonplussed. "Is everything okay?"

"Yeah. I'm talking to the hat. In my head." Julie tapped it.

"Less freaked out now?" Taylor grinned.

"Hey, I didn't grow up with rainbow unicorns, unlike some of us," Julie shot back.

Let's get out of here, the hat insisted.

Julie's belly clenched when they reached the Warehouse doors, but the elves gave her only a cursory glance. "Taking anything out?" grunted the shorter one.

Julie quelled *no* when it rose to her lips, forcing her grin into place. She ran a hand down the side of her body. "*All* of this."

"Still nothing," chorused both guards and Taylor, and the room echoed with laughter as they made it safely to the elevator.

CHAPTER EIGHT

"Dumbles," Julie suggested as the elevator rattled upward. "Dumb-Dumb."

Seriously? groaned the hat.

"He doesn't like either of those," Julie told Taylor.

He leaned against the back of the elevator, arms folded. The crease between his brows relaxed slightly. "I suggest you just go on calling it the hat."

"I identify as male," the hat said aloud. They were alone in the elevator.

"Fine. I suggest you go on calling *him* the hat." Taylor shrugged. "Since he doesn't like DumbleDork."

"I can't do that." Julie ran a hand over the hat's brim. "That's just mean. He needs a nickname."

"I need a nickname," the hat agreed.

"Dummy. Dork. Dorkas? That's a girl's name." Julie sighed.

"Just call him 'Hat,'" Taylor suggested.

The hat paused. "Actually..." His voice rose. "I like that."

Julie pouted. "You're not a hat, technically."

Hat wiggled. "No, but it's simple and straightforward, and I like it."

"Shhh." Taylor straightened. "We're stopping."

The elevator doors opened at Floor Delta and light poured over them, so bright Julie raised a hand and blinked against it. When her vision cleared, she was looking out at a huge stone balcony the size of her apartment, dotted with desks that held computers and files. Beyond, rocky red and gold crags towered on either side, and there was an expanse of azure sky. People in white coats were hurrying from desk to desk.

"What's *this*?" Julie gasped. Something enormous swooped from below. Its wings blotted out the sun. Talons clicked, and the creature perched on the balcony railing. An eagle as big as an SUV towered over them. It turned its head to one side and regarded them with a sharp, golden eye.

Roc. Giant bird of prey from the Middle East. Known for stealth and endurance. The knowledge bubbled up from wherever it was inside her brain that the orb had hidden it.

"Rocs? What are you doing with rocs?" Julie asked.

Taylor shrugged.

Studying them, Hat told her. *Trying to find out why they wouldn't take the hobbits to Mordor.*

Julie tried to figure out if he was serious or not when a familiar greenish figure appeared in the doorway. "Room for us?" Qtana asked. Behind her, the ever-faithful Gnerk clutched a clipboard.

"Sure." Taylor moved up, and the trolls stepped inside.

"Headed to the third floor, are you?" Qtana hit the corresponding button. "We had to get some data from the roc researchers, and we were just on our way there to talk to you, Meadows."

Shut up, traitor, Hat growled.

Julie smiled and ignored him. "Oh? Do you have my report?"

"We do." Qtana beamed. "Give it to her, Gnerk."

Gnerk plucked a piece of paper from the clipboard and handed it to Julie with a flourish. She glanced at it. Ten names.

Ha! Hat snorted. *I've got thirty just waiting for you.*

Clearly, getting you out of there was the right decision, Julie answered. She managed a smile for Qtana. "Thanks."

"The data's still messed up. Can you imagine the possibilities when we iron out the last of those wrinkles?" Qtana's eyes shone.

"I'm sure it's everything you need."

The elevator halted, and Julie hurried out, waving the paper at Qtana. "Thanks!" she called.

"Thanks?" Taylor hissed, following her to their desk. "*Thanks?* What are you thanking them for? There are only names on there. No addresses. Nothing!"

You don't need addresses, Hat chipped in. *I'll get them for you. We can use this as a starting point.*

Julie glanced around the office, hoping not to be overhead, then leaned forward. "Hat says..."

"It's okay." Taylor smiled. "I can hear him."

Julie raised her eyebrows. "You can?"

Of course he can. I'm not the IRSA 4000, Hat snorted. *I should think I can communicate telepathically with some elf sitting directly across from me.*

Okay, okay. Julie laughed inwardly. *So, tell me about these. Hey, can Taylor hear me?*

No, just me, Hat told her. *He can hear me, though. Show me the list.*

Taylor held it up, and Julie felt Hat scanning it through her eyes. She felt a sense of intense activity vibrating from Hat.

Hat laughed. *What is going on? These people shouldn't be in the PMA!*

What do you mean? Julie asked.

Well, just take Honeydew Gardiner. Hat pointed out a name. *She's a were-bunny. What do you think she's going to do to her enemies? Kill them with cuteness? She owns a coffee shop, for goodness' sake.*

Julie and Taylor exchanged glances, and Taylor grimaced. "The others have got to be better."

Hardly. Hat snorted. *Here. Frederick Dankworth. He's a warlock.*

Warlock? Julie perked up.

Yeah, with epilepsy.

Julie sighed, propping her chin on her hand. "I guess that disqualifies him from service in the PMA, then."

"You could say that." Taylor shook his head. "Why would the IRSA even put him on the list?"

Hat sniffed. *Because it's pathetic.*

"It's almost like it's trying to make you fail." Taylor ran a hand over his face. "Here's the next one. Kara Gutenberg."

Nope. Not going to happen. She's a pixie. Not quite six inches tall.

"Kaplan did say he wanted breathing paranormals." Taylor shrugged. "Maybe we should just go out there and try all of them. It's not your problem if they're bad agents as long as you get them to sign, right?"

Julie frowned. "No. That doesn't sit right with me."

"Julie, you remember what's going on here, right?" Taylor raised his eyebrows.

"Yeah, I do, but I'm also going to show Kaplan what I can do, not just what I need to do." Julie grabbed a pen and crossed out the first three names on the list. *Come on, Hat,* she begged. *Get me a good one.*

Fine. We'll go through the rest of the list, but I'm telling you, this IRSA has picked out the worst ones.

Julie's chest felt tight by the time they'd finished working through the list. She circled the last name, tapping it with her pen. "How about this Christos Papadopoulos?"

Firstly, he lives in Greece, Hat said.

"Yeah, so? There's email and stuff," Julie snapped. "What is he?"

"Julie..." Taylor started.

He's a satyr. They're big on alcohol. Hat chuckled. *Really big.*

"So? He could still be a good agent, right?" Julie paused. "When he's sober."

"Satyrs generally aren't sober." Taylor grimaced. "I went to college with one. It was, well, interesting."

It'd be a waste of time, Hat insisted. *Which we don't have a lot of.*

"No." Julie glanced at the time on her grainy computer screen. "We don't. We've only got two and a half days left."

"Oh!" Taylor looked up eagerly. "Is it lunchtime already?"

"Yep." Julie sighed. "It's lunchtime, and we don't have a good option for a recruit yet." She reached up and rubbed her aching temples.

Taylor got up. "Well, we're not going to find one while we're hungry. Come on."

"We don't have time to break for lunch, Taylor." Julie gave him a sharp look. "Some of us have something on the line here."

"I know." He grinned, grabbed her arm, and tugged her to her feet. "We can go on brainstorming, but it'll go much better over a plate of steak, don't you think?"

CHAPTER NINE

"You were right," Julie admitted as she shoved another forkful of mashed potatoes into her mouth.

Taylor smiled. "Told you." He grabbed a ketchup bottle and squirted a pool of it onto his French fries. "You can't concentrate when you're hangry."

"Excuse me, sir, but I was *far* from hangry. You haven't seen me hangry. You definitely wouldn't like it."

Taylor raised an eyebrow, fishing out a ketchup-soaked fry. "Yeah, I'll bet."

"What's that supposed to mean?" Julie asked. She sliced her steak, still impressed that the PMA could provide delicious food like this every day. Some sort of crazy magic. Her orb training told her that she wasn't wrong.

"It means you're cranky enough most of the time." Taylor ate the fry.

He's not wrong, Hat supplied.

You're supposed to be finding us new recruits while we eat. Julie frowned, taking a mouthful of the steak: butter-soft, medium-rare, just how she liked it. *Not eavesdropping on our conversation.*

I'm inside your brain, Julie. It's not like I can just put my fingers in my ears, Hat retorted. *Don't worry. I'm working on it.*

Julie sighed, looking around for a distraction and quickly finding one as Taylor plowed through lunch contentedly. "Dude, are you seriously going to put ketchup on a perfectly good steak?"

"Why not?" Taylor squeezed the bottle violently. "Ketchup is amazing."

"Aren't princes supposed to have better taste?" Julie teased.

Taylor grinned. "Just wait until you try my favorite: mayonnaise with chili."

"Gross." Julie fake-gagged.

Okay, listen up, children, Hat barked. *I've found a good little selection for you.*

Julie sat up, her steak forgotten. *Let's hear it.*

First, I've got you a Were working in the demolition business for peanuts. She's been a reliable employee, and she's obviously physically tough.

"Sounds good," Taylor murmured.

Then there's an orc down in Brooklyn. Runs a butcher shop, but he's not making much. Spends most of it on gambling. He also dabbles in amateur boxing, and apparently, he's unbeatable. His therapist thinks he could turn his life around if he used his strengths for a higher purpose.

"Joining the PMA might be just that purpose." Julie sipped her soda. *Anything else?*

Hat hesitated. *Well, yes, but I doubt it's worth trying.*

What is it? Julie demanded.

It's a kelpie that lives down by the harbor. It's going to be difficult to convince...

"A kelpie?" Taylor hissed. "No way."

Julie frowned, annoyed that the orb training still hadn't been integrated. "Which three would have the highest signing bonus for me?"

Taylor bit his lip. "Well, the kelpie," he admitted, "but the orc and the Were are very good choices too."

"Nope." Julie ate the last bite of her steak and put down her silverware. "We're going after that kelpie, whatever that even is."

Julie, think about this, Hat cajoled. *You need a recruit by Friday. Any recruit. Isn't it smarter to just go after the easiest one you can find?*

"He's right." Taylor sat back. "We need to get a recruit. Kaplan wants any para that breathes, right?"

Julie clenched her fists. "No. I'm going to show him what I can do. I can do better." She pushed back her chair. "Let's go get that kelpie."

Taylor was still protesting, and Julie ignored him as she led him to the parking garage.

"Julie, you don't understand. Kelpies—"

"No negative thinking, Taylor." Julie took out her car keys and unlocked the Mustang's doors.

Taylor stared at the car. "How old is this thing?"

"Genevieve is a classic, and you'll respect her as such." Julie opened her door. "Come on. Let's go."

"Do you even know how to drive this?" Taylor hovered by the passenger door. "Maybe I should—"

"No." Julie turned over the engine, goosebumps rising on her arms at the snarl of the V8. "Genevieve is my landlady's baby. Nobody touches her but me."

Taylor opened the door and stared at her. "You know you're impossible, right?"

She knows, Hat answered.

"I know," Julie echoed. "Now, come on."

Taylor sank into the bucket seat and buckled up nervously as Julie drove out of the gate. She waved at Fred. The GPS told her to turn right at the end of the driveway.

"'How old is this thing'?" she repeated, looking at Taylor.

"How can you not recognize a classic Mustang?"

Taylor shrugged. "I'm not that interested in cars."

"What do you drive, then? A Prius?" Julie sniggered.

"Actually..." Taylor turned the sickly gray, his Aether version of a blush. "I don't drive."

"You don't drive?" Julie gaped. "How do you get places?"

"Well, someone drives me if I need to go somewhere." He looked down at his lap. "A perk of being royalty."

Perk? Sounds restricting, Hat commented.

Julie silently agreed. "So, you're chauffeured into work every day?"

"Oh, no. I have a house close by. I walk to work." Taylor's grin was sheepish.

Julie laughed. "Well, princely prestige or not, it's not helping you become a man."

He drew himself up. "Excuse me! I am *very much* a man, I'll have you know."

"Plumbing doesn't make a guy or girl a man or woman," Julie told him. "It just says that the plumbing has matured. You have to be more careful with it."

Taylor folded his arms. "I'm exceedingly careful with my plumbing, I assure you."

Hat snickered. Julie tried to smother her smile by putting her foot down, and Genevieve roared across the road, making Taylor blanch and grab his seat belt.

A few minutes later, they were bumping along a narrow road just yards away from where boats bobbed by the docks. "Whoa." Julie glanced at her phone's GPS. "You guys weren't kidding when you said this kelpie lives right by the harbor."

"Not right by the harbor." Taylor glanced at her. "*In* the harbor."

"What?" Julie stared at him.

"You have arrived at your destination," the GPS's tinny voice announced.

Julie parked Genevieve in a small lot filled with trucks and boat trailers. A cool sea breeze yanked at her hair when she stepped out, and seagulls yipped as they circled above them. The harbor was gray and restless, and the boats constantly moved, their moorings creaking.

"Does it live on a boat or something?" Julie asked, slamming the door.

Not exactly. Hat sighed.

"Come on." Taylor headed along an empty dock. "Let's find your kelpie."

"Wait!" Julie jogged after him. "Where are you going?"

She caught up to him as he reached the damp wood at the very end. Panting, she struggled after him, cursing her high-heeled boots. Taylor shaded his eyes, looking out at the harbor.

"There's no one here." Julie's heart sank. "Is it not home or something?"

It is home, Hat told her. *In the harbor. In the water.*

"What?" Julie squawked. Damn her orb training for failing to give her anything useful. The sooner her mind integrated with the magic, the better.

"If you'd heard us out, you would have known that the kelpie doesn't move on land." Despite his chiding tone, Taylor's grin had an apologetic twist. "That's why they have such a high sign-on bonus. They're hard to find, much less talk to."

Just stay still, Hat instructed. *If it shows itself, Miss Silver-Tongue here might have a chance at recruiting it.*

Julie's heart hammered, and she drew deep breaths. "I'm going to show Kaplan what I'm made of."

"Shhh," Taylor whispered.

They stared at the sea for a few moments that stretched on for an eternity. Julie saw nothing but a few seals playing in the distance, their forms almost black against the gray sea. They disappeared, and Julie's legs began to cramp from standing still.

This is no use, she told Hat. *Maybe we should—*

Shhh! Hat gasped. *Over there! You're in luck.*

Julie squinted. A wake was spreading across the gray water, heading toward her. Her heart thudded. Something was coming toward them. Something huge.

"It's here," Taylor whispered.

What was a kelpie, anyway? The wake was enormous. Was it aggressive?

She opened her mouth to ask, and the water beneath her feet churned and slopped against the dock. Her words died on her lips, and she looked down through the water into the biggest, bluest eye she had ever seen. It was the size of her fist, and its color was neon-blue against the dark water, wide and intelligent as it stared up at her.

Julie's breath hitched.

Well, go on, recruiter, Hat commented dryly. *Do your thing.*

What do I say? She gulped.

Try flattery to start with. They're vain.

Julie's knees trembled with awe as the water stilled and she glimpsed more of the creature. A gigantic head was as long as she was tall and covered in silver skin like a dolphin's. A long neck and a streamlined body followed. The thing must be bigger than a city bus. She caught a glimpse of flippers beneath the ripples. Flattery would be easy.

Slowly, she crouched down on one knee. "I've never seen anything like you in my life," she blurted.

"Try to be professional, Julie," Taylor muttered.

It seemed to work. The kelpie's head broke the surface, and it sprayed water from its nostrils. It lay low in the water, regarding her with those amazing eyes. Its head had an equine shape.

Kelpie. Also known as the water horse, her training told her.

More information butted against her brain, but she pushed it aside. She needed to focus on her pitch.

The kelpie raised its nose above the water. Julie had expected sharp teeth, but the teeth she glimpsed were flat and square like a horse's.

"What's this?" it rumbled. "A human talking to me?"

"Hi." Julie couldn't suppress a smile, but she stopped herself from touching its velvety nose. "I'm from the Para-Military Agency."

The kelpie snorted, spraying them with seawater. "What does the PMA want with me? I don't want to hear any of its politics. We kelpies keep to ourselves."

I want to touch it, Julie groaned inwardly.

Under absolutely no circumstances! Hat barked.

"Oh, I'm not here to talk to you about politics," Julie told the kelpie. "I'm here to make you an offer you can't refuse."

The kelpie turned to the side to look at her with the other eye. Water splashed over the deck, soaking her boots. "I'm listening."

"I'm here to offer you a higher-paying job than you'll find with any human agency." Julie parroted the pitch she'd written and memorized yesterday. "There are great benefits and minimal training."

The kelpie made a deep rumbling sound. It took Julie a second to realize the creature was laughing.

"A job!" it boomed. "Where do you propose I keep the money I'd earn from this job? In my pockets?" It rolled, flashing its white underbelly.

Julie felt her cheeks warming. "Um, there's also the advantage of doing something worthwhile for the good of society," she stammered.

"I told you, human," the kelpie growled. "When it comes to society, I'm partial to my own."

"Maybe–" Julie began.

"Oh, look!" The voice made all of them jump. It came from the road. When Julie spun around, she saw an SUV had stopped nearby. The windows were rolled down, and a mom with a messy bun pointed at the kelpie as the kids hung out of the window.

"What?" Julie gasped. "Hat, how are they seeing the kelpie?"

Before Hat could answer, the mom turned to her kids, grinning. "Look, kids, it's a seal!"

"A *seal*!" The kelpie huffed out a cloud of spray. "A seal!"

Julie spun to it. "Don't worry about them. They—"

"All you humans are the same. They could see me as a majestic whale or a dolphin, but a *seal*!" shrieked the kelpie. It slapped a flipper on the water, eliciting giggles from the kids.

Taylor jogged toward the SUV, waving his arms and shouting gibberish about an endangered species. Julie knelt on the dock, desperate. "Never mind them. *I* don't see you as a seal."

"Clearly, you do," sniffed the kelpie. "Trying to recruit me like some common mermaid or something! Did you really think a creature like me would join your PMA?"

"Please—" Julie began.

With a final disgusted snort, the kelpie rolled onto its side, belly flashing for an instant, then disappeared in a curtain of bubbles.

"They're gone," Taylor panted, jogging up to her. "I'm sorry about that. Wait, where did it go?"

"It's gone." Hat spoke aloud. "No thanks to those humans."

"I don't understand." Julie sat back. "Surely humans have seen it and thought it was a seal before. Was it my pitch?"

"I don't think so, Julie." Taylor put a hand on her shoulder. "Kelpies don't like to get involved with other species. They barely even speak to other members of their own species."

"Yeah, and they're bound to water, anyway." Hat sighed. "That makes them hard to sign on, logistically."

"I'm sorry." Taylor bit his lip.

Julie ran a hand through her hair, her eyes burning. "You guys did try to tell me. I just... I thought my luck would hold after getting DumbleDork, you know?"

"We still have two days." Taylor gave her shoulder a squeeze. "Plus a couple of hours left in this one. Come on. Let's get back and get all the information we can on our other two candidates to get straight to recruiting tomorrow."

"I can help with that," Hat added.

Julie picked herself up and squared her shoulders. "Let's do it. It's not like giving up is an option."

She marched to Genevieve, Taylor close behind her, determined not to make the same mistake again.

It took the whole afternoon, but Julie had two files tucked under her arm that evening as she and Taylor headed to the parking garage. The files were thin, but they were real and solid. She wasn't skimping on her research this time.

Taylor glanced left and right as they stepped into the deserted garage. "What are you going to do with your hat?" he asked nervously.

Julie touched the brim. "He's coming home with me, of course."

"What?" Taylor hissed.

That was the deal, Hat added. *To get me out of the SPTM.*

"Julie, this is theft," Taylor whispered.

"It's more like a prison break. Hat is sentient. It wasn't fair to him to be locked up in that Warehouse." Julie shrugged. "Especially when he didn't do anything wrong."

"Debatable," Taylor muttered.

I heard that!

"You're going to get in serious trouble for this." Taylor sighed. "I'm starting to know better than to try to stop you."

Julie smirked. "You're learning. So, is your royal carriage here to pick you up?"

He huffed. "I walk home, remember?"

"Not today, you don't." Julie unlocked Genevieve's door. "I'll run you home."

"It's out of your way." Taylor hesitated.

"I don't care, dumbass. Now get in."

The drive was only five minutes, but it was in the opposite direction. As Julie drove, she couldn't help but gape. If she'd thought the Nox mansion was massive, the buildings in this neighborhood were gigantic.

"Here we are." Taylor gestured at a driveway leading between tall white walls on their right. Julie turned and drove slowly, staring. There were towering trees, brilliant in their pale green foliage, on either side behind the walls. It felt like she was traveling through a tunnel. Their leaves rustled overhead. In front of them, a palisade with a gate waited. A round sign hung at the top of the gate. Julie squinted, but it was like looking at something underwater. The colors and words rippled and blurred.

As they neared the gate, she peered at a sprawling mansion spread over green lawns. She saw a pillared wrap-around porch, multiple stories, and a swimming pool, but everything was fuzzy around the edges.

"Whoa. This isn't a mansion. This is a...a..."

"Compound," Taylor supplied. "The compound of the Aether Elves."

Julie rubbed away goosebumps on her arms. "It's magnificent. I'm also sure it's not the mansion I see here."

He stared at her. "Your genetic mutation must be weird for you to see, even a little, through an Aether illusion," he told her. "We *are* the Elves of Mystical Dusk, after all."

"Mystical Dusk, huh?" Julie grinned.

"Oh, shut up."

Julie brought Genevieve to a halt in front of the gates guarded by two enormous elves in black suits and sunglasses. Taylor opened the door. "Don't bother trying to get in. They're not friendly."

"I wasn't planning on it." Julie hesitated. "Can we meet earlier tomorrow morning? I could pick you up at seven?"

"Sure. We'll go for breakfast." Taylor smiled. "My treat."

Julie raised an eyebrow. "The last time a guy told me that, it didn't go so well."

"Pretty sure that guy wasn't an elf." Taylor laughed and closed the door.

Julie backed Genevieve out of the long drive. "One more stop before we go home, Hat."

Oh? Where's that?

"To see someone," Julie told him.

CHAPTER TEN

The Nox mansion was shrouded in darkness. Only Genevieve's headlights reflected against the solid gate. Beyond, Julie saw the glimmer of reflected streetlamps in the tall windows. No lights were on inside.

"Creeps," she muttered.

That's speciesist of you, Hat commented.

"Sorry." Julie rolled down the window and hit the intercom button.

"Nox residence," came the now-familiar voice of the butler.

"Hey, it's me. Julie. The human."

"Good evening, madam," purred the butler.

"I'm here to see Mr. Nox."

"Young Master Nox is not taking visitors right now, as he is still—" the butler began.

"No, not Malcolm." Julie grinned. "His dad."

Sire, Hat corrected. *Julius Nox.*

"Julius," Julie added.

The butler paused.

"His Grace will see you." The butler sniffed. "You may enter."

The gate opened, and Julie drove into the black courtyard,

almost crashing into a wall when Genevieve's headlights picked out the tall butler standing in the courtyard. "How did he get here so fast?" she whispered.

Well, he is a vampire, Hat snarked.

She parked Genevieve, feeling blind when the headlights went out, and she fumbled for her phone to turn on its flashlight and then got out. The butler was right by her elbow. Julie jumped but managed not to squeal.

"This way, madam," the butler intoned.

He glided off, and Julie scampered after him, trying to resist the urge to shine the phone flashlight in every direction. Her eyes adjusted to the darkness, and as he led her through the courtyard gate, she couldn't help but gasp in surprise. They were walking through a magnificent rose garden. The intense fragrance filled the air all around them, hundreds of glorious blooms luminous in the faint moonlight: white and blue with splashes of yellow and red ones so deep they were almost invisible in the dark garden. The path was flanked by what seemed to be millions of white roses.

I'm not sure what I was expecting, but it wasn't this, she whispered in her mind.

Oh, Julius has won plenty of prizes with his roses. Hat laughed. *I'll find you pictures.*

Julie struggled to comprehend the idea of Julius Nox exhibiting a bunch of roses at some country fair. She came dangerously close to giggling.

When she held up her phone, her flashlight illuminated the front of the mansion, and she couldn't help gasping again. The mansion was even more amazing up close. Its front doors seemed twice the height of any normal door, wide enough to drive Genevieve through them, and there were ornate golden locks and knockers. Fragrant jasmine and wisteria climbed over the facade. Blinking at her reflection in one of the vast windows, Julie realized they were made with one-way glass.

"This is epic," she whispered.

"The master is this way." The butler had turned away from the mansion and followed the rose-lined path around it. Julie hurried to catch up, eager to glimpse the Nox backyard. It took an absurdly long time to walk around the house.

When they finally reached the back of the house, Julie felt a breeze against her face and stared. The Nox grounds were bigger on the inside than on the outside. Vast lawns spread out in front of her, lined with budding trees and more roses. A tennis court and an Olympic-sized pool shimmered under the stars. Laughter came from the pool, and when Julie squinted, she saw a few small, pale figures pushing and shoving each other at the edge, squealing with joy.

The butler stopped, and Julie almost walked into him. She looked at a greenhouse bigger than Lillie's home, crowded with plants. The butler opened the glass door.

"Miss Julie Meadows to see you, Sire," he called.

"Turn on the lights, Perkins," boomed the elder Nox's voice. "Where *are* your manners? Don't you know humans can't see in the dark?"

Perkins muttered something inaudible, and a light switch clicked. The greenhouse was bathed in a warm glow from hundreds of light bulbs hanging from the roof. They lent a whimsical look to the greenhouse, filled with plants that Julie had only ever heard of—or never heard of.

The butler withdrew, and Julie stepped forward toward the voice, then stopped to stare in awe. A huge plant bloomed right in front of her. Its long, sharp leaves grew over Julie's head, and its flowers spilled toward her, palest yellow and speckled with blood-red. She reached out and brushed her fingertips over one of the petals.

"Beautiful, isn't it?"

Julie whipped around. Somehow, Julius Nox was behind her. He smiled and flashed his fangs, but it was difficult to take it too seriously, considering that he was wearing floral gardening gloves and carrying a bright blue watering can.

"*Grammatophyllum speciosum.*" Julie turned to the plant. "I've never seen one in real life."

"I'm not surprised. They're almost impossible to grow here, especially this time of year." Julius passed her and lovingly began watering the plant. "I *am* surprised that you know what this is."

"It's the biggest orchid in the world. People call it the Queen of Orchids." Julie shrugged. "My mom gardens sometimes. I liked helping her when I was a kid. Plus reading. A lot."

"Clearly." Julius set down the watering can. "This might interest you, then."

He led her among the jumble of plants to a section near the back of the greenhouse. "Do you recognize this, Miss Meadows?"

Julie tried not to let her jaw drop, but it dropped anyway. Growing directly out of the dirt without leaves or a stem, a flower spread deep red petals almost three feet across. It was the most bizarre plant Julie had ever seen, but there was nothing paranormal about it.

"The monster flower?" Julie stared at Julius. "It's supposed to stink of rotting meat."

Julius beamed. He lifted a spray bottle nearby and gave the flower a few spritzes. "You're right in that it looks like the monster flower, miss, but this isn't *Rafflesia arnoldii*. Have a good sniff."

Julie edged nearer and peered into the flower. A few dead insects floated in the interior. When she leaned down and breathed deeply, she blinked in surprise. "It smells like frangipani."

"Of course it does." Julius was glowing. "It's been crossbred with frangipani."

"What? How?" Julie gaped at him.

"I had supernatural help." Julius winked. "Beautiful, isn't it?"

"Amazing." Julie laughed. "You've got quite the green thumb there, Sire."

Julius inclined his head. "Well, I've enjoyed this little chit-chat with an unexpectedly intelligent human, but I'm sure you didn't come here to see my greenhouse, Miss Meadows."

"Well, no." Julie stopped, thinking. "Um, I mostly came to see Malcolm. I wanted to know if he's okay."

Julius cocked his head to one side. "You're interested in a young vampire who rudely tried mesmerization on you."

Julie shrugged. "We do crazy things when we're hurt, right?"

Julius chuckled. "Profound."

"Okay, so maybe I have another question, too." Julie tugged at Hat. "Maybe a more important one."

Julius set down the spray bottle. "I'm listening."

"Why...well, why would someone want to join the Para-Military Agency?"

"A complicated question." Julius pulled off his gloves. He eyed Hat for a few moments longer than necessary. "I think I may have your answer, though it might be longer than you expect. Come with me. This will be a more comfortable conversation in my library."

Julie's heart thumped briskly. Library! If this guy's greenhouse is like this, his library will be mind-blowing.

Quite literally, in some cases, Hat chipped in.

She followed Julius to the door, pausing here and there to lean in and sniff at some of the flowers they passed. He had everything: great red splashes of tropical hibiscus, impossibly delicate fynbos from South Africa, and purple lady's slippers that were almost priceless. She thought she saw him half turn back when she paused to smell the fynbos, and a smile tugged at the corner of his mouth.

Julius led her through the mansion's back door—still larger and more ornate than the nicest front doors in her part of Brooklyn—and up a flight of polished oak stairs carpeted in royal blue. He turned on the lights as he went. "We can see in the dark," he explained, "but we all have lights in our homes for our non-vampire visitors."

"You entertain a lot of humans, then?" Julie swallowed, suddenly conscious of the thud of her pulse in her neck.

Julius stopped to swing open an ornate oak door carved with galloping horses, leaping deer, and roaring lions. "Not usually, no."

He hit the lights and gestured for Julie to go first. The sight of the library was splendid enough to erase her fear. If she was going to be eaten by a vampire, at least she'd die happy. The room was round, and every wall was covered with bookshelves to the ceiling. Its carpet was cream-colored and luxuriously deep, and it housed a desk near the back. In the center of the room, leather couches curled around a coffee table, with fluffy pillows propped in the corners.

"I could live here," Julie blurted.

Julius laughed. "Let's sit at my desk."

Julie was still staring as she sank into a leather armchair on one side of Julius' desk. He took the office chair on the other side and steepled his fingers, looking at her over them. "You're not used to this finery, are you?"

"No," she admitted.

"I noticed. You might like the library, but the rest of the house makes you uncomfortable."

"I wasn't brought up around so much." Julie glanced at one of the shelves. "I think that that first edition of *A Tale of Two Cities* is worth more than the house I grew up in."

"Probably." Julius grinned. "Of course, it helps that I bought it myself when it first came out."

Julie bit back the pithy comment that sprang to her lips. He was a vampire. Of course he was older than he looked. The copy she'd read in middle school had been held together with sticky tape, but the words still held the same power.

Julius leaned back in his chair. "So, you want to know why someone would want to join the PMA."

"It's something my training didn't cover for some reason."

Because I didn't do your training, that's why. Hat snorted.

"Maybe that's why the PMA is so desperate for recruits." Julius chuckled. "Do you know what the PMA does?"

"It's like the police and the army," Julie guessed. "For your federal government."

"Close." Julius's eyes crinkled at the corners. "The PMA is the military and law arm that supposedly governs all paranormals. It doesn't work for a government like yours, though."

"So, it's international?" Julie asked.

"Well, yes. The paranormal world doesn't operate on the same borders that yours does," Julius explained. "Instead, we're divided into species and families. All of it is governed by the Eternity Throne."

"Sounds pretentious."

"Maybe." Julius smiled. "The Eternity Throne exists to keep the peace among paranormals and between paranormals and humans. It's been occupied by the Lunar Fae family for the past two thousand years."

"The PMA is how the Eternity Throne keeps that peace."

"Exactly." Julius nodded. "So knowing that, you'll know that people join the PMA for two basic reasons. Either for themselves or for the good of society."

Or because their other option is getting decapitated by Kaplan, Julie mused.

"Some people believe serving the Eternity Throne by joining the PMA is their purpose in life, and they'll do it because they believe in the royal family and its causes," Julius went on. "Others will join the PMA because it provides training, experience, or a job when they can't get anything else."

"Like our US Army posters," Julie commented. "Or maybe the Marines."

"Probably the Marines," the vampire admitted. "Building something in yourself in short order."

Julie nodded. "Thank you. That gives me a lot more background information than I had."

You could just have asked me, Hat grumbled.

I figured that talking to a breathing paranormal, as Kaplan demanded, would be more helpful, Julie teased.

"I'm glad I could be of some help." Julius' lip twitched. "Now we're even after you saved my foolish son."

"Speaking of which..." Julie bit her lip. "I don't suppose you'd let me check on him, would you?"

"Oh, he's fine." Julius sighed, waving a hand. "Perkins, take her to him."

"Yes, Sire."

Julie jumped clean out of her chair. The butler was standing directly behind her. "How long have you been standing there?" she squawked.

He regarded her steadily out of serene red eyes. "About three seconds, madam. This way."

Julie glanced over her shoulder as the butler glided to the door. "Thanks again, Sire."

Julius picked up a book and waved a languid hand.

The butler turned on lights this time as he led Julie up another flight of stairs along a hallway lined with portraits. Julie stared at the portraits—she could swear one Renaissance-looking equestrian portrait was of Julius—when an explosion rattled down the hall, followed by fluent cursing.

"What was *that*?" Julie asked.

The butler raised his eyebrows, the first sign of emotion Julie had ever seen on his face. "That would be young Master Nox."

CHAPTER ELEVEN

A crash shook the walls as the door swung open, and Malcolm's voice rose. "Shit, shit, *shit!*"

Julie almost echoed that sentiment when a giant face appeared on the other side of the room, with staring eyes and bloodied jaws. She stepped back before she realized the face was very much CGI.

The room was bathed in bluish light from a huge screen against the opposite wall. Malcolm's voice came from a couch facing it, along with the clicking of a video game controller as the CGI zombie received a knife to the face in stylized sprays of scarlet blood. It collapsed to the ground, and Malcolm spoke more calmly. "Where are you, Zee? You need first aid?"

What is this? Hat asked.

It's a video game. Julie looked around for the butler, but he'd disappeared. *Nothing to be scared of.*

Your elevated heart rate and blood pressure would say otherwise. Hat snickered. *Such a funny little system. It's primitive.*

Malcolm's character ran toward a figure lying on the ground nearby. "I got you, bro," he yelled. His character knelt beside the prone figure—ItzMeZee189, according to the tag over its head—

and there was a *plink* from the screen. The figure disappeared, then faded into existence, this time on its feet and clutching a shotgun.

"Yeah, baby!" Malcolm cheered. "C'mon. Let's go get those suckers!"

Gunfire rattled through the room. Malcolm's avatar and ItzMeZee took cover behind a broken-down wall.

Using the screen's light, Julie picked her way across the room and touched Malcolm's arm. "Hi there."

Malcolm uttered a curse in Ancient Greek. His arms jerked, and the controller sailed through the air and landed on the couch. On the screen, his avatar jumped to its feet. Bullets tore through its chest, and it stumbled to the ground.

"Crap! Sorry," Julie squeaked.

"Zee, save me," Malcolm yelped, grabbing the remote. "Yeah, sorry. Someone walked in." He hooked one earphone behind his ear and grinned at Julie. "Hello, human. How's it hanging?" He raised both hands and clapped them, and warm light flooded the room. Julie realized it was a whole suite. This living room was bigger than Lillie's and definitely more luxurious.

"I'd ask you the same question." Julie stared at him. "Looks like you're doing a lot better than the last time I saw you, though."

Malcolm laughed. "Takes more than a yeti swipe to keep a vampire down for very long." He was still almost translucent, but then again, so was Julius. He wasn't wearing any bandages, and his wounded shoulder moved freely.

"Magical healing powers or something?" Julie asked.

Malcolm gestured to an armchair, his eyes sliding back to the game. Julie sat.

I should hack into this system and cause some havoc. Hat snorted. *He's going to turn his brain into mush.*

Shhh. I'm trying to talk to Malcolm here. Julie shushed him.

Hat snickered, and Julie tried to ignore it.

"Oh, it only took me about twenty-four hours to heal with the right blood." Malcolm's fingers were dancing on the controller again, strangely elegant.

Julie raised her eyebrows. "The right blood?"

"By transfusion." Malcolm cocked a lazy eye at her. "Still not a barbarian, you know. What are you doing here, anyway?"

"I wanted to check on you."

"Check on me?" Malcolm gave her his full attention. "Why would you want to do that?"

"Because I helped pick you up the other night, moron!" she teased. "Believe it or not, you weren't just a bleeding Uber passenger."

He dragged his eyes to the screen, shifting his weight. "Oh, okay."

Silence hung over them like a thick blanket. Julie fished for something to say. "So, why are you playing this?"

Malcolm gritted his teeth and pulled a trigger on the controller. A staccato of gunfire roared through the speakers.

Yeah, why? Hat added. *It's not very good. I could do much better.*

We all know that, Hat, Julie responded.

"I don't know." Malcolm touched his headphones, turning off his mic. "I guess it's because all my supernatural reflexes and strength don't mean shit with video games."

"Humble-brag much?" Julie quipped.

Malcolm gave her a wry look and went on. "Sure, I can move the stick faster, but system speed and network lag barely make me better than good humans." His grin returned. "I can think faster. That's my real advantage."

Blood sprayed over the screen, which turned red. A skull appeared in the center.

YOU ARE DEAD!

"Until I do something stupid." Malcolm touched the headphones again. "Sorry, guys. I've got to go. Okay. I'll talk to you guys tomorrow. Bye."

After he pulled off the headphones, Malcolm tossed them and the controller aside and turned to face Julie. His eyes widened when they rested on her. They darted quickly up and down her body before he dropped them and a faint pink tinge crept into his cheeks.

The silence stretched. Julie crossed her arms.

"Nice hat," Malcolm croaked. He looked at her again, then nibbled the inside of his bottom lip and glanced away.

"Don't see a lot of humans, do you?" Julie smirked.

"Well, not a lot of humans like you." Malcolm managed a grin. "How did you get in here, anyway?"

"Oh, your dad let me in. He's super nice. We talked about his plants."

Malcolm gaped. "Sire *likes* you?"

"Who wouldn't like all this?" Julie teased, gesturing to herself, and Malcolm laughed. It was a strangely earthy, genuine sound, making him look like any other handsome college kid for a few seconds.

"Who is *this*?"

The feminine hiss came from behind her. Julie's fingers dug into her armchair, and it was all she could do not to jump. She stood up, forcing herself to do it slowly, and turned.

The girl behind her wore a figure-hugging black dress that barely covered what was necessary, revealing endless miles of legs so white and slender that they looked like porcelain. Julie almost expected them to crack as she walked across the room. Her lips were the brightest red against her moon-white face, and a cascade of black hair swayed over her elegant hips. She wore blood-red heels with a grace Julie envied.

"Julie. Julie Meadows." Julie held out a hand.

The girl gave her an elegant sneer that revealed delicate fangs and kept her hands on her pricey purse. She skirted around Julie and addressed Malcolm instead.

"Is this a *human*?" she hissed.

"Hello, Cassidy." Malcolm cast Julie an apologetic glance. "Julie's the one who scooped me off the sidewalk when I was hurt."

The girl threw herself on the couch beside him, keeping herself between him and Julie, and threw an arm around his shoulders. "How *are* you feeling, my love?" she purred, tracing her fingertips over the shoulder that had been wounded.

Malcolm shifted, his eyes darting to Julie again. "Um, I'm fine, just like I was when you asked this morning."

"I'm so glad you're all better." Cassidy draped herself over Malcolm's chest and kissed his cheek, leaving a smear of lipstick. "I was so worried about my precious one."

Well, aren't we possessive? Hat chuckled.

Just a little. Julie crossed her legs and interlaced her fingers over one knee, bouncing her foot. "Yeah, I'm glad I found him in time." She gave the girl a big smile.

Malcolm was trying to disentangle himself from her, but she was like an octopus, forever finding another tentacle to throw around him. "Julie, this is Cassidy Consta. She's..." He stopped.

"I'm from one of the vampiric noble families." Cassidy threw her glorious hair over her shoulder and shot Julie a look. "What are you doing here, anyway?"

"She came to check up on me," Malcolm protested.

"Oh, how sweet." Cassidy's smile revealed all of her fangs. "Your little pet human is rather loyal."

"Julie saved my life, you know." Malcolm's voice lost firmness as he went on. Cassidy grabbed one of his hands and intertwined her fingers with it, squeezing until the little color in Malcolm's hand faded to white.

"Wasn't that gallant of her?" Cassidy spoke flatly. "I'm sure she can see that you're just fine, though."

"I'm right here, you know." Julie laughed.

Cassidy's eyes narrowed. "What are *you* laughing at?"

At how absolutely ridiculous you are. Julie thought better of saying it out loud. She got up. "I think I'd better be on my way. It's good to see you're okay, Malcolm."

"Yes, I think you'd better," hissed Cassidy.

Malcolm's mouth turned down. "Thanks for coming."

Julie was not even remotely surprised to find that, when she reached the door, the butler was already holding it open for her. She thought she detected a savageness in his eyes when he glanced at Cassidy. Then he closed the door with unnecessary violence.

They retraced their steps to the courtyard in silence. When Julie unlocked Genevieve, the butler spoke.

"It's a sad night," he whispered, "when a human shows just how bitchy a vampire can be."

Julie couldn't help laughing at the word *bitchy* in the decorous butler's mouth. He shook his head as though he'd said too much.

You're not the only one who thinks Cassidy sucks, Hat observed.

The butler turned to go, but Julie held up a hand, stopping him. "Please, can I have your name?"

He stared at her. "Perkins."

She smiled. "Where I come from, we don't call people by their last names."

The butler's lip twitched. "Well, in that case, madam, you may call me Gerald."

Julie's visit to the Nox mansion had helped her to skip the traffic, at least. The streets were busy but flowing well as Genevieve rumbled toward home. Julie felt wonder and awe throbbing in her mind, and she suspected it wasn't her own.

It's been a while since you saw the outside world, huh?

A long time, Hat admitted. *Even before I was 'obsolete,' I spent most of my time on the fourth floor with those bloody trolls.* He gasped. *Look at these cars!*

Julie laughed aloud. *Not everyone drives a classic.* She gave Genevieve's steering wheel a friendly pat.

They halted at a red light, and Julie touched the accelerator a few times, letting Genevieve growl, ready to jump off the line as soon as the light turned green.

Hold up! On your left, Hat hissed.

Julie saw the hood of the police car peeking from a side street, watching. She slowly let go of the accelerator.

"Thanks, Hat." She patted the dashboard. "Look at the trouble you almost got me into, Genevieve!"

CHAPTER TWELVE

It was past nine when Julie brought Genevieve to a halt in the garage, stifling a yawn. She picked up Hat and planted him on her head.

"Easy!" Hat barked.

"Shhh. You'll wake Lillie, my landlady. She's always asleep by this time." Julie pulled out her backpack and closed the car door, traipsing across the garage.

"Landlady? Don't you even own this ramshackle place?"

"That's my home you're talking about, and no, I don't own it. This is New York City. Do I look like a trillionaire to you?"

"That's got to be an exaggeration," Hat muttered.

When she reached the top of the stairs, Julie flicked on the lights. "Home sweet home."

Hat paused, and she sensed Hat staring at her apartment. He seemed at a loss for words and retreated to her mind. *You live here?*

Julie took off Hat and set it down on the kitchen table, then rummaged in a cabinet for bread. *Yes, I do live here, and I happen to like it.*

It's...not much, Hat tried diplomatically.

It was a relief to have someone to talk to as she started assembling a ham sandwich. *It's all I want. My own space, you know?* Hat turned on the table. *I do like the bookshelves. Pity about the view. And the kitchen. And the space. And—*

I get it, I get it. Like I said, I just needed my own space, Julie told him. She added some lettuce. She'd probably die if she didn't eat something green at some point.

Your own space? Why? Hat asked.

Well, you know. I needed to move out. Spread my wings. Julie snorted as she cut her sandwich in half. *Get away from my mom.*

Your mother treats you poorly? An edge crept into Hat's voice.

No, nothing like that. She's just... Julie flapped a hand. *She drives me crazy sometimes. I wanted to see if there was more to life than the 'burbs.*

Hat hopped to face her as she sat at the table. Was *there more to life?*

Julie's cheeks warmed. *Not until recently, to be honest. I did more reading than anything else, not unlike in high school.*

I did notice your excellent grades. I wondered why you didn't try to pursue higher education with your 4.0 GPA.

Hey! Have you been snooping in my records? Julie raised an eyebrow.

Hat's brim curled like he was shrugging. *It's what I do. So, why didn't you?*

I don't know. I guess there wasn't anything I was invested in studying. My mom said she wouldn't let me go into student debt just to learn things for the sake of learning. Julie grinned. *Even though that's one of my favorite things.*

I noticed in the greenhouse. Hat cocked to one side. *I detect a message from someone named Sam on your mobile device.*

Julie had almost forgotten about Stingy Sam. *Ugh. Don't even ask. One of my few and unsuccessful forays into dating. I should've stayed home reading. I love learning, and making friends with people is hard.*

Really? Hat quipped. *That's not what the data shows.*

What data? Julie bit into her sandwich.

Well, you do *have an Aether prince.*

Sixth in line, Julie argued. *It's not that special. Not even Taylor thinks it's that special.*

It is *special.* Hat leaned against his brim. *You're picking him up for a date tomorrow.*

Hat, no! Julie groaned. *That's not a date!*

You set a time. You set a day. By definition, that's a date.

No. It is not. You're being ridiculous. Julie laughed. *I'm glad you're an ancient magical artifact and not a life coach.*

If life was a sport, I would be a fantastic coach. Hat snorted. *You're definitely going on a date with Taylor.*

No, I'm not. Picking someone up for work isn't a date!

Well, what exactly defines a date, then?

Julie rubbed her chin. *It's when you make an appointment to see someone you're romantically involved with.*

Like you and Sam? Hat shot back.

No! Okay, so it's when you make an appointment to do something fun while seeing someone you want to get to know better, Julie attempted.

So. Tomorrow is a date, Hat stated. *Recruiting is fun, and you want to get to know Taylor better, right?*

Not like that, Hat. Julie shook her head. *Besides, I bet it's against PMA policy or something.*

Is that the only reason why you won't admit it?

What's it to you? Julie retorted.

Come on, Julia. I've been stuck in the Warehouse for years. Forgive me if I want to live a little.

I told you not to call me Julia. Julie grimaced. *It's such an old lady name.*

One day, you will be an old lady, Hat pointed out.

Ugh, whatever. Julie finished her sandwich and got up. *I'm going to shower and get to bed. It's been a long day.*

I win. Hat smirked.

Julie flipped him off as she stumbled to the bathroom.

Profanity is a sure sign of losing! Hat called.

When she returned from her shower, Hat was on her nightstand, and he had made himself comfortable.

Do you sleep? Julie sat down on the edge of her bed and stretched.

Hat turned to face her. *I'm a magical artifact that has existed for several thousand years. What do you think?*

I don't know. Julie shrugged. *I try not to make assumptions. Whenever I do, people call me 'speciesist,' which isn't a label I like.*

Trying to avoid prejudice and stereotypes, are you?

Exactly. Julie flicked a piece of lint from her nightgown. *All this is foreign to me, you know. The huge Nox house, all the fancy stuff at the PMA...it's not something I'm used to.*

Hat snorted. *Clearly.*

Hey, I didn't have a ton of stuff growing up, but that doesn't mean it was bad. Julie yawned and lay down on her side, stuffing a pillow under her head.

I'm sure Malcolm Nox would argue that luxuries are a big part of making life fun. Or at least bearable.

Maybe he would. Or maybe he would do better if he stood up to his bitchy girlfriend and did something with his life. Julie laughed. *My life might be a train wreck, but at least I'm trying.*

You got that first part right.

Hey! Julie shook her head. *I didn't ask to get drafted into the PMA and forced to do Kaplan's bidding on pain of death, you know.* She sighed. *Not that my life was all put together before the PMA.*

Admit it, Hat wheedled. *You're enjoying your new world.*

Maybe I would if the threat of decapitation wasn't hanging over my head. She tugged down her covers. *It's exhausting, you know.*

Hat said nothing.

Night, Hat. Julie crawled into bed and pulled the covers up to her shoulder.

Goodnight, Julie.

She closed her eyes and rolled over, and fell asleep almost instantly. She didn't see Hat turn into an old-fashioned custodian helmet and stand guard over her in the moonlight.

Genevieve's engine bellowed the next morning as Julie gunned it down the road, her knuckles white on the steering wheel. Her eyes darted to the speedometer, the needle twitching up to forty-five.

"Why did you let me sleep in?" she squawked.

The cute purple beret on the passenger seat twitched. *You were tired.*

Yeah, and now I'm late to the job that might kill me if I fail to perform!

You're not late, Hat pointed out. *You're just a little less early than you wanted.*

Julie slowed, tapped the brakes at a stop sign, squealed around a turn, and stomped on the accelerator. Genevieve surged forward, tires screaming.

Uh-oh. Hat spoke a second before the yip of a siren. *We've got company.*

Julie squinted into the rearview mirror, greeted by spinning blue lights. She gritted her teeth, slowing down marginally.

I told you this was a thirty zone, Hat grouched.

"You also stopped my phone from waking me at six like it was supposed to!" Julie barked aloud.

A smaller engine whined beside her, and Julie gasped, grabbing at the wheel as a smooth black sedan hissed and swished down the road. The siren behind her yowled as the cop passed her, pursuing the black sedan.

Julie felt her shoulders relax, though she did ease off the accelerator. *Crap. That was close.*

Maybe drive a little more carefully, Hat suggested.

No shit. Julie frowned. *Is it just me, or is this car getting a lot of attention from the cops?*

Girl, I've been in the Warehouse for years. How am I supposed to know?

Valid. Julie shrugged. *I'll have to ask Lillie. She did say something about being a hellion.*

They made it to the long Aether driveway in one piece, and to Julie's surprise, when she reached the palisade gate, it swung open. She drove forward, squinting at the mansion, which still had that fake, blurry look. A boom and the guardhouse were just past the gate. They pulled up at the boom and a hulking Aether elf with a suspicious bulge on his right hip came up to the car and tapped on the window.

Julie rolled it down. "Hey. I'm Taylor's coworker. Here to pick him up."

"It's her, Victor." Taylor brushed past the bulky elf and made for the passenger door, but Victor seized him by the arm.

Victor didn't let go. "Security protocol, Your Highness."

"Seriously?" Julie raised her eyebrows. She grabbed the purple beret and put it on her head.

Aether Elves are a little paranoid, Hat told her.

Clearly.

The Aether elf looked her up and down, then walked around Genevieve, inspecting her.

"My dude. What *are* you doing?" Julie demanded.

Victor glared. "Security check, ma'am."

She stared.

"Step out of the car, please, ma'am." Victor moved back.

"What are you gonna do, strip-search me?" Julie cracked the door.

"Just have to ask you some questions, ma'am."

"What, like, what are my intentions for your daughter?" Julie raised an eyebrow.

Good one. Hat snickered.

"Full name and surname. True name, if you please." Victor had produced a clipboard from somewhere.

"I'll tell you mine if you tell me yours."

Victor stared at her. "Victor Barkhands."

"Fine. Julie Meadows." Julie crossed her arms. "What do you want with Taylor?"

"Julie," Taylor groaned.

"I'm his security guard, ma'am. I want to keep him safe." Victor scribbled on his clipboard. "Destination?"

"Breakfast. Then recruiting." Julie tipped up her chin. "So, where are you from, Victor?"

"The Aether catacombs in Slovenia, ma'am."

"Slovenia, huh? Seems suspicious to me."

Not really. Aether Elves often live underground, and Slovenia has an extensive cave system that houses a whole Aether Elf colony, Hat told her.

"Does it?" Victor raised one eyebrow.

"Hey, sue me." Julie spread her hands. "I'm just trying to ensure you're not a spy for another family. You might be setting me up to do something stupid to a prince."

Victor sighed, lowering his clipboard. "My family has served the Woodskins for sixteen generations."

She shrugged. "Fine. If you're trying to protect Taylor, I'm happy to help you."

Victor gave her another long stare.

"Welcome to my life, Victor." Taylor huffed. "Can I go with her now?"

"As you wish, Your Highness." Victor stalked off.

Taylor scrambled into Genevieve and slammed the door as Julie joined him. "What were you playing at?" he demanded.

"Oh, just giving old Vicky a hard time." Julie turned the car around.

"*Why?*"

"Why not? He was treating you like a prisoner."

Taylor grimaced. "It's not as bad as my older siblings have it. The Crown Prince hardly ever gets to leave the compound."

"I still don't think it's fair." Julie accelerated gratefully down the drive. "So, where do you want to go for breakfast?"

"I have no idea." Taylor turned faintly gray. "I don't get out much."

Julie grinned. "Then I'm taking you to the best breakfast in the city."

Taylor stared at the cardboard container Julie shoved into his hands. "What's this?"

Julie led him to a bench in the small, scruffy Brooklyn Park. The food truck stood on the corner. Sweet, creamy, fatty aromas gloriously filled the air surrounding it. She raised her cardboard container to her nose and sniffed deeply, then answered. "I told you. This is the best breakfast in the city."

"Yes, but what *is* it?" Taylor picked up his plastic fork as they sat down and prodded the monstrosity.

"It's a Belgian waffle with cream, strawberries, fudge, syrup, caramel bits, and nuts. You're not allergic to nuts, are you?"

"Nuts are the ancestral food of my people." Taylor sniffed at it. "I've never had...street food."

"You have not lived." Julie shoveled a heaping forkful of her waffle into her mouth and groaned with pleasure.

Do you want to know how many calories that contains? Hat queried.

No. I do not want to know. Julie took another bite for good measure.

You should know. You're not going to live forever, you know. That's diabetes on a plate, Hat protested.

Shhh. Julie filled her mouth with heaven.

Taylor scooped up a forkful and nibbled suspiciously. His eyes widened. "Wow," he moaned with his mouth full.

"Right?" Julie laughed. "Good, isn't it?"

Taylor took a huge bite, leaving his upper lip smeared with whipped cream. His eyes closed in ecstasy.

Julie let him enjoy most of the waffle in silence before she got down to business. "Okay, let's get one thing out of the way. I screwed up with the kelpie yesterday."

Taylor shrugged, dabbing at his upper lip with a paper napkin. "That doesn't matter now. We need to get to work on the others. Who do you want to go after first, the Were or the orc?"

"Who seems like the surest bet to you?" Julie asked. She sighed, her appetite waning as nausea lurched in her belly. "I only have until tomorrow. Wait..." She tensed. "How does the paperwork work? Does it take a long time?"

"I don't know," Taylor admitted. "I've, uh, never signed anyone." He was graying again.

"What? How long have you been recruiting for the PMA?"

Taylor shrugged. "A year?"

Julie rubbed a hand over the back of her neck. "I don't have that luxury."

Taylor looked away. "I know. Hat, you've got to know how the paperwork goes."

Don't worry, Hat reassured. *It doesn't take long. They just need to sign the form in the files you've got there, Julie. It's a magical form they can't touch if they're under the influence of mind-controlling magic, like mesmerization. They can sign it themselves, or if they're too young, their guardians have to sign on their behalf. Then it needs to be uploaded to the database in the PMA.*

"Okay." Julie's shoulders slouched, and she put her waffle to one side. "Wait, why would you sign a minor? What's a kid going to do in the PMA?"

"Legal majority age varies from species to species," Taylor

explained. "Take your friend Malcolm Nox, for example. He's not of age yet, even though he's forty-five."

"Forty-five!" Julie blinked. "He doesn't look a day over nineteen."

Taylor shrugged. "Don't even ask how old *I* am."

Julie didn't want to know. "So, if I wanted to sign Malcolm, I'd have to get Julius to sign on his behalf?"

That's a good summary, Hat admitted. *You're not brainless.*

"Thanks. I think."

"That was a compliment I never thought I'd hear," Taylor added.

I was talking to the lady. Hat sniffed. *The jury's still out on you.*

Taylor scoffed and rose to his feet, then tossed the empty container into a nearby garbage can. "To get back to your earlier question, Julie, I think it's best we start with the Were. The orc might be harder to convince. Sounds like he's a tough guy."

"Oh, great." Julie huffed and threw out her half-eaten waffle. She hurried over to Genevieve. "I'm going to be outclassed in both strength and beauty."

As usual, Hat snarked.

CHAPTER THIRTEEN

The GPS led them deep into the heart of Staten Island suburbia. As Genevieve rolled down a wide street shaded by trees with delicate green spring leaves, Julie peered at the elegant family homes on either side. They were surrounded by green lawns and broad sidewalks, with people walking dogs or babies in strollers. Giggling kids bounced on a trampoline outside one house.

"This place is nice."

Taylor glanced around. "Better than Brooklyn, anyway."

"Hey, I like my home!"

Taylor raised his eyebrows. "You live in *Brooklyn?*"

"You're saying it like it's a slum or something."

Taylor shrugged.

"I grew up here." Julie gestured around her.

"What? Really?"

"Not in this part of Staten Island, obviously." Julie laughed. "I grew up in West Brighton. Not quite in the projects, but not far from them, either."

"Oh." Taylor stared at the houses like he didn't know what to say.

"Weird to meet part of the 99%, huh?" Julie teased.

He grinned sheepishly. "I'm sorry. I don't mean to be snobbish or anything."

"You're not." She laughed. "Just a little weird."

They left the suburbs behind and passed several shopping centers before they reached an old, run-down mall. The building was surrounded by danger tape, chain-link panels, and KEEP OUT: CONSTRUCTION signs. Julie parked Genevieve across the street, and she and Taylor sat looking at the building.

"Why are they demolishing it?" she asked. "It looks good on the outside."

"They're not," Hat explained. "They're knocking down the interior walls. Turning it into a parking garage for a new mall they're building."

"Oh." Julie wiped her damp palms on her tasteful purple slacks.

"How are we going to get in?" Taylor peered at a temporary office that had been erected at the corner of the lot. A burly man in a hard hat stood at the door, arms folded, talking to a couple of gawking teenagers. He gestured sharply, sending them on their way.

Julie rubbed her chin. "I think I have an idea." She took off the purple beret. "Hey, Hat, can you turn into a hard hat?"

"A *what?*" Hat snorted.

"A hard hat. Like that one." She pointed to the site manager, or whatever he was.

"Ugh. So blue-collar." Hat sighed.

"Come on. For me?"

"Okay, fine." *Poof.* Julie held a plastic yellow hard hat exactly like those worn by the builders moving around the site. With a second, smaller *poof*, a big pink heart appeared on the front.

"Dude! Why?" Julie groaned. "Stop it."

"It's bad enough that I have to be a hard hat. I might as well be a fun one," Hat retorted.

"Whatever." Julie donned Hat and pushed the door open. "We'll have to find you one, Taylor."

"Leave that to me." Taylor grinned.

They crossed the street, and Julie threw back her shoulders, strutting across the street with all the sass she could muster. She strode up to the site manager as he was about to return to the office.

"Excuse me, sir," she barked. "We're here to see Sheila Johnson."

The manager raised an eyebrow, his eyes dwelling on Hat. "You are...?"

"That's irrelevant." Julie tipped up her chin. "We need to come in. Now." Out of the corner of her eye, she saw a hard hat lift itself from a pile at the corner of the office and float gently toward Taylor's outstretched hand.

The manager sighed. "Ma'am, this is a demolition site. No one's coming in."

Julie's heart fluttered. Was this going to be another repeat of the kelpie? Was she going to walk away from this in defeat, too? The pressure of time slipped past her. Seconds slid against her skin, and—

"I don't think you want to stand in our way." The deep, important voice behind her made her jump. She gaped as Taylor stepped forward, flashing his PMA ID badge too quickly to see it.

The manager's eyes widened. "Who are you people?"

"Let's just say you don't want to cross us." Taylor brushed a hand over his hip like he was armed. "We need to speak to Ms. Johnson immediately."

"Why are you here?" The manager stepped back. "What's she done?"

"Nothing wrong," Julie chipped in quickly. "It's important that we see her at once."

"What's all this about?" the manager demanded.

"That's classified information." Taylor tucked his ID inside his well-cut black jacket. "Now, do you want to obstruct our investigation, or are you going to cooperate?"

The manager was sweating. "I-I didn't know..."

"I suggest you fetch Sheila Johnson. Immediately," Taylor barked.

"Okay. Okay. I'll...I'll be right back." The manager turned and scurried into the construction site, glancing nervously over his shoulder as he went.

"Thank you." Julie's shoulders slumped. "Where did that even come from, anyway?"

Taylor shrugged, his cheek twitching to stifle a smile. "Being important is just acting. That's all royalty is, acting."

"I thought you weren't important," Julie teased.

"I'm not." Taylor's shoulders sagged, and he looked away.

"I'm sorry." Julie bit her lip. "I didn't mean..."

Taylor's carefree smile bounced easily back. "Of course not."

Well, this is awkward, Hat commented.

Before Julie could say something, a woman strode to them. She was head and shoulders taller than Julie and wore a sleeveless coverall that revealed rippling muscles under deep bronze skin. Her brown eyes were large and soft, and she moved with heavy, powerful grace. Those eyes rested on Taylor for a few moments longer than necessary, then darted to Julie.

"What's all this?" She frowned at Julie.

"Are you Sheila Johnson?" Taylor asked.

The woman regarded him, taking her time traveling up and down his slender figure. "Yes."

Julie held up her PMA ID. "We just want to talk to you for a moment."

Sheila's eyebrows rose. "You're human."

That's getting old. "I just need a few moments of your time," Julie said aloud.

Sheila shrugged amiably. "Okay."

"Can we talk somewhere private?" Julie suggested.

"Not too far. The boss won't be happy if I disappear."

"We could just stand by the car." Taylor gestured. "No one will overhear us there."

They crossed the street, and Taylor leaned against Genevieve, watching as Julie turned to Sheila. Before she could speak, though, the burly Were gave her a curious look up and down. "Seriously. Are you really from the PMA? Are you really human?"

"Yes, I am." Julie sighed. "It's not that shocking, you know."

"Actually, I've never even heard of a human being in the PMA." Sheila blinked. "Is she really human?" She turned to Taylor.

Taylor gave her a winning smile. "Oh, yes. As human as they come. They're trying something new." He grimaced.

Amazing how she thinks he'd know your species better than you do. Hat snickered.

Shhh. I've got to concentrate, Julie hissed.

"Trying something new?" Sheila asked. "What do you mean?"

Julie interrupted. "I'll get right to it." *I don't have time not to.* "Sheila, we're recruiters for the Para-Military Agency, and we thought you would be an excellent candidate."

Sheila's eyebrows shot up. "Me? In the PMA?" She folded her arms, biceps bulging. "I'm not sure."

"We feel you have the potential to be so much more than a blue-collar worker." Julie smiled. "You have strengths the PMA needs."

A little flattery went a long way. Sheila unfolded her arms. "I'm listening, but I like my job."

"Maybe you do, but what does it pay you?" Julie fished for the recruitment form and held it out, trying to stop her hand from shaking. She tapped the figure at the bottom of the page. "I'm sure this would be a much better income for you."

Sheila sucked in a breath and ran a hand over the back of her neck. "That *is* a lot better, but, well, I'm not much of a fighter."

"We will provide training, of course." Julie took a deep breath and forced her smile to stay in place.

"Yeah, well. I don't know if you can train someone to be a fighter if they just aren't." Sheila shifted her weight from one giant foot to the other.

She looks like she could run through a brick wall, never mind a rebel troop. Hat laughed. *What does she mean, she's not a fighter?*

"PMA agents are more than fighters," Taylor added. "They're keepers of the peace."

"I don't always know about that." Sheila glanced at the demolition site. "You're not wrong, though. I feel...stuck."

"Maybe this would give you the sense of purpose you've been looking for," Julie suggested.

"Maybe." Sheila gave a short, rumbling laugh. "I'm sorta shocked that anyone would ask *me*." Her eyes darted to Taylor again, her cheeks reddening.

Why? You must be two hundred pounds of muscle. Julie decided against saying it.

Taylor smiled so his eyes crinkled and then spoke. "You would be a huge asset to the PMA. I know you would."

"Okay. Look, I've got to get back to work, and I'm just not sure." Sheila's eyes were glued to Taylor. "I want to think about it. Maybe you could give me a card?"

Julie's heart plummeted, and she patted her pockets. A card! Why hadn't she thought to take one?

Taylor made an elaborate movement with his right wrist, and a card materialized in his palm. Sheila's giggle was disproportionately high-pitched as she took it. "Aren't you a talented man?"

"Not as talented as you would be as a PMA agent," Taylor purred.

"I'll be in touch," Sheila simpered.

"I'm counting on it." Taylor winked.

Tittering again, Sheila strode across the street, and Hat burst out laughing in Julie's head. *"I'm counting on it?"* He chortled.

"Oh, shut up." Taylor turned gray. "It worked, didn't it?"

"Hey, no argument from me." Julie held up her hands. "The Captain did say to promise *whatever* we need to."

"I'm not a piece of man-meat!" Taylor argued.

Julie opened the driver's door. "Debatable."

"Besides," Hat added, "you could do far worse than a six-foot gentle giant."

Taylor shot Julie and Hat a glare. "This prince is not in the market for a Princess Charming right now, thanks."

"Why not? You definitely need to be rescued from your dark tower," Julie teased.

Taylor snorted. "Cut that out and let's get lunch and then look for this orc of yours. I'm not going to be bait for any more recruits, okay?"

Julie slipped into the driver's seat and typed the address into her phone's GPS. "It's a shame. While I'm not willing to get on the pole yet, I'm willing to let you dance if it helps." Her cheeks blazed, and she clapped her hand over her mouth. "Did I say that out loud?"

Taylor doubled over, chuckling.

CHAPTER FOURTEEN

Taylor pulled out a smartphone as they drove away. "This time, I'm picking our lunch spot."

"Wait, you didn't like breakfast?" Julie stared. "You have a phone?"

"Of course I have a phone. This is the twenty-first century." Taylor was calmly typing.

"I thought paras weren't allowed to connect to the internet for security reasons."

"Oh, we're not allowed on social media as paranormals." Taylor grinned. "As long as we keep the conversation strictly human, we can use the internet like anyone else. All I want to do is put in the address for a nice lunch spot outside Brooklyn."

"I looked you up on Facebook but couldn't find you anywhere."

"Oh, you were Facebook stalking me?" Taylor looked up from his phone.

"Not like that." Julie gave him a playful shove.

"Well, I can't very well use my Aether Elven name, can I?" Taylor set down the phone. "Anyway, you're going to love this little place."

"In six hundred feet, turn left," announced the GPS.

"Fine." Julie leaned back, clenching her fists on the steering wheel. "I'm not sure I have much of an appetite, anyway."

"You made good progress with Sheila." Taylor smiled. "You never know. She might sign before tomorrow afternoon."

"Yeah, but I can't count on that." Julie rolled her neck and worked the tight knots from her shoulders. "I definitely can't stake my life on it."

The GPS guided Julie over the bridge and back into Brooklyn, stopping in the parking lot of a little restaurant overlooking Lower Bay. Julie looked around in appreciation as Taylor led her inside. It was decorated in sea blues and greens and dotted with rusty anchors and old cannons, each with a historical plaque beside it. The salty smell of fresh fish filled the air.

"Stacy's Seafood," Taylor announced, leading Julie to a balcony overlooking the beach.

"I'm surprised you're familiar with the Brooklyn dining scene." Julie sat down, trying not to think about how late it was. *One and a half days left.*

Taylor grinned. "There's a lot about me that may surprise you."

A portly woman distributed menus and garlic rolls. Taylor munched his with energy, and Julie sipped water, looking at the menu without interest. "I'll just have whatever you're having."

"Come on, Julie." Taylor nudged the menu toward her. "It's going to be okay. We'll get someone."

"We'll have to." Julie put Hat on the table and ran a hand through her hair. "I should have brought that orc's file to look over it."

"You've already memorized it," Taylor pointed out. "You know what to tell him."

She nodded. "I'll draw attention to his boxing skills. Tell him there's a way to use them for good. Better than gambling money, anyway."

"Exactly." Taylor shrugged. "Hey, if all else fails, you could just draft someone."

"That's an option?" Julie raised an eyebrow.

"Of course it is."

"I thought I wasn't allowed to compel anyone. They're supposed to sign of their own free will."

Technically, so were you, Hat chipped in. *Then you turned out to be human.*

"That makes no sense." Julie shook her head. "How can drafting someone still allow them to use their free will?"

"Well..." Taylor grimaced. "Like Hat said, if you'd been a Fae or a Were or an orc or anything but human, Kaplan technically couldn't have forced you to become a recruiter."

Julie stared at him.

The drafting was a smokescreen, Hat explained. *They wanted to scare people into coming into the PMA for breakfast so recruiters could make their pitches. Kaplan was desperate.*

"So everyone keeps telling me." Julie ran a hand over her face. "So you're saying that if I'd just tossed that letter in the garbage, none of this would ever have happened?"

Taylor winced. "Yeah. Sorry."

Julie stared out at the rippling sea. If only she'd thrown away that letter, the threat of her "termination" wouldn't be hanging over her head. She'd be safe in her apartment, reading something. With no idea that elves and orcs existed. No idea that Lillie owned a muscle car named Genevieve. She'd have no idea that there were talking hats, vampires, or elf princes in her world.

"You okay?" Taylor peered at her.

"I'm fine." Julie squared her shoulders. "Just thinking."

"We could easily type and print a fake draft notice. You could send it this afternoon, get some people in for breakfast tomorrow morning," Taylor suggested.

It would take me ten minutes, Hat offered. *I could do it right now.*

Julie shook her head before he finished the sentence. "This

drafting bullshit is nothing more than a timeshare marketing plan. I will no way and no how cheat people into making this decision like I was!"

Even if it is your life? Hat asked.

Julie snorted. "I'm in this pickle because the trolls 'drafted' me. It's dishonest, and it's wrong. I won't do this to someone else."

"Paras wouldn't be obligated to be mind-wiped like you are." Taylor held up his hands. "They could just walk away."

"No." Julie shook her head violently. "I'm not going to scare and lie to people. It's wrong."

The waitress arrived with the sodas they'd ordered. Taylor asked for calamari and fries. "Same for me," Julie muttered.

When the waitress had left, Taylor leaned across the table toward her. "Do you *want* to be terminated?" he hissed.

Julie popped open the can and poured her soda into her glass to keep her hands busy. "I think people should join the PMA for the right reasons, whether from loyalty to their ideals or because they want to learn or grow. Not because someone 'drafted' them and coerced them."

Took Julius seriously, didn't you? Hat chuckled.

"Julius?" Taylor frowned. "What's he talking about?"

"I'll tell you later." Julie sighed. "Taylor, I don't want to be terminated, but I'd rather that happen than some poor idiot get suckered into joining the PMA and killed in the line of duty or whatever because of *my* bad ethics. I wasn't brought up to do shit like that."

Clearly, Hat commented.

Taylor sat back, ignoring his soda. She felt his dark eyes on her and dropped her gaze to the table.

It was a long time before Taylor spoke. "For what it's worth, that's refreshing."

"What is?" Julie grumbled.

"Your morality." Taylor finally unfroze and poured his own

soda, putting the plastic straw aside. "In the royal lines, you're taught to think like that from the day you're born."

"Think like what?"

"Like a power-grabbing ass." Taylor sighed. "We're taught that we're entitled to whatever we want. If something doesn't fall into our laps, we're supposed to take it by any means necessary. Maintaining the family's power is the priority of our existence."

"Why aren't you a total dick, then?" Julie countered.

Taylor smirked. "Was that a compliment?"

Coming from Julie, probably, Hat teased.

"Just answer the question," Julie huffed.

Taylor shrugged. "Sixth in line, remember? My other siblings had all the attention. So by the time my tutors and parents got to me, they were happy to let me watch the morning cartoons as long as I didn't cause any trouble."

"So you became an expert at not causing trouble," Julie guessed.

"Invisibility would be my superpower."

"Wait, so you *can't* turn invisible?" Julie placed a hand over her heart in mock amazement.

Taylor snorted. "No, but I'm good at staying under the radar. Until I was saddled with a troublesome little human, that is."

The arrival of some truly excellent calamari brought a sharp end to that conversation.

An hour later, Julie squeezed Genevieve between two ancient, beat-up sedans and peered through the window. "Is this it?"

"Yep." Taylor glanced at the shady butcher shop. "This is it."

"It's not much," Hat observed.

Julie couldn't help agreeing with him, even though she felt more at home in this part of Brooklyn than in Stacy's Seafood.

The narrow street was crowded with buildings. Some soared high above them. Others, like the row of shops on their left, squatted together as if for safety. Graffiti was splashed against the nearest alley and was the only real color on the street. On a litter-strewn sidewalk, a homeless man was curled up on a piece of cardboard, gazing at the world with jaundiced eyes that seemed to be staring into another dimension.

Julie stepped from the car and flipped him a dollar. He barely noticed.

"Here." Taylor gripped Julie's arm protectively. "There's the butcher shop."

"Let me go." Julie shook him off. "I don't need a bodyguard."

"Sorry." Taylor grayed. "It's just, this place is…"

"Like home," Julie snapped. "It's just like where I live."

Taylor's face was pale, and he dropped his eyes to the sidewalk. "Sorry."

Our little prince is out of his depth here. Hat snorted.

Just a little. Julie gave Taylor a sharp look. He didn't give the beggar anything.

Take it easy, Mother Teresa. He's rattled, Hat told her.

Why are you defending him? Julie demanded.

I'm not. I'm just saying that he doesn't get out much. Hat chuckled. *Not like some of us.*

You're one to talk. You've spent the last who knows how many years in a warehouse.

"What are you two talking about?" Taylor hissed.

"Nothing." Julie looked up at the sign over the grimy storefront. "Rossini Meats," she read.

"Stan Rossini." Taylor glanced at the file. "That sounds about right."

"Okay, then." Squaring her shoulders, Julie stepped inside.

The butcher shop was empty. Large display fridges hummed along the sides of the tiny shop, handwritten signs proclaiming low prices. Behind the counter, Julie caught a glimpse through an open cold room door of whole carcasses hanging from meat hooks. The place smelled of raw meat, salt, and spices.

"Hello?" Julie called, making Taylor jump.

A massive creature came plodding from the cold room with a heavy grunt. No amount of fantasy movies could have prepared Julie for the appearance of Stan Rossini. His stooped shoulders were broad enough that his grubby white t-shirt strained to cover them. A bloody apron stretched over his broad belly, and he carried a side of ham in one hand and a butcher knife in the other. The blade glimmered in the faint sunlight filtering through the dirty windows.

Scared? Hat mocked.

Julie ignored him, taking slow breaths as Stan hung up the ham and leaned on the counter, putting down the enormous knife. The orc's bare arms were covered with tattoos. The most prominent one, on his left bicep, showed a caricature of Tolkien with a red circle and slash obscuring the author's face.

Sacrilege, Julie thought.

Hey, you can't blame orcs for disliking their depiction in his books, Hat pointed out.

Of course, he didn't know they were real. Julie would defend her favorite writer to the death.

She raised her gaze to the orc's face, which was chiseled with high cheekbones. His eyes burned gold.

"How can I help you today?" he asked in a rich, round New York accent.

It was the last thing Julie had been expecting him to say. She stammered for a few moments before words came out. "Uh, good afternoon. Actually, we're not here to shop. We're here to talk to you."

Stan's eyes narrowed as they rested on Taylor. "Are you PMA?"

"Yes, we are." Julie fished her ID out and showed it to him.

"Well, I've done nothing wrong, and I didn't see nothing." Stan picked up the knife again. "So unless you want some lamb chops or ground beef, I suggest you all just piss off."

"We're not agents." Julie forced a grin. "We're recruiters. According to your file, Mr. Rossini, you'd make a perfect PMA agent."

Stan rumbled a laugh. "Me? In the PMA? You're wasting your time, lady."

"You're one of the best amateur boxers in the city," Julie insisted.

"Yeah, well, it's not difficult to beat humans." Stan raised an eyebrow as he glanced at her, then picked up the ham, slammed it down on a marble slab, and began carving it. The knife ran through the chilled meat like it was butter.

"Still. Your skills could be an asset to the PMA and Eternity Throne." Julie stepped forward.

"Eternity Throne?" Stan snorted. "What have the Lunar Fae ever done for me? What did they do for my grandpa when he came up from the Amazon, chasing the American Dream, and got gunned down by vamps in his own store?"

"You could change that," Julie replied. "You could be an agent that looks out for your own people."

"No. I couldn't." Stan slammed the knife into the ham again. "Agents are just puppets for the PMA. I'm not interested in politics. Leaders come, leaders go. Real people like me just have to look out for ourselves."

"Whatever you believe, you can't argue with the salary." Taylor showed Stan the figure on the signing form.

Stan snorted. "A pretty little number, to be sure, but what's that number going to do for me one day when Her Majesty kicks the bucket and we're plunged into a dynastic war? I'd rather be here in the shop than stuck in the military when that happens, thanks."

"That could be decades away," Taylor shot back. "This contract is only for three years."

"Sure." Stan barked a laugh. "If something happens in the next three years, you're stuck until the dynasty changes, or you're dead. Thanks, but no thanks."

The orc turned away and started packaging the sliced-up ham in a plastic bag. Julie stepped forward. "You could improve your military training," she attempted. "It could change your life."

"It could *end* my life," snapped Stan. He shoved the end of the bag into a vacuum sealer and turned back to them as the buzz of the machine filled the air. "Give it up, lady. You're wasting your time."

What he doesn't know is if he doesn't sign, it could end my life. Julie sighed.

"Come on, Julie." Taylor gripped her elbow and steered her toward the door, shooting a last glance at Stan. "This is a lost cause," he added loudly.

"Don't," Julie grouched. "It's not his fault."

They stepped outside, and Taylor glanced nervously at Genevieve like he'd half expected her to be gone. He ran a hand through his hair as they trudged to the car. "We'll find another candidate."

I'm already running a search, Hat told them. *We can go back to the PMA and assemble a few more files for tomorrow.*

"Tomorrow is the last day I've got." Julie slipped into the driver's seat, gripped the steering wheel, and leaned her forehead against it with a groan.

"A lot can happen in a day." Taylor got in. "We'll get someone. We'll just have to."

"Yeah." Julie sighed. "You've got that right." She blinked away the exhaustion stinging her eyes and started Genevieve, then drove back toward Staten Island in the thickening traffic. Pink came on the radio, and Julie turned it loud. The car was filled with the thudding beat, and nobody said a word.

The afternoon's frantic research had yielded only one measly file. When she glanced in the rearview mirror, Julie saw it lying in the backseat. It was just an ordinary file with a photograph of a strikingly gorgeous blonde girl paper-clipped to the front, and it was hard to believe that it held her last hope of survival.

Julie stifled a yawn as she stopped Genevieve outside the Aether Compound gate. Taylor got out, then paused to peer at her. "Hey, are you okay to drive home?"

"I'm fine. Just—tired." Julie rubbed her temples. "We've got to sign someone tomorrow, Taylor."

"We will. I mean, DumbleDork uncovered a hive of Fae at that fashion modeling agency." Taylor grinned. "One of them will definitely want to join up. Her whole family served the Eternity Throne. It's in her blood."

"Don't look so excited about visiting a hive of Fae models." Julie winked.

Taylor grayed, grinning sheepishly. "Whatever. I'll see you at six tomorrow morning?"

"Six?" Julie raised her eyebrows. "Look at you, taking initiative and everything."

"Yeah, whatever." Taylor shook his head.

"Six it is," Julie agreed. "See you."

Traffic thickened as Julie drove toward Brooklyn. She pulled off the purple beret and gently placed him on the passenger seat, where he shuffled around, getting comfortable. "Now, that was a long day. I haven't been on a head all day in a while."

"Get used to it." Julie sighed. "Or don't. I might not have a head to put you on anymore by tomorrow night."

"Don't say that." Hat bounced around to face her. "You're going to sign someone tomorrow. I know you are."

"I'd better." Julie squeezed the wheel, crawling over the bridge after a long train of cars. Honking horns surrounded them. "I don't know what my mom would do if I failed," she murmured.

"I wouldn't worry about that just yet," Hat offered. "You've still got time."

"Yeah. Well." Julie reached for the radio and flipped through the channels until she found a suitably angry rock number playing and turned it up to the top.

You know that's not going to shut me up, right? Hat informed her.

Not now, Hat. Julie groaned, and he fell silent.

Genevieve's speakers still thudded when she turned down her street. She turned the volume down as she pulled into the garage, but the back door was open, and blue light from the TV flickered in Lillie's living room.

"Let's say hi to Lillie," Julie muttered, pulling on Hat.

He wisely remained silent as she locked Genevieve, closed the garage door, and went up to the living room. She popped her head inside and saw Lillie slumped on the couch, lighting up another cigarette as usual.

"Hey, Lillie," she called over the cacophony of the TV.

Lillie reached for the remote and muted the sound, looking up at Julie. She grinned. "Hi, sweetie. You have a nice day at work?"

"Yeah, it was fine," Julie lied. "Do you want me to fix you something for dinner?"

"Oh, I'm okay, dear." The paper-thin skin of Lillie's brow furrowed. "Are you okay? You look peaky."

Julie managed a faint smile. "I just had a long day, that's all."

"It's an adjustment, starting a new job," Lillie soothed. "Are you home this weekend?"

I might not be alive this weekend. Julie pushed the thought away. "Yeah, I guess so."

"Oh, lovely. Well, why don't we do something fun?" Lillie's eyes crinkled with her grin.

Julie smiled. "Why not? What did you have in mind?"

"Maybe we could have a nice dinner." Lillie's eyes strayed to the chaotic kitchen. "I could clean everything up, and we'll set the table, and we could cook something nice."

"Here's a deal for you. I'll help you clean up the kitchen, and then I'll order something delicious, and you can pick a movie."

Lillie's eyes lit up. "That sounds wonderful, dear. Saturday night, then?"

"Saturday night," Julie agreed. "Sleep tight, Lillie."

"Sweet dreams, Julie."

She dragged herself up the stairs to her room, put Hat on the kitchen table while she boiled the kettle, and started assembling some pasta for dinner. Hat was quiet for an uncharacteristically long time.

"Hey, you still alive?" Julie quipped.

"Yes." Hat sniffed. "I thought you wanted me to be quiet."

"Sorry. I'm just tired and stressed." Julie poured boiling water over the pasta and turned on the burner. "I'll feel better in the morning."

"Lillie seems nice," Hat offered.

"Oh, yeah. She's cool. Cooler than I thought." Julie laughed. "I wonder what she'll pick for the movie on Saturday."

Hat chuckled. "Something tells me it won't be *The Sound of Music*."

"Yeah, me too." Julie yawned. "I'm looking forward to it. Assuming I'm still alive on Saturday, that is."

The implication hung over her head like a guillotine. She prodded at the pasta with a wooden spoon. Hat was conspicuously silent, and Julie reached for her phone.

Hat stirred. "What are you doing?"

"I'm going to call my mom."

"I thought you came to the city to escape your mom."

Julie shot Hat a sharp look. "That doesn't mean I don't love her, you know." She scrolled through her phone, realizing she'd forgotten to answer the last few texts from her mother. A twinge of guilt prickled the pit of her stomach. She tapped on her mom's contact and pressed the phone to her ear.

Rosa answered on the first ring. *"Juliiiaaaaaa!* Honey! It's so wonderful to hear from you!"

Julie gritted her teeth. Rosa's voice, as usual, sliced through her brain like a missile. "Hey, Mom."

"How are you doing? How's the new job?" Rosa fired a new round of questions. "Made any new friends yet?"

Julie laughed uneasily. "I guess. My partner is nice."

"Tell me everything, darling!"

Julie rubbed the bridge of her nose. "You know, Mom, I'm tired. I don't want to talk about work right now."

"Oh, okay. Is everything okay at work, honey?" Rosa's voice softened.

Julie sank into her chair at the kitchen table, staring at the wall. No, it's not okay. I don't know if I'll ever see you again because if I don't achieve my goals at work, I'll die.

"Julia? Hello? You there?"

"Yes. Sorry. I think I lost connection for a minute there." Julie forced a smile into her voice. "Yeah, work's fine. Anyway, tell me about your day. How's Ernesto?"

"He's wonderful as always, honey. You know, you should come over this weekend. I think you and Ernesto can work things out if you spend more time together." Rosa laughed. "He loves reading, too, you know."

"Mom, there's nothing to work out. Things are fine between Ernesto and me."

"You've always seemed so resistant about him, Julie."

"I guess I've never been ready to let go of Dad." Julie swallowed the rising lump in her throat.

"Well, sweetheart, why don't you ever come to the cemetery?"

The question brought Julie up short. She picked at a piece of peeling paint on the table.

"I should go," she decided. "You're right."

"What?" Rosa teased. "Me, Rosa Hernandez? I'm *right?*"

Julie huffed. "Cut it out, Mom."

"Okay, okay. Why don't you come to the cemetery with me on Saturday morning? I'm going anyway. We could have lunch afterward. Or dinner."

"I have dinner plans." Julie bit her lip. "Lunch sounds good, though." *If I'm still alive by Saturday.*

"Wonderful!" Rosa chirped. "I'm so excited! I'm going to order a new crate of aloe vera juice right now. I was reading up on it, and I think you should increase your daily intake, Julie. It's got all sorts of benefits that will help you in your new career..."

Julie opened her mouth to protest but sat still, listening to her mom's voice washing over her. The sound brought back memories from when she was a kid. Her mom was forever trying to make cough syrup from pineapples, or telling everyone she met about the healing properties of turmeric, but she was also always *there*. On the sidelines of every soccer game and debate competition, sitting across from Julie at the dinner table even on the nights when dinner was just sandwiches or ramen noodles, offering hugs and ice cream after teenage breakups.

Rosa was always there. Julie thought of Taylor and realized that she might count herself lucky to have a mother who was around enough to drive her crazy.

"And if this doesn't work out, the juice will still keep on improving your figure to the point where the pole still isn't an impossibility—"

"Hey, Mom?" Julie interrupted.

"What?"

Julie hesitated. "Is everything okay with you and Ernesto?"

"What? Yes, honey! Everything is fine. Why would you ask that?" Rosa squawked.

"Oh, nothing. Forget I asked." Julie cleared her throat. "What were you saying about the aloe vera juice?"

Rosa took the bait. "Oh, yes. It assists in weight loss, so…"

Julie got up and turned off the pasta, listening to her voice without hearing a single word. At least her mom had Ernesto.

So if it all went wrong tomorrow, she wouldn't be completely alone in this world.

CHAPTER FIFTEEN

"Sup, Victor." Julie rolled down her window and smirked at the tall elf. He was even more imposing in the pale dawn light.

Victor gave her one of his trademark impassive stares, then walked around Genevieve. Taylor, leaning against the guardhouse, caught Julie's eye and shrugged.

"Seriously, Victor." Julie poked her head out of the window. "What are you doing?"

"Security protocol, ma'am." Victor stepped back. "Kindly step out of the vehicle."

"You want my license and registration, too?" Julie sassed.

"You know back-chatting Victor only makes this process longer, right?" Taylor called.

"That won't be necessary, ma'am," deadpanned Victor.

Julie got out, held out her arms, and spun slowly. "See? Same as yesterday. Still Julie Meadows, still Taylor's coworker."

"Please sign here." Victor held out the clipboard.

"Don't you think Taylor can sign himself in and out?" Julie scribbled on the page anyway. "He's not a package, you know."

"Actually, that's what they call me on the few occasions I've been moved around in high-risk situations." Taylor sauntered past and opened the passenger door. "'The package.' As in, 'the package is secure.'"

"Really?" Julie patted Victor on the shoulder. "Can't you come up with something more original?"

"Don't touch him," Taylor called from the passenger seat. "He doesn't like it."

"It goes against protocol." Victor took the clipboard. "Destination?"

"More breakfast. More recruiting. Are we going to do this every day?" Julie stifled a fake yawn.

"Yes, we are, ma'am." Victor wrote on the clipboard. "Be safe, Your Highness."

However will he do that without Victor to protect him? Hat simpered.

Julie was still chuckling at him as she got back into Genevieve and drove away. "He's so funny," she told Taylor. "He practically begs to be mocked."

"I know. You can imagine the jokes we used to make when we were kids. There are six of us, after all." Taylor shook his head. "Victor's a good guy, though. Just..."

"Robotic?" Julie suggested.

"Yeah."

"His military record is exemplary," Hat informed them. "He wasn't wrong when he said his family had been serving the Aether royals for generations. Pity he's so boring."

"Maybe he isn't." Julie grinned. "I thought Lillie was boring too." She patted Genevieve's dashboard, then sighed. "We have a dinner and movie date for tomorrow if I make it to tomorrow."

"You're going to." A lump rose in his throat.

"Yeah, depending on if I get a recruit or not." Julie shifted in her seat. "Either I'll have a big check, or Kaplan will have decapitated me by the end of today."

"Oh, I spoke to Kaplan." Taylor held up his phone. "He called to ask what we'd been doing yesterday since he didn't see us around the office."

Julie winced. "Is he mad?"

"Mad? Oh, no. I think he was sort of impressed, to be honest."

"Impressed?" Julie stared at him. "*Kaplan?*"

"He growled something about how he was happy we weren't 'goofing around like a bunch of IT trolls,'" Taylor told her. "Something like that. Hard to tell with all the snarling."

"Well, okay. That's good news." Julie rubbed her chin. "Hey, I keep meaning to ask you because I just can't figure it out. What kind of a Were is Kaplan?"

"Sorry." Taylor held up both hands. "Really, I am, but I'm not going to tell you without his permission."

"What? Is it speciesist or something?"

"Well, no. A little rude, though. But that's not why I won't tell you." Taylor grimaced. "Captain doesn't like his other form to be the only thing that defines him."

"Pretty sure his massive biceps, angry eyes, and short temper already define him," Julie retorted. "What he *is* would just help to explain it. Hat, help me out here."

"No, thank you." Hat sniffed. "I don't want to get 'terminated' either. You'll just have to find out for yourself."

"Fine. Kaplan can keep his secret for now." Julie made a right turn, heading for a food truck she'd seen on her way here. "Let's talk about that Fae hive we found yesterday."

"Give us the run-down again, Hat," Taylor instructed.

"Okay." Hat stirred, preparing himself. "Woodland Fae tend to congregate in hives until they form their family units. This particular hive is a group of young Fae who spend all of their time together. They live together, go out together, and they all work together at this modeling agency."

"Is the agency run by Fae?" Julie asked.

"No. It's human-run. They think they just got lucky to employ eight of the most beautiful people in New York City all at once." Hat chuckled.

"Beautiful?" Julie glanced at Hat in the rearview mirror. The wind was nippy today, and he was a fetching little beanie with a pom-pom on the top. "So, what good will they be in the agency?"

"All Fae are naturally gorgeous," Taylor told her. "It doesn't mean they can't be natural fighters or peacekeepers, either."

"Yeah, Julie," Hat mocked her. "Don't be so superficial."

Julie huffed at them both. "Yeah, yeah."

"The royal family has been Fae for two thousand years," Taylor reminded her. "The Lunar Fae are some of the smartest people around."

"What was Stan saying yesterday about the queen?" Julie asked. "Is she really old or something?"

"She's old. She's been on the throne for three hundred fifty years," Taylor explained.

"Wait… three hundred fifty?"

Taylor grinned. "Paras age differently, remember?"

Julie shook her head. "That's a long time to be in power. I bet she's sick of it."

"Seems like it, but she still has to choose a successor," Taylor told her.

"The Eternity Throne isn't strictly hereditary," Hat added. "Well, it can't be, not right now. The Lunar Fae are dying out. Except for the three that abdicated, obviously."

"Sounds like a whole lot of politics to me." Julie sighed. "I can see why Stan was so eager to stay out of it."

"Focus." Taylor rubbed his hands. "We're not thinking about grumpy old Stan today. We're going to get you a recruit."

"We're going to see some sexy Fae," Julie teased.

Taylor grinned. "Well, that *is* an added bonus."

Julie's phone buzzed in its holder. She glanced at it and a second text popped up on the screen as she did.

Hey baby! Have a nice day at work! Can't wait to see you this weekend! Love and miss you so much. Mom xoxo

"Who signs their name on a text?" Julie muttered, locking the phone. Her belly churned queasily. How would her mom find out if she was decapitated?

P. S. Remember to drink your extra aloe juice for performance and concentration-enhancing benefits!

"Who is that?" Taylor asked her. "A boyfriend?"
"Worse." Julie grimaced. "My mom."
"She texts you?" Taylor raised an eyebrow.
"What, doesn't your mom text you?" Julie countered.
"Well, we live in the same house." Taylor grimaced. "Sometimes she yells at me from her suite."

Julie laughed to cover the tension in her chest. *Would she be seeing her mom this weekend?*

She wished she knew.

Despite it all, a thrill ran through Julie as they headed into Manhattan. Here, the buildings that blotted out the sky on either side all had sharp, clean lines and shimmering windows. They reeked of affluence. Dog walkers with packs of designer mutts struggled down the sidewalks. Women in business gear, smoking expensive cigarettes, toted Calvin Klein handbags while they yelled at their personal assistants over the phone. The food trucks here were trendy and stylish instead of being run-down, with calligraphy on chalkboards instead of handwritten paper signs.

For once, when Julie brought Genevieve to a stop outside the glossy Manhattan building, the flashy Mustang didn't look out of place.

The parking lot was filled with sleek, shining cars, the likes of which Julie had never seen. She wasn't a car person, but she knew enough to recognize the little rearing horse emblem on the bright red sports car beside hers.

"That's a Ferrari, isn't it?" she asked.

"Never mind that." Taylor was practically drooling over a gleaming silver vehicle beside him. It was slung even lower than Genevieve, and its lines and curves were dangerous and irresponsible. "This is a Bugatti Chiron. It has more than three times the horsepower of your old girl."

"Hey!" Julie put a defensive hand on Genevieve's hood. "Watch it." She sniffed, tossing her head. "Genevieve can hear you. Besides, I bet we'd smoke that ugly modern monster, don't you, Genny?"

"You have no idea what you're talking about." Taylor laughed. "Come on. Let's go get you a recruit."

They walked up to one of the gleaming skyscrapers lining both sides of this elegant street. Julie could practically smell the money oozing from the building as they stepped inside. Its lobby was all plush and velvet, with exotic plants in the corners that would have made Julius Nox purr. The elevator played classical music when they stepped inside and checked the modeling agency's website address.

"Eleventh floor." Taylor looked up. "That's high."

Julie raised an eyebrow. "Don't like heights?"

"Aether Elves prefer being underground."

Julie hit the button. "I hope we're not going to fetch up in Switzerland this time."

Taylor laughed uneasily, and the elevator swished upward.

Julie opened her phone again, looking at the photos from the modeling agency. "Which Fae was it?"

That one. Second photo from the top, Hat told her. *The blonde girl.*

"She's more than blonde. She's drop-dead gorgeous." Julie guessed she could see the pointed ears and foxy features because of her genetic mutation. She was an impossibly tall and elegant young woman poised on a pedestal. She had her head turned to the side, with her lips parted, her expensively-curled strawberry-blonde hair cascading down her back.

"Mmm," Taylor murmured appreciatively. "I hope *she* joins up."

"Oh, stop it." Julie swatted him with the file. "We're here to recruit this…" she checked the name "Natalie Furfoot, not flirt with her."

Natalie Fergus, Hat corrected. *Remember to use her human name. The owner of the agency is a human.*

"We'll get her." Taylor nodded. "If we don't, we'll recruit one of the others. There's a whole hive of Fae here, remember?"

"Yeah, and they're all equally gorgeous." Julie scrolled through the website. "Gorgeous and, I'm willing to bet, super-rich."

"Judging by the cars we saw outside?" Taylor raised his eyebrows. "Yeah, their salaries probably make my trust fund payouts seem ordinary."

"I don't know about this." Julie tucked her hair underneath the beanie. "Look at these people, Taylor. They're extravagantly rich and wildly good-looking. They must have everything they could possibly want. What could the PMA possibly offer them? I know this Natalie's family were military, but maybe that gives her all the more reason not to want to join."

"You might be surprised." Taylor smiled faintly. "Money and looks aren't everything." His grin widened, and he smoothed down his hair. "I would know."

Julie chuckled. "Yeah, yeah." She sighed. "You're not wrong, though. I didn't grow up with much, but I guess I was happy."

"Then why were you so desperate for a job?" Taylor cocked his head.

"Well, I couldn't exactly just sponge off my parents," Julie pointed out. "Mom wouldn't let me go into debt to study unless I was sure about what I wanted to do. I just wasn't. All I've ever liked doing is reading." She shrugged. "I wanted to be left alone to read, that's all."

"Maybe having to step out into the world isn't such a bad thing." Taylor grinned. "You've forced me to do it, and worse things have happened to me."

Julie scoffed. "You're forgetting the part where you still have a choice."

"So, what would you want if you didn't have to be a recruiter?"

The elevator stopped, the doors opening with a genteel *ping*.

She would want to be left alone to read again, obviously, Hat chipped in.

"I don't know," Julie answered. "I don't care too much, as long as I don't have to drink aloe vera juice and dance on a pole."

"Wait, that was an option?" Taylor's eyes widened.

Julie slapped him with the file again. "Focus!"

"Okay, okay." Taylor cleared his throat as they walked down the hall to the door at the end, with a sign bearing the modeling agency's name. "So, what will we offer these people to get one of them into the PMA?"

"Purpose," Julie decided out loud.

A higher cause to serve, Hat suggested. *Something more important than themselves. It's our only chance.*

"Your pitch is to appeal to the unselfish side of a bunch of Woodland Fae working as models?" Taylor grimaced.

"What else am I supposed to do?" Julie retorted.

"It's the only idea we've got," he admitted.

They knocked on the door, which was answered by a plump, harassed, and human woman in a floral dress. She had huge, thick glasses with bright red frames and blinked at them. "Who are you?"

"Good morning, ma'am." Julie flashed her ID. "We're here to speak to Natalie Fergus."

"What's this about?" Her eyes narrowed.

Julie wavered, glancing at Taylor. *Time for the royal prince routine?* she wondered.

No. Wait, Hat instructed. *I'm scanning this woman's records. She was a model herself, but she quit after an eating disorder nearly killed her. She volunteers at a bunch of organizations supporting young women's mental health. I bet she'd be open to a different career path for some of these models.*

She's just a receptionist, Julie protested. *What if we go in there, and the manager or someone sees us and has us thrown out?*

Trust me and try it, Hat insisted.

Julie widened her smile and lowered her voice. "We're from a recruitment agency. We're looking for someone to join us to do good things in the world."

The woman glanced over her shoulder, then grinned. "Well, Mr. Russo won't like it, but he doesn't own these models, contrary to what he might think." She stepped back, holding the door wide. "They're taking a water break in the studio. I'll be in my office."

She disappeared down a side door, and Taylor and Julie stepped into a roomy studio. Its floor-to-ceiling windows looked out over a thatch of skyscrapers, and the snaking freeway below glimmered with cars. Taylor averted his eyes from the window, but Julie suspected this wasn't just because of his fear of heights. His gaze rested on the young women in the room.

Chairs were scattered in one corner of the studio, clustered around a mini-fridge and coffee table, and the chairs contained some of the most beautiful people Julie had ever seen. The photographs didn't do them justice. Fox-faced Natalie Fergus was there, running her fingers through her luxurious hair. Beside her was a girl with slender limbs and the giant, dark eyes of a doe.

The third girl sat on a chair near them. Even slumped over her phone, she was stunning.

Julie, for her part, tried not to stare at the three guys lounging opposite the girls. They were all wearing shorts and robes. The biggest one, with skin the color of an ancient oak, had allowed his robe to fall open to reveal a glimpse of smooth, sculpted abs.

Julia! Hat barked. *Concentrate!*

Crap! Yes. Julie drew a deep breath, fumbling with the file. She stepped forward. "Natalie Fergus?"

The model looked up, a lazy smile tugging at her expertly made-up face. "Who are you?"

"My name is Julie Meadows." Julie walked up to her, glancing around. *Are there any humans within earshot, Hat?*

None, he responded. *You can speak freely.*

"I'm from the Para-Military Agency." Julie opened the file as she reached Natalie. "I know you're busy, so I'll get right to the point."

"Oooh," mocked one of the guys. "Nat's in trouble again."

"Oh, shut up." Natalie glared daggers at them. "I'm not in trouble."

"Sure you aren't." The girl beside her sneered. "You definitely weren't hanging around with that dryad that got you into trouble last time, were you?"

"He's a changed man." Natalie tipped her chin, glaring at Julie. "So, are you here to arrest me?"

"No, no." Taylor beamed. "We're here because of your incredible talents."

Julie elbowed him in the ribs. "We're not enforcers, Natalie. We're recruiters. We want you to join the PMA."

Laughter burst through the studio; two people weren't joining. The first was a girl she'd barely noticed when they walked into the room, smaller and younger than the others. She sat on a pouf at the back of the room, sipping a bottle of water and watching. Natalie cracked a smile, but she didn't laugh.

"You can't be serious." One of the guys smirked openly. "You want *Natalie* to become a PMA agent?"

"There are plenty of advantages." Julie stood her ground.

"Yeah, like earning no money." Natalie snorted and tossed her hair over her shoulder.

The lady doth protest too much, methinks, Julie muttered inwardly.

Oh, you like Shakespeare? Hat asked.

Yes, but let's talk literature later. Julie pasted her smile back into place. "The money might not be as good as it is in modeling," she conceded, "but like I say, there are other advantages." She glanced at the young men. "Can we talk privately?"

"I've got five minutes." Natalie glanced at a watch worth more than Julie's apartment.

"Nat, come on. You don't need to talk to these people," protested one of the guys.

"I'm just humoring them, so they'll leave sooner," Natalie stage whispered.

She led Julie and Taylor to another corner of the studio and turned to them, folding her arms. "You'd better make this quick."

"Sure." Julie drew a deep breath and went out on a limb. "Natalie, when was the last time you felt that your work meant something?"

Natalie's eyes narrowed. "My work means I take more money home every month than most people can ever dream of. Second, it means that everyone who's anyone knows my face."

Julie watched her closely. "Then why does it feel like you're thinking up as many excuses as you can not to join the PMA?"

Natalie looked away, absently twirling one of her curls around her index finger.

Talk to her about her family, Hat whispered.

"Your entire family served the Eternity Throne." Julie paused. "They spent their lives keeping peace and ensuring justice in the kingdom."

"Listen to you." Natalie tipped her chin. "Aren't you naïve!"

"I don't know. Your family didn't seem to think that my point of view was naïve."

Natalie folded her arms, but her shoulders were sagging. "Fine. So, my family made a different career choice. That doesn't mean I have to follow in their footsteps."

Julie saw her chance. "Then why am I getting the sense that you might want to?"

Natalie chewed on an elegantly outlined lip. Then her eyes dropped to the floor, and a faint pinkness flushed her cheeks.

"Okay, so you've seen through me." A sigh tugged the corners of her lips downward. "Maybe modeling isn't everything I thought it would be when I ran away from home and joined the hive. What am I supposed to do? I can't leave now. If I do, they'll never talk to me again."

Julie blinked, about to protest, but she stopped when she saw tears pooling in Natalie's sapphire-blue eyes. She turned away, dabbing at them to avoid smudging her expensive makeup.

"I just can't," she choked. "I'm sorry." Sniffing hard, she turned and walked away. Her voice was strong and playful when she fell back into her chair. "Never mind them. They seriously wanted to recruit me as an agent."

The others laughed, and this time, Natalie joined in, even though there was something false about her laughter. The girl in the back still didn't smile. Instead, her eyes followed Julie and Taylor as they slunk, defeated, out of the room.

Taylor steered Julie into an upscale restaurant several blocks away, choosing a quiet table in a corner by a bay window overlooking the bustling street. Julie flopped into a chair, only managing a weak smile for the server who appeared with menus, water, and breadsticks.

"She wanted to join, Taylor. Did you see?" Julie pinched the bridge of her nose, holding back the headache that pounded at the back of her temples. "She wanted to join."

"Yeah. I thought so, too." Taylor barely glanced at the menu and then set it aside. "I can pick up this check. This place isn't exactly cheap."

"Well, it *is* Manhattan." Julie looked up. "What does it matter, anyway? It's lunchtime. I have maybe three, maybe four hours to sign someone. Then I'm dead. I might as well blow some of my sign-on bonus cash on a pricey last meal."

"Don't say that." Taylor's jaw hardened. "Come on, Julie. We're going to get someone to sign."

Julie tugged at the beanie, adjusting it on her forehead.

Hey! Easy there, Hat grumbled. *It's not my fault you haven't signed anyone yet.*

What kind of messed up world is this, Hat? Julie demanded angrily. *How come I'm going to be killed for not performing a task I didn't ask to do? It's just wrong!*

Oh, unhappy that life is unfair, are you? Hat shot back.

Yes, actually, I am! Julie snapped. *You know what I'm going to do if, by some miracle, I manage to survive the rest of this day?*

What? Hat stirred.

I'm going to change this. I'm going to ensure this can never happen to anyone else ever again. Julie picked up her menu as if to hide behind it. Her fingernails dug into the edges as she stared at the words without seeing them.

Oh, so you're single-handedly going to change the world, are you? Hat snorted.

Maybe I am, Julie ranted. *Maybe I'm not. I'm sure going to try. Someone's got to.*

"Hello?" Taylor waved a hand over the menu. "Julie? Are you and Hat having fun in your head without me?"

"Sorry." Julie lowered the menu and rubbed her eyes. "What did Natalie mean about being unable to get back into the hive if she left?"

"Well, DumbleDork explained how Woodland Fae form hives when they're young adults." Taylor gestured vaguely in the direction of the agency building. "They support young people until they mature and either form a family unit or decide to pursue some other career."

Woodland Fae are known for forming very strong connections, either to each other or to a specific cause or goal, Julie's orb training supplied.

"If only my training would kick in at more opportune moments," she grumbled, slapping the side of her head as though to shake some knowledge loose. "Anyway, what's the issue with Natalie leaving for the PMA?"

"Hives don't take kindly to those who leave them." Taylor sighed. "Once Natalie leaves the hive, none of her friends will talk to her. It's Woodland Fae culture. Harsh, I guess, but that's how it is."

"Seems dumb, not allowing second chances." Julie mustered a smile at the waiter as they both ordered coffee and chicken salads.

So, you believe in second chances? Hat asked.

"Obviously I do, but the paranormal world doesn't. Otherwise, I'd have more than an afternoon left to live." Julie rubbed her eyes. "Taylor, do you think I could still convince Natalie to sign if I go back, even with this whole hive thing?"

"I think it's possible. She wanted to join. We both saw it." Taylor shrugged. "I don't know if it's a sure-enough bet to keep chasing this afternoon."

"What other option do we have?" Julie drummed her fingers on the tabletop. "There's got to be something toxic about the hive's dynamic, given how they treat people who leave. If we can't persuade Natalie to join us for the benefits of coming to the PMA, maybe we can get her to come so that she can get away from something. Everyone wants to get away from something."

"Even you, Miss I-Just-Want-To-Read?" Taylor smirked.

Julie glared. "Yeah. Why do you think I came to the city? I just needed to get away from my mom." She sighed. "Don't get me wrong, though. I love her. Maybe I should have stayed in the suburbs and flipped burgers like she wanted."

"Don't say that. You're going to turn this around." Taylor sat back in his chair. "That's why I became a PMA recruiter too. To dodge my family."

Well, aren't you two little rays of sunshine? Hat scoffed.

Lunch arrived, and they ate in silence. Julie tried not to look at the digits on her phone, counting the time until five.

"Everyone in the hive seemed to love Natalie, though." Taylor dabbed his lips with a napkin. "She's the popular one. I'm not sure we'll be able to convince her to leave since I don't know that the hive is something she wants to get away from."

Julie rubbed her chin. "Maybe one of the other Fae in the hive. Someone who seems more 'out' than the others..."

Taylor sat bolt upright. "The girl in the back!"

"Who?"

"You noticed her. I followed your eyes." Taylor grinned. "The small one with dark hair."

"Oh!" Julie sat back. "I remember her. She didn't laugh, even when all of the others did. She looked sad that Natalie didn't join us."

Taylor grinned. "Maybe someone who's not that into the hive, don't you think?"

"Maybe." Julie's heart thudded. "Someone who wouldn't mind leaving it, right?"

This could work. Hat squirmed on Julie's head. *If I can find her human name, I might be able to download more information on her.*

Hold on, how do you download things off the human internet? Julie frowned. *Taylor made it clear that paras aren't allowed on the internet.*

Paras aren't. Hat huffed. *I'm not a para. I'm an extremely advanced magical artifact. I think I can manage hacking into the* humans' internet and hiding my true identity. *I might not be able to connect to the PMA database from here, but if we can find her human name, I can look up her human employment history and social media.*

Taylor must have been in on the conversation because he was already scrolling through his phone. "Here!" He held it up. "She's listed under 'Junior Models.'"

Julie leaned forward to peer at the screen. The photograph showed the small, dark-skinned girl peering at the camera, her lashes lowered alluringly over huge amber eyes.

"Ellie Featheringham," she read.

"Her true name is probably Feathertouch," Taylor observed. "It's a common Woodland Fae name."

Wait. Hat paused. *This is strange.*

What is? Julie asked.

Ellie Featheringham is listed in human databases going back to her childhood. She attended a human school.

Taylor met Julie's eyes. "That's very unusual. Paras normally go to schools for our own species."

"Maybe it's the wrong Ellie?" Julie bit her lip.

No, her school photos match the picture on the website. Hat stirred. *Wait. I see it now. Ellie's records show she's not a pure Fae. She had a Fae father and a human mother.*

"Oh, wow." Taylor stared. "So much for keeping paranormals a secret, right?"

It seems Ellie's mother never found out the truth about her father. He was never part of the picture, Hat explained. *Though her mother gave her father's last name, she grew up human. Ellie was also Sighted, able to see beyond the Veil into the paranormal world. As soon as she graduated high school, she joined this modeling agency.*

"She must have known these models were Fae like her all her life," said Julie. "She always knew that she was Fae, too. As soon as she could, she joined these people who were like her."

"Ellie's not looking for fame." Taylor tapped the picture on his phone screen. "This girl is looking for a connection to the paranormal world."

Their eyes met.

Records show Ellie enjoyed fencing when she was in school. What's more, she was passionate about advocating for various causes in high school, Hat went on.

"She's perfect." A grin blossomed on Taylor's face.

Julie grabbed her phone. 14:15.

"We've got less than three hours." She swallowed.

Taylor held up a hand to the waiter. "Check, please!"

They hurried to Genevieve, and the intoxicating hum of the engine filled the air as soon as Julie turned the key. She gritted her teeth and stomped down, hard, on the accelerator.

They had no time to lose.

Julie and Taylor were breathless when they jogged up to the door of the modeling agency. Taylor hammered on it. Julie's pulse pounded in her temples as they waited.

The door swung open, and the plump woman from before regarded them, her full-lipped pout as red and round as a rose in her face. "I don't think you're going to have any luck. Natalie spent her lunch hour eating celery and talking about how she'll never leave the agency. I doubt—"

"We don't want to talk to Natalie," Julie interrupted. "We want to talk to Ellie Featheringham."

"Ellie?" The receptionist's eyebrows rose. "Well, all right, if you want. Be quiet. The models are working."

She stepped back, and Julie went into the studio. Natalie stood front and center, wearing a pale blue dress that flowed over her body like water. She worked the camera, turning, tossing her hair, casting come-hither looks at the photographer, who was bent over his tripod and shouting orders in a harsh tone.

Taylor gazed at her, open-mouthed. Julie planted her elbow in his ribs. "I don't see Ellie."

With an effort, the elf prince dragged his eyes away from the foxy Fae. He glanced around the studio, frowning. "Those must be the junior models." He pointed at a group clustered around the back of the room. "Where's Ellie?"

Hat, any help? Julie looked at her watch, her heart thudding. It was 14:51. Getting to the agency from the restaurant in the ever-thickening traffic had taken far longer than she'd hoped.

I can try to locate her cell phone. Her number is on her social media profile, lucky for us. Hat was busy for a few seconds. *Got it! She's at the Starbucks on the corner, two blocks away.*

Julie gazed out the window with dismay. The street below was packed bumper-to-bumper with traffic.

"Come on!" Taylor grabbed her arm. "We don't have time."

Those words beat against her mind as they rushed from the studio. *We don't have time. We don't have time.*

Genevieve was still parked at the modeling agency, and a trickle of sweat ran down Julie's back despite the chill spring air as she ran down the sidewalk. The Starbucks was just in front of them, and there was a line out the door. She scanned it quickly with her eyes. No sign of Ellie.

Inside! Hat panted. *She's inside!*

Julie increased her pace, brushing past annoyed shoppers. *Why do you sound like you're the one who's just run two blocks in heels?*

Hat scoffed. *Hey, I've been running multiple processes here for you to find your recruit, little miss. Don't get snippy with me.*

"There!" Taylor pointed.

Julie skidded to a halt on the smooth tiled floor. Customers sitting at tiny, crowded tables gave her disapproving looks. A barista behind the polished wooden counter clipped the lid onto a large latte, looking at her warily like he *knew* she would be a difficult customer.

Julie followed Taylor's finger to where the dark-haired girl was perched on a stool by the counter, waiting. Julie started forward. The barista scribbled on the latte and set it down. "Ellie!" he shouted.

"Here!" Ellie pushed off the bar stool and stepped forward.

The barista was packing latte after latte into three cardboard holders. He raised an eyebrow as Ellie approached. "You alone, miss?"

"Yes, but don't worry." Ellie hooked some of her glossy hair behind her ear. "I'll be okay."

Taylor and Julie exchanged glances.

"Seems like she's less of a junior model and more of a personal slave to the senior models," Julie muttered.

Taylor stepped forward. "Come on. Let's help her."

Ellie had balanced one tray of drinks in the crook of her left elbow, and she reached for the second one, trying to clutch it awkwardly in her left hand. The tray wobbled. Julie grabbed it just as the coffees were about to tip onto the floor.

"Oh!" Ellie looked up. "Thanks!"

Julie smiled. "Let me help you."

"I've got this one." Taylor grabbed the third tray.

"That's sweet of you, but I'm sorry." Ellie shook her hair away from her face. "I have two blocks to go in this cold wind. I'll be okay. I've done it before."

Julie picked up the tray. "Actually, Ellie, I was hoping to talk to you. Do you mind if we walk back to the agency with you?"

Ellie blinked. "How do you know my name?"

"We're recruiters." Taylor shuffled out of the way as other customers pressed forward for their drinks.

Ellie's eyes flickered to him, then to Julie. "Well, I guess, but I can't see why recruiters would be interested in me."

"You've got nothing to lose." *I have everything to lose*, Julie added silently. "Worst case scenario, at least you've got someone to help you with all these."

Ellie's cheeks flushed. "Well, okay. Thanks."

Carrying a tray apiece, Julie, Taylor, and Ellie headed out of the Starbucks and started the walk back toward the modeling agency. Honking horns filled the air. Julie didn't have a free hand to check her phone, but she felt the pressure of time slipping by.

15:12, Hat supplied. *Get moving.*

"You said you were recruiters?" Ellie's eyes darted to Taylor again. "From where?"

The hubbub of the street covered Julie's voice. "From the PMA."

Ellie stared at her. "The...the paranormal police?"

Taylor smiled. "It's okay. Julie's with us. We're from the Para-Military Agency."

"Wow." Ellie stared down at the drinks in her hands. "The others have talked about the PMA, but I've never talked to anyone from there. Is it true that the PMA is supposed to act as the law and military enforcers of the Eternity Throne? Do you really keep the peace all around the world?"

"That's the idea." Julie smiled. "You haven't been among other Fae for long, have you, Ellie?"

The young Fae shook her head. "No. When I was a kid, I would go to other paranormals and ask them questions, but they always avoided me. They treated me like I was lesser because I'm half-human." She glanced at Julie. "It made me give up for a long time, even try to ignore my Fae side and fit in with the human world. When I saw the chance to audition as a junior model for this agency, knowing that I'd seen Fae models for years, I figured it was worth one last shot."

"How's it working out for you?" Julie tugged at Hat, partially for comfort and to protect her ears from the wind.

"Well, it's better than denying who I am." Ellie shrugged. "It's good to be among my own people, you know? Natalie and the others? Wow. They're so sure of themselves and know so much about this world. I feel like an idiot sometimes. Like I can barely tell a Woodland Fae from an elf or whatever you are."

"Aether Elf, actually." Taylor smiled with crinkled eyes.

"You're royalty?" Ellie gasped.

Julie glared at Taylor. "He's sixth in line to the throne. It's not that big of a deal. So, did you do much modeling before you joined the hive?"

Ellie laughed. "Oh, no. I hate modeling. It was the only way I could get close to my people." Her eyes sparkled. "I don't care how much modeling I have to do. It's just good to be near them."

"Seems like maybe they take advantage of you." Taylor gave the drinks in their hands a pointed look.

Ellie's cheeks flushed again. "Well, maybe. What does it matter? At least they allow me near them. They've accepted me despite my human blood when nobody else would. They're my new family. They're...my hive."

They had reached the building, and Taylor led them into the lobby. It was empty. Julie's heart thudded. *My new family. My hive.* How was she going to get Ellie to see things differently?

"Could we go somewhere to talk some more?" Julie tried to hide the desperation in her voice.

"Oh, well, it would be interesting, but I should get back to the hive." Ellie looked at the elevator.

"Tell you what." Taylor stepped forward. "I'll take all of these drinks up to the hive. You girls chat."

Julie caught his eye, mouthing, *Thank you.*

"Would you manage?" Ellie grimaced at the trays of drinks.

Taylor glanced around again. Seeing that no one else was nearby, he waved, and the three trays stacked themselves neatly on top of each other in his arms. "I'll be just fine."

"Okay, then." Ellie watched him go.

Julie touched her arm, gesturing to a corner of the lobby

where a pair of leather couches were pushed up against the wall. "Shall we sit?"

"Okay." Ellie followed her, her arms wrapped around her body as if against the cold despite the heating that flooded the big room.

They sat, and Julie smiled at the Fae. *Hat, help me here. We've got to make this work!*

I've got you, Hat told her. *You're doing great. Try to establish a connection with her.*

Julie licked her lips. "So, you grew up human, right?"

"Yeah." Ellie shrugged. "My mom still doesn't know I'm Fae. I tried telling her when I was little, but she never believed me. Lucky for me, probably, since we're supposed to be secret from humans."

Lucky for your mom, more like, Julie thought. "Do you like the paranormal world so far?"

"Oh, yes. It's interesting and wonderful to embrace a part of me that I had to deny for so long! Natalie and the others have been so good to me. They've opened doors for me that have been slammed shut in my face for my entire life."

Julie thought of Ellie wrestling three trays of drinks on her own from the Starbucks to the agency, and she thought of the derisive laughter of the other Fae.

They're using her, Hat interjected.

Julie squared her shoulders. *So, I still have a chance.*

"Why exactly did you come to me?" Ellie cocked her head to one side, her glossy hair spilling over her shoulders.

"I'll get right to the point." Julie drew a deep breath. "Ellie, we're recruiting new agents for the Para-Military Agency, and we came to you because we think you would make an outstanding PMA agent."

"Me!" Ellie sat back, her eyes wide. "Why? I'm half-human!"

She's breathing, so she meets Kaplan's criteria, Hat reminded Julie.

"You're Fae enough to know all about the paranormal world."

Julie smiled. "What's more, you're smart. You had an excellent GPA in high school, and you liked fencing, didn't you?"

"Well, yeah." Ellie's shy grin struggled to escape her serious expression. "I was good, too."

"Those are all things we're looking for in a PMA agent." Julie leaned forward, her hands resting on her knees. "There's an excellent salary and benefits, too. You'd be doing something that matters. Something that will immerse you in the heart of the paranormal world."

Ellie's eyes were wide and shining, but she sat back, folding her arms. "I don't know. It would mean leaving the hive, and once I leave it, there'd be no going back."

"You're not happy being just a part of the hive, are you?" Julie checked her phone. 15:36.

Ellie lowered her head. "I guess not. I just...I had to go it alone for so long. I don't want to be on my own again."

"You won't be." Julie leaned forward and rested a hand on Ellie's knee. "I'm not. I've only been a recruiter for a week, and Taylor's had my back every step of the way. In the PMA, you'll have a hive of sorts. Only it won't be structured and toxic like this one. You'll have people to support you, but you'll still be able to go in whichever direction you please after boot camp."

"Boot camp?" Ellie's eyes widened. "There's a boot camp?" Her grin had almost escaped now.

Is there a boot camp? Julie's stomach clenched.

Give me one second, Hat told her.

The elevator doors pinged, and Taylor strode into the lobby. "Yes, there is," he announced when he reached them. "It's only three days long, but we have a magical orb that will download weeks of training into your brain. You'll know more about the paranormal world than you could ever have dreamed of all in a matter of days."

"Wow." Ellie laughed. "Good thing the US military doesn't know about that."

Julie blinked at Taylor, wondering how he knew so much about their conversation.

You're welcome. Hat chuckled.

Thanks! Julie turned her attention to Ellie, who was nibbling on a fingernail.

"I know it's scary to leave everything you know behind." Julie smiled at her. "I think you're ready for more than this. I think you're capable of more than this."

Ellie lowered her hand. "You know what? You're right." She squared her shoulders. "Where do I sign up?"

"Right here." Taylor produced her file from under his arm.

Please don't want to read the whole thing first. Please don't read it all, Julie begged. The young Fae was grinning with excitement, and she practically snatched the paperwork from Taylor's hands, plucked a pen from her pocket, and signed in a happy little flourish: *Elspeth Feathertouch.* "It's my real name," she admitted. "I found it in a letter my father left for me."

"Thank you very much." Julie shook Ellie's hand, dizzy with relief. "We'll see you at the PMA on Monday, I'm sure."

"We will. The details and address are all on your copy of the form." Taylor grabbed Julie's arm. "We've got to go now, though. Bye!"

He hauled Julie from the building while Ellie waved after them, looking bemused.

"We did it!" Julie squealed as Taylor dragged her to Genevieve. "We did it!"

"Not quite yet!" Taylor checked his watch and blanched. "We need to hand in this paperwork before it counts."

Julie's stomach lurched. "What? Seriously? At the PMA? We'll never get there in time, not in this traffic!"

It doesn't have to be physically at the PMA. Hat wriggled on her head. *It needs to be recorded in the next,* he checked the time, *hour and twenty minutes if it's going to count.*

Well, connect to the PMA and upload the paperwork, then! Julie huffed.

It's not that simple. The PMA's connection works differently, remember? We have to keep the humans out. Hat groaned.

"So, we have to be closer." Taylor gestured at Genevieve. "A *lot* closer."

"Shit. *Shit!* Okay." Julie grabbed the keys and flung herself into the car. The engine roared, and she peeled out, tires squealing, into the street. Almost immediately, she slammed on the brakes. A wall of traffic greeted her, shimmering in the fading sunlight.

Julie banged a flat hand on the steering wheel. "It's almost like someone is out to get me!"

"Or it's a Friday at almost four, and everyone is ready to start their weekend." Taylor ran a hand through his hair, churning it. "There's got to be another way to get closer, fast."

A long silence followed. All Julie heard was the rushing of blood in her ears.

Then Hat spoke. "I have an idea."

CHAPTER SIXTEEN

"Line of sight?" Julie shrieked. "What do you mean you need a line of sight?"

"Bite me, okay?" Hat shot back. "I'm doing my best with the IRSA's pathetic connection here. It's absolutely useless."

"Okay. Sorry." Julie clutched the wheel, staring at the crawling traffic. She allowed Genevieve to inch forward a couple of feet. "So, you need to be able to see the PMA, basically, to transmit the forms to them?"

"That's right."

Julie looked at Taylor. "We're in Manhattan. The PMA is in Staten Island. How are we supposed to do that?"

Taylor checked his watch. 15:42. "Well, we need to climb a tall building. A really tall building."

"A really tall building between Manhattan and Staten Island." Julie stared at him. "Taylor..."

"No." Taylor gaped. "Absolutely not."

"It's perfect!" Julie grabbed her phone, steadied the wheel with her knees, and typed into the GPS. "Even in this traffic, we'll make it there in an hour."

"Think about this, Julie," Taylor implored. "You need a reservation to go to the crown. There won't be any room."

"Wait, *what* are you two talking about?" Hat barked.

Julie pulled the beanie off her head and set him on the dashboard. "The Statue of Liberty."

Hat was silent, then perked up. The pom-pom on the beanie bounced. "Yes! Yes, it can work!"

"You're both crazy!" Taylor protested.

"Better crazy than dead." Julie revved Genevieve into gear and took the next left as hard and fast as she could, the big engine growling in protest when she had to stomp on the brakes behind the next bumper as this street crawled forward at the same snail's pace.

"It's our best option, Taylor." Hat cocked his pom-pom toward Julie. "We'll never make it to the PMA in that time. We have a chance—a tiny chance—of reaching Liberty Island."

Taylor groaned as Julie squeezed Genevieve between a semi and an SUV with bare inches to spare. "You're going to get us killed!"

"I'm trying for exactly the opposite," Julie snapped.

She sliced through the traffic, sending Genevieve through gaps that looked too small for the Mustang. She was grateful for every ounce of torque the engine offered, weaving between stationary cars, ignoring the angry honks surrounding them. Hat slid around on the dashboard, yelping. Taylor grabbed him and clutched him in both hands. They both screamed as Julie threw Genevieve around a corner. The Mustang skidded wildly, then squealed to a halt a hair's breadth from the car in front of them.

"The ferry!" Taylor cried, pointing. "It's leaving!"

"No, it's not." Hat wriggled. "I'm pulling a few strings. Causing a delay."

"Hat, you're my hero." Julie meant it.

With seconds to spare, Genevieve roared into the ferry's

parking lot. Julie threw the car haphazardly into a space and checked the time. 16:21.

"Good girl, Genevieve!" Julie slapped the car's dashboard. "Good girl!"

"Let's all be grateful that your elderly landlady had a muscle car hiding in her garage." Taylor kicked the door open and scrambled out. "We'd never have made it here in this time if we were driving something ordinary."

"I think I'm going to be sick, and I don't even have anything to be sick with," Hat groaned.

Julie jogged around the hood of Genevieve, Hat grabbed, and rammed him down over her ears again. "Come on. We're nearly there!"

Following the start-of-weekend crowds, Julie and Taylor ran up to the ferry, snagging the last two tickets. They stood at the railing as the ferry rumbled across the water. The afternoon sun skipped and danced, reflecting brightly on the wake. Julie squinted at the statue that towered over the bay, one arm outstretched, crown raised high.

"You know it's actually not called the Statue of Liberty?" She turned to Taylor.

He stared at her. "What?"

"It's actually called Liberty Enlightening the World."

Taylor continued staring. "Why are you thinking about that at a time like this?"

"I don't know. I've got to take my mind off it somehow." Julie checked her watch as the ferry cruised to a halt at the terminal. 16:47.

"We're cutting it fine!" Taylor whimpered as they hurried off the ferry.

Julie looked up at the shining copper-green of the statue rising beyond the gardens and manicured walkways in front of them. "Come on. Run!"

Their feet hammering on the pavement, they bolted past the

crowds. Julie's arms swung to drive her forward faster. Her breaths heaved, and she ignored their burning, struggling to keep pace with Taylor as his long legs covered the ground.

A long line wrapped around the tower's base, and Julie's heart faltered. "Taylor!" she yelped. "Time for that royalty bullshit!"

"On it," Taylor barked. He ripped his PMA ID from inside his coat, skirted the line, and ran straight to the security guard. "Hot pursuit!" he yelled at the guy, waving the badge too quickly for the man to read. "Let us through!"

"What?" The guard stared at him.

"Listen, mister, there's a serial killer on the loose, and he's inside that statue!" Taylor pointed up at Lady Liberty. "Now, unless you want everyone here to be murdered, you'll get out of my way!"

The security guard pursed his lips. "Yeah, beat it, sonny. Nice try."

"Did he say *serial killer?*" shrieked a voice in the crowd.

Julie turned. The queue of sightseers was getting restless. People were looking this way and that, standing on tiptoe to peer at Taylor and Julie.

"That's right!" Julie called. "He's out for blood!"

"Blood?" squealed a woman in the front of the crowd. "Blood!" She howled the word like a bad actress.

"Now, ma'am, there's no reason for this." The security guard held out one hand. "It's all just a misunderstanding. There is no murderer. These people are intruders."

"Intruders!" a man near the back screeched.

"No, you're not listening!" another crowd member yelled. "*Murderers!*"

The crowd broke ranks. The security guard stepped forward, holding out both hands. "Wait. Calm down!"

Taylor put a flat hand on Julie's shoulder and gave her a shove. "Go! Go!"

The security guard didn't even look around, struggling to

control the crowd. Julie bolted past him and into the pedestal lobby. She'd been here for a school trip before and headed for the stairs dead ahead. Shouts rose behind her.

Run! Hat tugged at her head. *Run, Julie!*

She was already breathless, but she tackled the stairs two at a time, Taylor right next to her. The double helix staircase waited in front of them, all curves of shining metal, and Julie grabbed the smooth railing and began climbing as fast as her limbs would carry her.

16:49, Hat barked. *Get moving!*

"It's easy for you to say!" Julie rasped, bounding up the stairs. "You're a hat! Can't you change into a bird or something?"

Taylor huffed along behind her. "That would definitely be helpful."

Hat scoffed. "I can't change into living things."

"Then change into a plane or something!" Julie yelled.

"How am I supposed to know the atomic structure of a plane? I've never been close to one!" Hat shot back.

"Never mind." Taylor brushed past her, his long legs making short work of the stairs. "We can do it. Come on, Julie!"

They'd reached the lower platform, and sweat trickled down Julie's skin. She ripped off her jacket and tossed it down the stairs. Taylor was going faster, much faster, as though he never tired.

Elves are known for unusual speed and stamina, the orb training informed her helpfully.

"You should go on ahead," Julie gasped. She ripped Hat from her head and held him out to Taylor. "I can't keep up."

"Of course you can. We're doing this." Taylor grabbed her arm. "Almost there!"

For the next few minutes, Julie was plunged into a world of breathless effort. Every fiber of her body strained. Her lungs were afire, her muscles ached relentlessly, and her feet felt as though they weighed a ton. She tripped twice, but Taylor hauled her upright again, and then somehow, the staircase opened up around them, bright sunlight stabbing her eyes, and they were in the crown of Lady Liberty.

Julie stopped, looking around wildly. She was surrounded by arched windows with elegant wooden frames. "Where do we need to go? The torch?"

"No. This is fine!" Hat wriggled. "Open the window!"

Taylor flung the window wide. "What time is it?"

"16:58. Hurry!" Hat cried.

Julie rushed to the window, gripping Hat tightly, and held him out. Below was the speck of Liberty Island. Beyond were the endless sea ripples and the perfect Manhattan skyline. Behind them, yelling. Here, at this moment, there was just her heart pounding in her ears.

Hat cursed. "No. *No!*"

"What?" Taylor gripped the windowsill as if for support.

"I need to be higher. It's not working!"

Julie looked at Taylor, feeling like she'd just been drenched with ice water. "That's it, then," she whispered. "It's over."

Taylor was ashen.

"Throw me." Hat stiffened in her hands.

"What?"

"Throw me in the air!" Hat ordered.

Julie shook her head. "What if you fall?" When she looked down, the bay's water was a very long way away. White flecks of the waves crashed against the edges of the island.

"Just do it!" Hat shrieked. "Trust me!"

Julie realized she did. Gritting her teeth, she leaned as far out the window as possible and bent her arms.

"Do it. High!" Hat yelled.

Julie threw him with all of her strength, and for a breathless few seconds, she and Taylor stared at the pom-pom beanie floating through the air. The world moved in slow motion. Hat tumbled toward her. Julie flung herself against the windowsill and stretched out her hands. Hat plummeted toward the earth, and her arms were too short. She wasn't going to make it.

"No!" She sobbed.

Poof!

The beanie became a straw hat with a wide brim. The edge of the brim slid into her fingers as her feet left the ground, and her balance tipped her out the window. Buttons on her blouse snagged on the windowsill as she slipped forward.

"Julie!" Taylor yelped, and a firm hand latched onto the back of her belt. Julie grabbed the straw hat, clutching it to her chest as Taylor hauled her into the crown with all his might. She shot through the window, slamming against him, and they all collapsed in a heap on the floor.

"Hey! Get off me," Hat grumbled.

Julie sat up, pulling Hat from under her backside. "Are you okay?"

"You weigh more than an overweight unicorn. Do you know that?" Hat sputtered.

Taylor seized him. "Did you get it? Did it go through?"

Julie pulled out her phone. 17:00.

"Yes." Hat laughed. "It went through in time. Congratulations, kid. You've got your first recruit!"

Julie sagged back against the staircase railing, unsure whether she was laughing or sobbing. Taylor grinned, his eyes almost vanishing as his cheeks lifted. "You did it!" He held up a hand.

Julie high-fived it. "*We* did it." She took Hat gently from Taylor and placed him on her head. "It could never have happened without you two."

Taylor's eyes met hers. "What are friends for?"

Friends better be for getting out of this statue as quickly as possible. We've got company!

"Oh, crap!" Julie scrambled to her feet and leaned over the railing to peer down at the staircase. She caught only a faint glimpse of security guards thundering up the stairs toward them.

Taylor gave her a wide-eyed look. "What now?"

"Now we'd better run...again!" Julie burst out laughing, high on a giddy tide of relief. "What's the worst that can happen now?"

Two guards appeared on one side of the staircase in the crown. "You!" barked one. "Stop there!"

"Go!" Julie squealed, bolting down the double helix as fast as her legs could carry her. They felt like noodles, but they were living noodles, which was better than they might have been if they'd reached the top of this statue five minutes too late.

"I think we've lost them," Julie panted as they entered the lobby. Her feet ached fiercely.

Taylor looked around, sweat trickling down the sides of his face. "We've outrun them, but they're right behind us. There will be other guards at the door."

Julie groaned. "Are we really going to end this day with being arrested for trespassing?"

Taylor cracked his knuckles. "Not if I can help it. Come on!"

He rushed the doors, and Julie followed at the best run she could manage. The same harassed guard from earlier was outside, shouting over a milling crowd trying to decide whether they were gawking or panicking. He spun around when the doors opened, a hand going to the pepper spray on his belt. "Don't make me use this!"

"Run, Julie!" Taylor rushed at the guard, batting the pepper spray as the man yanked it from his holster.

"Taylor!" Julie squeaked, slowing down. "It's not his fault. He's innocent!"

"I know." Taylor grunted, and with a deft maneuver Julie could barely see, Taylor spun the guard and sent him stumbling into the arms of the gawking crowd. They caught the guard before he tripped.

Julie didn't look back for more details. She pushed through the crowd, holding Hat firmly on her head. Taylor was close behind her. The mob, still distracted by the infuriated guard, had swallowed them in a few seconds.

"*Now* we've lost them." Taylor grinned as they both slowed to a walk and headed back toward the ferry terminal.

"That was intense." Julie mopped her brow and shifted the straw hat back. "Those were some slick moves back there, cowboy."

Taylor shoved his hair from his eyes. "You think so? I've never tried any of that in real life. Just sparring with my teacher."

Julie grinned. "Maybe your teacher needs to spar with me, too."

"I wouldn't worry." Taylor chuckled. "I think you can take care of yourself."

The ferry people were blissfully unaware that Julie and Taylor had caused any trouble. They boarded and sat by the rail, still breathless and sweaty. Julie pulled Hat off her head and put him down in her lap. *Hat, are you okay? Are you sure it went through?*

I promise. Hat's brim curved as if in a smile. *It's all done now.*

Julie leaned back, enjoying the sunshine on her face. "I can't believe it. I'll visit my mom tomorrow, have dinner with Lillie, and spend Sunday in bed…alive."

"What about Monday?" Taylor shaded his eyes, not looking at her.

"I haven't thought as far as Monday yet." Julie grinned. "It's just good to be alive and not running."

"Yeah, I could do with never seeing stairs again in my entire life," Taylor admitted. "I'm glad there's an elevator at the PMA. I can't wait to see Kaplan's face when he realizes we actually did it."

Julie wrapped her arms around herself against a cold breeze rushing over the bay. "I can't wait to rub his nose in it."

Taylor's eyes widened. "I wouldn't recommend it."

Julie's legs protested when they reached the terminal, and she got off the bench. She groaned her way into the parking lot. "I feel a hundred years old after this week."

"I *am* a hundred years old, and I feel a lot older." Taylor rubbed his lower back as they limped to Genevieve.

"What? Really?"

"Wouldn't you like to know?" He smirked.

Julie spotted a white rectangle flashing on Genevieve's windshield. She hurried up to the car and snatched it up. "Seriously?" she hissed. "A parking ticket?"

"Well, you did double-park it," Taylor pointed out.

In the middle of rush hour on a Friday afternoon.

Julie slapped the ticket down on the hood. "Neither of you is being helpful. I wish I could just...magic this shit away or something."

"Okay, okay, I'm helping." Taylor plucked his phone from his pocket and snapped a photo.

"What are you doing?"

"Sending this to my lawyers." Taylor tucked his phone away. "It's for the job. They can take care of it. It's not magic, but it's close."

Julie smiled. "You're learning to delegate, Your Highness."

This time, when she started Genevieve's engine, she leaned back in her seat and enjoyed the mighty rumble in leisure as she pulled the car from the parking lot and joined the bumper-to-bumper traffic back to Staten Island.

The PMA was almost empty when they left Genevieve in the parking lot and headed to the elevators. They'd been jamming out to Green Day, and Julie's body still buzzed with adrenaline, like the music had somehow gotten into her bloodstream.

"I still can't believe you almost fell from the Statue of Liberty!" Taylor threw up his hands. "How skinny *are* you?"

"More desperate than skinny." Julie gave him a shove with her elbow. "At least I didn't drop Hat."

You can both be grateful you didn't drop me, Hat sniffed. *I wouldn't have been happy if you had had to fish me from the drink. I think I'd have gone back to the Warehouse.*

"So you would have survived it?" Julie touched the brim.

Of course I would. Do you think it would have been my first time being thrown off a tall building?

"Well, Hat might have made it, but you wouldn't," Taylor smirked. "I saved your life, you know. You basically owe me forever now."

Julie scoffed. "Oh, please. I would have figured out a way not to plummet to my doom."

"Sure you would."

At least the police have stopped looking for you, considering you didn't actually hurt anyone or take anything. Hat sounded smug. *I did some scrambling when it came to their radios, so now they're arguing over your descriptions. They'll have forgotten about you by tomorrow.*

Thanks, Hat. Julie patted him as they reached the elevator. "You've been amazing," she told them both.

"We did it on your terms, too." Taylor folded his arms, leaning against the wall. "No drafting, no lies, no false promises."

"That's the best part." Julie's cheeks hurt from grinning. "I think the PMA is going to be good for Ellie, and what's more, I think she's going to be an incredible agent."

Taylor raised an eyebrow. "The best part? Better than the part where you saved your skin?"

"There are better things than my skin, you know." Julie ran a hand seductively down her cheek and neck. "Although not many."

Taylor burst out laughing.

He was still laughing when the elevator reached the third floor, and they stepped into the communal office. It was empty. Every desk was abandoned, and all the lights were turned off. A warm glow of fading sunlight came from Kaplan's open office door.

"Wait." Julie stopped. "Why's Kaplan's door open? He doesn't seem like the my-door-is-always-open kind of boss."

"He isn't." Taylor bit his lip.

I have a bad feeling about this. Hat squashed himself against Julie's head. *A really bad feeling.*

Julie squinted through the open door. "Who's that in his office?"

Even across the room, they heard Kaplan yelling. As they moved closer, Julie saw a large, heavy figure standing in front of Kaplan's desk, head bowed.

Taylor gulped. "The guards from the Warehouse."

Julie caught a glimpse of sunlight sparkling on pale green skin. "The IT trolls." She looked at Taylor. "This can only mean one thing."

Taylor's eyes widened. "Oh, *shit.*"

"I got this." Julie patted his arm. "I did this."

"Nope." Taylor shook his head. "You're my partner. *We* did it."

"Hey, that's my line," Julie retorted, which got a faint smile from Taylor.

No point in delaying the inevitable. They marched to the office. Kaplan's eyes lanced through the door and pierced Julie, narrowing. His bushy brows lowered dangerously over the bridge of his nose. His lip curled even more savagely than usual.

"Here they are!" The taller of the two elf guards whipped around, pointing. "They're the ones who did it, Captain!"

The other guard eyed Julie and Taylor like he wanted to fry them on the spot and then skewer them over coals. Qtana, Gnerk, and a taller troll Julie didn't recognize clustered in one corner of the room. Qtana was wide-eyed. The other troll, however, had a file clamped under his arm and cold, hard eyes that flashed instantly to the straw hat Julie was still wearing.

"Meadows. Woodskin." Kaplan sat back, folding his enormous arms. "You've been busy."

"Yes, sir." Julie marched to the desk, plucked Ellie's file from under her arm, and slapped it in front of him.

Kaplan opened it delicately with a finger and thumb. Julie noticed that his nails were unusually pointy, and the thought of decapitation flashed through her mind again.

"Elspeth Feathertouch," Kaplan read. "So it *was* you."

Julie squared her shoulders. "It was me, sir."

Taylor stepped up beside her, shooting a glance at the trolls. "It was *us*."

"It was we," Julie corrected.

Taylor shook his head. "No, that just sounds wrong."

"Yeah, you're right." Julie rubbed her chin. "That sounds even worse. The grammar just doesn't seem right either way."

"Enough!" Kaplan slammed a massive fist down on the desk, making everyone in the room jump. His amber eyes scanned the room, from the elf guards to the trolls, and a low snarl rumbled deep in his chest.

Julie swallowed. What's the penalty for stealing an important magical artifact?

Termination, Hat supplied. *Sorry. I probably should have mentioned that earlier.*

You think? Julie gulped, feeling like she was tipping from that narrow little window again, looking down at certain death.

Kaplan returned his gaze to Julie. "Qbiit and the other trolls here have a serious complaint." He pronounced the name "Qbiit."

The unfamiliar troll stepped forward, adjusting his glasses. "There it is!" He pointed at Hat. "There's that useless old system!"

WHAT? Hat roared loud enough that Julie's head stung.

"I don't know what you're talking about." Julie pulled off the straw hat and held it in front of her. "It's just a hat, my dude. You on something?"

"She's lying, captain!" Qbiit spun to face Kaplan. "She's lying, and I know it! That old system was used *without our permission.*"

"Instead of the IRSA!" Qtana chipped in.

Bugger. Hat groaned. *They must have identified me as active when I sent the files through. I'm sorry.*

It's okay. Julie tipped up her chin, meeting Kaplan's eyes. *It's not like you had time to hide it somehow.*

"Now, I wouldn't think it was possible for the old system to be used or even activated." Kaplan steepled his fingers, pinning Julie in place with a glare. "Considering that DUMB LE Dork is safely inside the Shrine for Previous Technology and Magic."

"That's what we just said!" one of the guards burst out. "DUMB LE Dork isn't in there anymore. *She* took it!"

Him, if you please, Hat muttered.

"Are you certain that the old system is active?" Kaplan asked without taking his eyes off Julie.

Qbiit clenched his fists. "Yes!"

"Active *and* taken from the Warehouse!" spat one of the elves.

Well, now we're in deep shit. Julie clutched Hat tightly.

Qbiit stepped forward, jabbing a finger at Julie. "This *human* came into our world, stole our artifacts, and activated dangerously senile ancient systems!"

Dangerously what? Hat jeered.

"She's a danger to paranormals everywhere. She's a disgrace to the Eternity Throne!" Flecks of saliva were gathering at the corners of Qbiit's dark green lips. "Captain, she needs to be *flogged!*"

"We haven't flogged anyone for two hundred years." Kaplan still had his unnerving stare fixed on Julie.

An elf shook his fist. "Never mind flogging! She should be terminated. She should be mind-wiped!"

Decapitation. The word played in Julie's mind, and she swallowed.

"Now, hang on a minute!" Taylor stepped forward.

Kaplan snarled. "Woodskin, shut up!"

Taylor fell silent, his eyes darting back to Julie.

"What is your involvement in all this?" Kaplan growled.

"His Highness cannot be blamed for the things that this human forced him to do." Qbiit smiled simperingly at Taylor. "Perhaps a fine or suspension would be appropriate for him, sir."

"Termination for the human!" The elf slapped his clenched fist into his other hand.

The other elf raised his chin. "Perhaps exile or banishment would be an appropriate punishment for her, sir."

"Termination!" thundered the other.

Kaplan finally turned his eyes from Julie to the elves. "You are in no position to prescribe how I will punish one of my own people."

The elves stuttered into silence.

"She's putting our entire world at risk," Qbiit spat. "She could expose us. She could drag us into war with the human world." He strode across the room, wagging a furious finger at Julie. "For all we know, she's a spy sent by the humans or the rebels, and she's come here to bring down the PMA and leave the paranormal world helpless!"

Julie stared at him, her blood turning to ice in her veins. If Kaplan believed Qbiit, then all this would have been for nothing.

Decapitation was practically inevitable.

CHAPTER SEVENTEEN

Julie opened her mouth to defend herself, even though she couldn't think of anything to say. Nothing that they would believe, anyway. Every argument seemed to shrivel within her throat in the face of Kaplan's glare. He had one hand resting on the desk, and as Julie stared at him, she thought she saw the nails lengthening, digging into the woodwork.

"Now, just you wait a minute!" thundered a deep, powerful voice beside her.

Julie jumped, whipping around. It was Taylor. He strode right up to Qbiit, getting nose to nose—or more accurately, nose to neck—with the troll. Qbiit was so much shorter than the elf prince that he had to tip back his head to look Taylor in the eye.

"None of what you just said is accurate." Taylor pointed at Julie. "That human was dragged into our world unwillingly and forced to take a job she never asked for. She's never quit, never given up, never slowed down, and never even considered the dishonesty you take for granted."

Qbiit sputtered. "But...but she's *human!*"

Taylor's hands flexed like he wanted to wrap them around the troll's throat. "Yes, and how did she end up here at HQ in the first place?"

Qbiit pressed his lips together.

"Oh yes, that's right. It was because of a glitch in *your* precious system." Taylor snarled, inches from Qbiit's face. "This mess is your fault, troll, and mark my words. I will not allow this innocent human to go down for your mistakes!"

Qbiit swallowed and stepped back.

"That doesn't change that she stole DUMB LE Dork." One of the elf guards folded his arms. "As did you, Your Highness."

Taylor whipped around. "Julie would never have needed DUMB LE Dork if the IRSA 4000 hadn't been so useless!"

"Hey!" Qtana blinked behind her glasses, hurt.

"I'm sorry, Qtana. I know that that system is your baby, but it's no use at all," Taylor barked. "It's probably why our recruiting numbers have been so poor lately! The IRSA has proven that it's not reliable, it's not fast, and not providing our recruiters with the data required to keep the PMA floating, and, in Julie's case, to keep from getting terminated." The elf prince threw up his hands. "She had no choice but to find a better system. If it had been up to *your* system, she would have been terminated by now!"

Kaplan was staring at Taylor with an open mouth. *She* was staring at Taylor with an open mouth.

I had no idea he had it in him, Hat mused.

Julie blinked. *Me neither! Look at him!*

"Say what you will, but she still stole it!" snapped the elf. He stepped forward, grabbed a computer screen on Kaplan's desk, and turned it around to face Taylor and Julie. "How else would you explain *this*?"

Julie felt her stomach lurch like it was falling through the ground. A loop of security footage played on the screen. The entrance to the Warehouse. The two elves standing guard. The elevator doors opened, and Julie and Taylor stepped out, that cocky little fedora on Julie's head.

The guard's tinny voice spoke through the screen. "Anything to declare?"

Julie grimaced, knowing what was coming next, as she watched herself on the screen, running a hand down her curves. "Just this."

"Still nothing!" chuckled the guard.

Kaplan raised an eyebrow at Julie. She winced. The guard in question, standing beside her, had gone gray.

The other guard jabbed at the screen. "There! Fifteen minutes later."

Everyone watched silently as the security footage showed Julie walking out of the Warehouse.

"All of this!" Again, Julie gestured on the screen. Kaplan raised the other eyebrow as laughter filled the room.

"Your point?" the captain snarled, looking up at the guards.

"Wait, sir. One more clip." The guard clicked through to the next video. This time, it showed the Warehouse and Hat in his wizarding form as Julie walked up to him. Hat turned into the perfect copy of the fedora she wore...and the switch.

Julie wasn't sure if she would die of fear or embarrassment, but it was one of the two.

Kaplan's eyes nailed her to the wall. "I see, Meadows, that you wore the old system on your head as you left?"

"Sir—" Julie began.

Taylor stepped forward, arms crossed. "What you two are clearly unaware of," he addressed the elves, "is that Julie had permission from Captain Kaplan to take DUMB LE Dork to aid in her work."

Kaplan's jaw dropped. He snapped it shut, narrowing his eyes. "Woodskin—"

The elf guard turned to him. "Is this true, sir?"

"Yes, sir." Taylor was staring daggers at Kaplan. "Why don't you tell them?"

Julie looked from Taylor to Kaplan and back. *What is*

happening right now? Why does it feel like Taylor has the upper hand here?

Hat chuckled. *I have no idea, but I'm enjoying this.*

Yeah, well, your life isn't the one on the line. Julie wiped her sweaty palms on her pants.

Kaplan slowly dragged his furious gaze from Taylor to the elves. The silence stretched for an eternity before he spoke. "Yes. I gave Meadows permission to use DUMB LE Dork."

"What?" Qbiit squawked. "*Why?*"

Kaplan gave him a long look.

"Why, *sir*," Qbiit muttered.

"Because, as Woodskin kindly pointed out, the IRSA 4000 has not been delivering results. Bringing in a human was an experiment." Kaplan shrugged shoulders that moved like rocks. "Bringing DUMB LE Dork back was another part of the experiment, and since Meadows here accomplished in a week what a whole army of recruiters have been failing to accomplish in an entire month, I would say it was a resounding success."

Julie let out a breath. Taylor shot her a grin, and she had to resist the urge to sag into the nearest armchair.

"And another thing." Kaplan sat back in his chair. "I also instructed Woodskin and Meadows to test the security system at the SPTM."

The elves both froze. "Sir?" squeaked the shorter one.

"You heard me. That's why you weren't notified the old system would be removed from the Warehouse. I wanted to see how hard it would be for someone to steal something." Kaplan's last word ended in a long, rumbling growl.

The elves shuffled their feet.

"It's the fact that it transfigures, sir," protested one. "How were we supposed to—"

"Oh, and DUMB LE Dork is the only thing in the SPTM that changes shape?" Kaplan leaned forward, slamming both hands down on the desk. "Are you telling me you can only guard *non-*

magical things in the Shrine of Previous Technology and Magic? Is that what this is?"

"No, sir." The elf gulped. "Sorry, sir."

Julie was doing her best not to let her mouth hang open. *Well, this is amazing.*

I'm enjoying it. Hat giggled. *If I was human, I'd want some popcorn now.*

Qbiit stepped forward. "That's all fine and good, *sir*," he spat, "but why didn't you tell *us* the old system was going to be activated?"

"I think you should give the IRSA a chance, sir." Qtana blinked behind her thick glasses. "There are still things that need to be changed, but I'm confident we can improve it to the point where—"

Kaplan held up a hand, silencing them both. "We will address your failings later." He turned back to the elves. "Now, I will speak to the security manager, and I expect a full report on how the building's security can be tightened on my desk by lunchtime on Monday. Is that clear?"

"Yes, sir." The taller of the two elves gulped.

"Good. You're both dismissed."

The guards shuffled to the door, but the shorter one paused and turned to Julie before leaving. His cheeks were pale gray. "We didn't know. You were just doing your job."

"Hey, no hard feelings." Julie smirked. "None of *this* holds a grudge." She ran a hand down her side and hip.

The elf cracked a smile and his color normalized. He followed his colleague from the office.

Qbiit walked up to the desk and leaned his hands, coming closer to Kaplan than Julie would care to be. "Sir, with respect, this is ridiculous. I'm the IT manager around here. You should have come to me with this rather than trusting in some wet-behind-the-ears recruiter and a system that's become senile and completely unreliable!"

"Hey! I'm right here." Hat popped off Julie's head and landed on the desk with a faint thump. "Captain, you know as well as I do that I wasn't decommissioned because of senility. I was decommissioned because these young upstarts couldn't deal with my attitude!"

Qtana was wide-eyed. Qbiit pretended Hat hadn't spoken. Kaplan's lip curled, revealing a row of shiny pointed teeth. They seemed to lengthen as Julie watched. "You're out of line, troll. I suggest you return to your office and focus on doing your job."

Qtana stepped forward, turning to Julie. "You know, I was trying to help you."

"I know." Julie stared at her. Were those tears in Qtana's eyes? The troll blinked before Julie could tell.

"You might not have been desperate enough to take the old system if you'd known the truth," Qtana added.

"The truth?" Julie frowned. "What do you mean?"

Qtana drew a deep breath, glanced at Kaplan, then shook her head and turned back to Julie.

"The truth is you could have returned safely to the human world any time you wanted. You can still do it."

CHAPTER EIGHTEEN

Silence hung over the room like smoke, choking Julie. It felt as though the floor was tipping underneath her feet. Qbiit's frown was still in place. Kaplan was still; not a muscle moved. He might as well have been a hulking statue carved from bronze.

It took Julie several moments to regain control over her voice. "Say...say that again."

"This whole thing was a farce, Julie." Qtana gestured at Kaplan. "We've never killed any humans for discovering paranormals exist."

"Did you think you were the only foolish human to stumble upon us in history?" Qbiit laughed, but it never reached his eyes. "If we had to kill every human who found out about paranormals, you lot would be halfway extinct by now."

"But...but..." Julie turned, and her eyes snagged on Taylor. "Is this true?"

Taylor was putty-gray. He lowered his head.

"So, you knew." Julie's mouth was dry. "You all knew."

"I never said you'd be killed, you know." Kaplan unfroze, sitting back in his chair. "I told you you'd be mind-wiped and terminated, which is true."

"Wait, what about *decapitation?*"

"It was a joke, Meadows." Kaplan smirked. "I make them sometimes."

This time, Julie did sink into an armchair. She ran her fingers through her short hair and stared at the trolls. "What is mind-wiping, then?"

"A painless process," Qbiit explained. "It's expensive, but it's easy. I've wiped out plenty of humans in my time. If Kaplan had followed protocol on this, you would have carried on with your day as usual on Monday, blissfully unaware trolls, Weres, or Aether Elves ever existed."

Julie's eyes darted to Taylor again.

"That's *Captain* Kaplan to you, troll," Kaplan snarled.

"Don't you understand what this means, Julie?" Qtana sat down beside her, perching on the edge of her chair. "It means you're free."

Julie swallowed. "Free?"

"Yes. Don't you understand? Without the threat of execution, which was never real, hanging over your head, well, you can do whatever you want. You've still got the sign-on bonus, which will tide you over until you can find another nice, human job."

Julie's mind raced. A nice, human job, no poles involved. Thanks, Mom. One where she didn't have to worry about death or trespass in the Statue of Liberty or scoop up bleeding vampires from the pavement.

"Everything could go back to normal," Qtana went on. "No, *better* than normal. You have the car now, don't you? Plus, more life experience. I think the least the captain can do after this fiasco is to write you a good reference. You'd easily get a job."

Julie pressed her fingers into her aching temples. She tried to imagine going back to the apartment. Sleeping in. Spending the weekend reading. Applying for more jobs. Maybe something online she could do from home. Data entry or copywriting or something. It'd be peaceful. She wouldn't have to talk to humans, which was always nice.

She would have no idea a dangerous world full of mythical creatures existed beyond the Veil.

Hat sat still on the desk as though he was made of nothing but straw. Taylor still wouldn't look at her, but his cheeks were pallid.

"None of this was fair, Julie." Qtana cocked her head so her ponytail spilled golden over her shoulder. "You should be allowed to return to the things you enjoy. You could read more, maybe even spend more time with your mom. Keep on building your relationship with Lillie. I think she needs you."

"Wait." Julie's eyes narrowed, and she looked up at Qtana. "How do you know about my mom and Lillie?"

Qtana straightened, faint pinkness crawling into her cheeks. "Well, in your file—"

"That doesn't explain the landlady." Taylor looked up. "Julie told me about her, but I know she didn't tell *you*, Qtana."

"We, um, we had... You see..." Qtana looked helplessly at Qbiit.

Julie pushed back. "Spy much? It's like you're afraid of what I might do to you, being the odd duck here."

"You don't understand." Qbiit stepped forward. "You're human. Tracking you was essential for security reasons."

"Oh, it was, was it?" Kaplan almost purred the words this time, but his eyes were dangerous. "Interesting, then, that you chose to spy on Meadows here without receiving any order to do so from me."

"Hey, don't try to play nice now, Captain." Julie jabbed a finger at him. "I'm not forgetting you're the one who lied to me."

Kaplan waved a hand as though this was irrelevant. "Who performed the surveillance on Meadows?"

Qtana was even pinker now. "I did, sir."

"Who told you to do that?"

Qtana said nothing, but her eyes darted to Qbiit.

Kaplan rounded on the older troll. "Is this true? Did you order surveillance on Meadows?"

"She's *new!*" Qbiit waved his arms. "She cannot be trusted!"

Kaplan half rose from his chair. "You are out of line, troll!" he thundered. "Did you place surveillance on Woodskin when he first joined the PMA?"

Qbiit blanched. "No, but he's an Aether elf and royalty. She's *human!*"

"Now, who's speciesist?" Julie hissed.

"Allow me to make one thing abundantly clear." Kaplan's voice was a low, dangerous purr again. He slapped an open hand on the desk with a force that made the floor tremble. "You will never be spying on any of my people, regardless of their species. Do you understand?"

Qbiit squirmed. "Sir—"

"Let me state it simply since you are incapable of understanding this basic concept." Kaplan's eyes burned. "You are not to do anything to Meadows you would not do to Woodskin."

Qbiit's eyes popped. "Captain Kaplan, Taylor Woodskin is a *prince!*"

"Sixth in line," Taylor smirked. "It's not number one, but it's better than nothing." He glanced at Julie, and his shoulders relaxed when she gave him an encouraging smile.

Kaplan leaned over the desk, eyes fixed on Qbiit. His words came out in a growl so loud Julie could barely make them out. "Same...as...my...other...recruiter."

Julie gave Qbiit credit. He held Kaplan's eyes much longer than she would have dared. Finally, he faltered under the captain's burning stare and dropped his gaze to the carpet.

"Yes, sir," he muttered.

"Good." Kaplan sat back in his chair, steepling his fingers. "Now that that's cleared up, you two are dismissed. Qtana?"

"Yes, sir?" Qtana jumped to her feet.

"I expect you to do better when you know better, even if someone in management tells you otherwise." Kaplan raised an eyebrow. "Understood?"

Qtana nodded, her ponytail bouncing. "Yes, sir."

"Good. Now go, both of you." Kaplan flicked a hand at them. "Dismissed."

Qbiit stalked past Julie, giving her a long, sideways sneer as he left. Qtana scurried through the door, flashing Julie a sheepish smile.

"Now." Kaplan leaned forward. "It's high time I dealt with you, human."

Julie folded her arms. "Let me guess. Mind-wiping, but not by decapitation?"

Kaplan snorted, shaking his head. "Don't think I *won't* decapitate someone if I have a good reason to do so."

Julie held his gaze. "Have I given you good reason?"

Kaplan, for once, blinked first. He sat back. "No. In fact, Meadows, you've exceeded expectations."

"So, it was *you* setting me up for failure?"

Kaplan stared. "What do you mean?"

"I know someone was trying to stop me." Julie tipped her chin. "I don't know who they are, but they were tinkering with the IRSA, making it give me bad results."

Kaplan snorted. "Why would I do that? Like I told you, I *need* recruits." He lifted a file from his desk, and Julie recognized Ellie's picture clipped to the front. "I told you I wanted breathing paranormals."

"Sir." Taylor stepped forward. "She might be only half-Fae, but—"

"Woodskin, I truly believe it is time you shut up," Kaplan growled.

Taylor shut his mouth.

"Like I said. All I wanted was someone *breathing*." Kaplan quirked an eyebrow, flipping the file open. "Someone strongly motivated, with some fighting skills already. Excellent grades and a high IQ? That's a bonus."

Julie opened her mouth to defend herself, but her brain registered what Kaplan had just said. She shut it.

"So, I have a better idea than mind-wiping." Kaplan set down the file. "I want you to join the PMA as a recruiter full-time. No pretenses. No threats." His lip curled, but this time, his eyes crinkled.

"S-sir?" Julie stammered.

Taylor was staring at her with wide eyes. Hat, too, wriggled on the desk, turning to face her.

"Come on, Julie," Hat blurted. "Say you'll stay."

"Silence." Kaplan made a swift, cutting motion with one hand. "This time, there will be no smoke and mirrors. No drafting. If Meadows is going to become a bona fide recruiter, she needs to do it on her own steam." He met Julie's eyes. "You still have the chance to walk away. Qtana isn't wrong. You can go back to your human life, and sure, I'll write you a reference."

Julie stared at Taylor, then at Hat. She thought of her mom. Her apartment. Her books. Lillie and Genevieve. If she walked away from all this, she would not remember it. She wouldn't remember Taylor's quips, Malcolm the gamer vampire, or Julius Nox's incredible greenhouse. She would have no idea she'd come face-to-face with a yeti and recruited a half-human, half-Fae, or that she'd hung out of the window of the Statue of Liberty.

"On the other hand, if you stay..." Kaplan spread his hands. "This world is more complicated and dangerous than you can imagine, Meadows."

Julie laughed. Once she started, she found she couldn't stop. The laughter rippled and burst out of her like bubbles. Kaplan, Taylor, and Hat stared at her like she was insane, and maybe she was, but her mind was made up.

"I can't walk away from all this. From all of you." Julie smiled. "I don't want to leave this team behind."

Taylor's face lit up like a kid on the first day of summer. Hat bounced on the desk.

Kaplan sat back. "Well, Meadows, I'm pleased to hear that. You'll—"

"I'm not done." Julie raised a hand.

"Excuse me?" Kaplan growled.

"I have one condition," Julie added.

"What would that be?"

Julie scooped up Hat from the desk and held him in front of her. "I want Hat. He's not allowed to go back into the Warehouse."

"He?" Kaplan raised his eyebrows.

"You heard me." Julie clutched Hat. "It's not fair. He's sentient, you know. He's much better than the IRSA 4000. Besides, we would never have found and recruited Ellie without him."

Kaplan stared at her, then waved a hand. "Fine. The hat stays."

"What about my sign-on bonus?" Julie added.

"What about it? It'll be paid to you, obviously."

"Nice." Julie grinned.

"You'll remain her partner, Woodskin." Kaplan raised his chin. "I'm not saying I was pleased with your little outburst earlier, but it's interesting to see you have developed something resembling a spine."

Taylor glanced at Julie, trying to smother his grin. "Yes, sir."

"Good." Kaplan's cheek twitched as though he was hiding a smile. He hesitated, raising a finger. "One more thing, Meadows."

"Yes, sir?"

Kaplan paused, frowning, locked in an internal battle. Finally, his features relaxed. "I would have told you about the termination clause."

"When?" Julie raised an eyebrow.

Kaplan gave her a steady glare.

"When, *sir*," Julie corrected.

"Tonight." Kaplan sat back in his chair and had the decency to look sheepish. "The trolls might have been the ones to tell you, but I would have done it. Like I say, we were desperate for recruits." He shrugged. "I was willing to try anything, and even if I may not be proud of what I ultimately tried, it still had the desired effect."

Julie smirked. "In that case, I want a bigger bonus, sir."

Kaplan's glare returned. "Don't push it."

"What if I get someone in the top three?" Julie folded her arms. "You know, vampire, warlock, drow?"

"You haven't, though, have you?" Kaplan snorted. "I'd like to see you try."

"I know I can do it. I know I can do better, actually." Julie grinned. "I can get you something even rarer than the top three."

"Rarer than the top three?"

"It's not impossible, you know. I almost recruited a kelpie."

"A kelpie!" Kaplan shook his head. "Useless. I think I might just have decapitated you if you'd done that, Meadows."

"You've underestimated me once," Julie argued. "Don't you think you should avoid doing so a second time?"

Kaplan huffed. "Tread lightly, human. You've already tested my generosity. Don't test my patience."

Taylor could tell this verbal sparring match would last a while. He slipped from the office door without either of them noticing, allowing his shoulders to sag, and crossed the communal office toward their desk. With only mild shock, he reached it, only to find it was no longer a desk in the middle of the empty floor. Walls had been erected around it, and when Taylor opened the door and stepped inside, the cheap old desk had been replaced with two new ones, both polished mahogany. It had a carpet, too, and a painting on the wall. It was boring. Taylor recognized it as a Renaissance depiction of a mermaid draping herself over a rock with a winsome expression on her face; the artist had provided her with some strategically placed seaweed. It was definitely nicer than the communal office had been.

"Always sly, huh, Kaplan?" Taylor muttered, going over to his desk, and sinking into a cushy new office chair. "You knew she wasn't going to leave."

He opened Minesweeper on his computer and clicked around, hardly knowing why. It was half past six already. He didn't think he had ever stayed at work late. The moment that clock hit five, he headed outside. Maybe he should just go. It would be much easier to face Julie on Monday after she'd had the weekend to cool off.

Somehow, though, Taylor closed the Minesweeper window and picked up the file from which they'd been selecting names the previous evening. He grabbed a pen and circled a few he could talk to Hat about next week.

Someone tapped softly on the door, and it opened enough for Julie to pop her head around it. "Whoa. How did this happen? Do we have a real office now?"

"Seems that way." Taylor searched her face. "I guess Kaplan wasn't surprised you decided to stay."

Julie sat in her own chair. "Ooh, squishy." She spun it. "Where did all this come from in a few hours?"

"Magic." Taylor wriggled his fingers, making a few little green sparks float off them.

Julie rolled her eyes at his party trick. "Kaplan thinks he has us all figured out, doesn't he?"

"He often does." Taylor gritted his teeth. It was now or never. "Um, speaking of which, I have some explaining to do."

Julie stopped spinning and met his eyes.

"I obviously also knew you were never going to be killed." Taylor bit his lip. "Kaplan told me to let you stay under that impression because he wanted to put pressure on you. I went along with it, and it was stupid and cowardly. You deserved to know. I'm sorry."

"It was cowardly." Julie grinned. "It ranked quite high on the stupid scale."

"Hey!" Taylor laughed. "I'm trying to give you a heartfelt apology here."

"For the record, *I* didn't tell you because I believed it was some new policy." Hat was perched on Julie's head again. "So, I agree. Let's be mad at Taylor."

"Monday Taylor wasn't the same person as today Taylor." Julie got up. "What are we still doing here? It's the weekend!"

"I was working on finding the next contestant on 'Who do we recruit this week?'" Taylor closed the file.

"Well, we can do that on Monday, dumbass." Julie lifted Hat from her head. "Can you give me something fun and chic for post-work drinks?"

"As you wish, milady," Hat mocked. *Poof!* Julie was holding a stylish black vintage hat with a neat satin ribbon.

"Perfect." Julie donned it, turning to Taylor. "Hey, you want to go get a drink?"

"Is this a date?" Hat interrupted. "Because there are formalities."

Taylor grinned, getting to his feet. "It's going for drinks with my partner. Can you drink, Hat?"

"Wait, I'm considered a partner?" Hat asked in a small voice.

"Aw, of course." Julie pulled Hat off her head and ran a hand over the top of him as if he were a cat. "You had my back."

Hat squirmed. "Well, hrrm, of course I did. That was the deal."

"You went above and beyond." Julie put him on her head and flashed Taylor a grin that made her eyes seem brighter. "So, are you coming?"

Taylor switched off his computer. "Okay, but I'm buying."

"We'll see about that."

"Oh, we will, will we?" Taylor offered her an arm.

She raised her eyebrows. "What are you doing?"

"Sorry." Taylor felt his cheeks turn gray and lowered his arm. "It was automatic. Old-fashioned royal manners, you know. My tutors practically beat them into me with a stick. I didn't mean—"

"Taylor, chill." Julie laughed, grabbed his arm, and threaded hers through it. "There's something to be said for chivalry." Her mouth tightened, and she wagged a finger at him. "Not for patriarchy, *capisce*?"

"That's something we can agree on."

They headed to the elevator after closing the door of the fancy new office behind them. Julie raised a hand to her mouth, stifling a yawn. Taylor noticed the back of her usually immaculate pixie cut was standing up. Wind from the top of the Statue of Liberty, no doubt. His stomach lurched as he remembered the sickening feeling when she'd started falling from the window.

He wasn't sorry he'd called Kaplan out the way he had. The elevator doors slid open, and they stepped forward. "Figured out where to put your filthy money yet?" Julie looked at him, mischief dimpling her cheeks.

"Well, no, actually." Taylor cleared his throat. "I'm sure they'll just pay it into my trust fund account."

"So even your salary goes where your accountant can see what you're doing with it?"

Taylor shrugged.

Julie's brow furrowed. "That won't do at all, will it, Hat?"

Hat chuckled. "Well, I don't see how His Royal Highness has much choice."

"Of course he has a choice." Julie fumbled Genevieve's keys from her pocket. "When I convinced you to help me, Taylor, I told you I was going to help you get some money that belongs to *you*, not your trust fund. I'm going to make good on that."

Taylor laughed at the fierce determination in her voice and gently disentangled his arm from hers as they reached the car. "It's okay, Julie. Don't worry about it."

"No, it's not." Julie grinned. "You need your own bank account."

Taylor opened Genevieve's passenger door and plopped into the bucket seat. "I don't even know where to get one."

"Don't worry." Julie started the car. "I do."

Genevieve let out a throaty roar that reverberated around the parking lot. Taylor gripped the handle above the window, not quite ready for a repeat of that afternoon. When they reached the PMA's gate, Taylor noticed two black SUVs parked outside. They flashed their IDs to the gate guard—Fred, Taylor reminded himself, feeling guilty he'd had to think about it when Julie had asked earlier—and drove into the street.

"Hey, wait a minute." Julie glanced into the rearview mirror. "Those two SUVs drove after us. I think they're following us."

Taylor grimaced. "I'm sorry. I don't get to go out on weekends without security." He glanced at Julie. "It's okay if you'd rather not go out for drinks with a bunch of bodyguards looking over your shoulder."

Julie laughed. "Nah, that's not necessary." Her fingers flexed on the wheel, and she tapped the accelerator, eliciting a lusty growl from the 375 horses under the hood.

"What are you doing?" Taylor gripped the handle more tightly.

Julie's grin turned wicked. "Let's see if they can catch up!"

"Yee-haw!" Hat squealed.

"Julie, Julie, don't—" Taylor began.

Julie slammed her foot to the floor. Genevieve leaped forward, her tires shrieking on the asphalt.

"*Nooooooo!*" Taylor yelled.

His protest was lost in Julie's laughter, Hat's whoops of encouragement, and the dizzying roar of the powerful engine as Genevieve surged into the bustling city.

CHAPTER NINETEEN

Sunlight shone on Julie's face, the gentle kiss of warmth on her cheek lifting her from the most delicious sleep she'd had in weeks. A pulse of anxiety ran through her before she remembered it was Saturday, she was sleeping in, and she was still alive. Her lips twitched in an involuntary smile.

"Finally! You're awake."

Julie sat up with a yelp at the sound of the faintly British, masculine voice. Hat sat on her nightstand, still the attractive vintage hat she'd worn last night. When Julie groaned and flopped back into her pillows, pulling her sheets up to her chin, Hat waddled closer to her and plopped onto the bed.

"Go away," Julie mumbled, snuggling down into her pillows. "I'm sleeping in."

"Oh, so you're not going to the cemetery?"

Julie's eyes snapped open. "What time is it?"

"Just after ten."

She groaned. She'd agreed to meet her mom at the cemetery at eleven. Pulling a pillow over her head, she contemplated the excellent wine Taylor had splurged on last night.

"How much of that bottle did I drink last night?" she wondered aloud.

"Not an irresponsible amount," Hat replied. "Although the same can't be said for Taylor."

Julie snickered. "Idiot."

"So, are we going or staying?"

Julie muffled a yawn, considering her options. On the one hand, her bed was wonderfully comfortable, and every inch of her ached like it had been beaten with a stick. She'd read somewhere there were a hundred and sixty-two steps from the pedestal to the crown of the Statue of Liberty.

On the other...

Julie sighed, pushing back her covers. "I promised my mom. There's nothing like a perceived near-death experience for new resolutions, right?" She got up and padded over to the kitchenette to boil the kettle.

"New resolutions?" Hat hopped back onto the nightstand and watched her. "What do you mean?"

"I just mean, maybe she isn't so bad." Julie fished for a packet of that disgusting instant coffee. "We need some real coffee, anyway."

With a *poof*, Hat turned into an attractive white sun hat with a cheerful orange bow. "The forecast is high 60s today. I'll bring the floral pattern to that midi dress you like."

"You're a creep."

"Just doing my research."

"What, like the trolls did?" Julie raised an eyebrow.

Hat huffed. "No, not like that."

She yawned again. "It's too early in the morning for debate, but you look nice."

Hat's bow perked up visibly. "Thank you!"

Julie laughed and poured the coffee. Here she was, stroking the ego of a magical hat, about to visit her mother of her own accord. She wasn't sure which was weirder.

Rosa's lips were pressed tight when Julie stopped Genevieve in the cemetery parking lot. It was immaculately groomed and surrounded by beds of spring flowers, with the memorial garden's name on an elegant plaque over the gate.

"Julia, what is *this*?" Rosa's strident voice resounded around the parking lot as Julie got out.

"*Her* name is Genevieve." Julie ran a hand along the hood affectionately and then walked over to her mom. "My landlady's letting me use her."

"It looks like a deathtrap on wheels. Did you know these old cars don't have enough safety features? You could get yourself killed."

Well, she's charming, Hat commented.

Shut up. I'm trying to be nice here. Julie plastered a smile as she reached her mother, noticing the redness around her mom's eyes that her heavy makeup didn't quite hide. She wore her thick, black hair short enough to brush her shoulders, and as a cool wind rushed through the pale green leaves of the pine trees surrounding the parking lot, she drew her knitted cardigan more tightly around her.

"It's nice to see you, Mom," Julie offered.

Rosa lowered her hands from her cardigan like she wanted a hug, then tucked them under her arms instead. "It's freezing out here. Did you bring flowers?"

"Yeah." Julie had gotten them from a hawker at a red light. She retrieved them from the passenger seat.

"Thank you." Rosa's smile flickered. "I like your hat. It's new."

"Thanks, Mom."

Okay, I take it back. I like her.

Shhh, Hat!

"I mean, the orange is bold." Rosa raised an eyebrow. "Do you really think you're going to attract an upper-class man with that?"

"Mom!"

"I'm just saying if your new job doesn't work out and you keep refusing to use your considerable assets to your advantage, you might want to consider marrying well." Rosa spread her hands. "Your cousin Emelie did, and—"

"Mom, Emelie married a total sugar daddy." Julie fell into step beside her mother as they made for the cemetery gate.

"It's always an option, honey."

Julie opened the gate and held it. As Rosa stepped through, she paused, squinting at Julie's face. "Is that a pimple on your chin?"

"Mom!"

"You know, if you were drinking your aloe vera juice, you'd have clearer skin, too."

Julie groaned. "Do we have to do this right now?"

"A skin blemish is the first thing a man notices about a woman." Rosa patted Julie's cheek. "You're such a beautiful young lady, sweetheart. Make sure to let your healthy inner beauty shine through."

"You get that off a moisturizer bottle or something?"

Rosa tossed her hair back and strode into the cemetery. "Your clients will notice it, too. It's important to present a professional appearance, honey. You need to take this job seriously if you want to succeed."

Julie considered strangling her but latched the gate and followed Rosa down the familiar path instead. A pang of guilt ran through her. When had she last been here? Had she visited Dad's grave since moving to the city?

Dad's headstone was granite and very plain. The cheapest one they could get, Julie remembered. Its lettering read simply, DAVID MEADOWS. BELOVED FATHER AND HUSBAND.

Julie crouched and laid the flowers at the foot of the headstone. She wanted to say something but didn't know what.

Rosa's voice was rough around the edges. "Your father loved yellow roses."

Julie traced a finger around the outline of a bright yellow petal. "I know."

Rosa cleared her throat. "Thank you."

Julie got up, searching her mom's eyes. Tears welled in them. She wanted to apologize, but she couldn't verbalize what for.

"I don't want you to think I let go of him too soon," Rosa blurted. She turned away, dabbing at her eyes with a sleeve. "It's been six years, Julie."

"Mom, no." Julie swallowed. "That's not what I think. I just… I miss him."

"So do I. Every day. Every single day."

Julie smiled, blinking away her tears. "He would have loved Genevieve, you know."

Rosa laughed softly. "Yes, he would have." A muscle jumped in her cheek. "It's just so unfair, honey. He gave his life to looking after people, you know. I don't know how he could give his whole heart to that hospital and us at the same time. It's not fair he would die so—so senselessly."

Julie didn't know what to say to that. She bent and brushed some dust from the face of Dad's headstone. "Dad would have said life wasn't fair, but that doesn't mean we don't have to be."

Rosa put a hand on Julie's shoulder. "You're quite right, honey. That's exactly what he would have said." She squeezed softly. "I see a lot of him in you, you know."

Julie looked up at her. "You do?"

"Yeah. He wouldn't drink aloe vera juice either, no matter how many times I told him it would do an excellent job of cleansing his colon. Your father was always constipated. If he'd just listened to me, he could have been as regular as I am." Rosa slapped her belly proudly.

Julie stopped herself from rolling her eyes. She straightened, laughing. "Did he refuse to become a stripper just to make more money?"

"Oh, really, Julia!" Rosa grasped her hand like she was a little girl. "Come on. Lunch is waiting."

Julie wanted to gently disentangle her hand from her mom's. Her mother's palm was sweaty, her fingers trembled a little, and she smelled abundantly of lavender essential oil. But she didn't. Just once, she let Rosa hold her hand all the way to the parking lot.

Taylor sat on the couch in his suite, splashing a spoon around a bowl of Cheerios and ignoring the fact that it was half past eleven on a Saturday morning. A chick flick played on the huge TV in a cabinet opposite the couch. He'd opened the expensive oak doors and turned it on first thing this morning after rolling out of bed.

His usual weekend routine, although normally his Saturday mornings didn't include a pounding headache in his temples. He guessed that wine from last night was responsible. He scratched his ass contentedly, let out a magnificent belch, then slurped the rest of his Cheerio milk straight from the bowl.

Super princely, as usual. That was one advantage to his suite being tucked away in the back corner of the compound, where his parents could barely even see it from the main castle.

They also couldn't see his secret love, *Notting Hill*. Setting the empty bowl aside, Taylor mouthed the last few lines alongside a doe-eyed Julia Roberts. The credits rolled, and he reached for the remote to put on the next one. *Pretty Woman*, perhaps.

With a faint chirping sound, a small creature buzzed through the open window and perched on the brim of the empty bowl. It was one of those annoying fledgling firebirds. "Shoo," he grumbled, waving a hand at it.

It chirped, a tiny flame the size of a birthday candle's flickering around the back of its head.

"Ugh, fine. Whatever. Just don't set my curtains on fire again."

The firebird pecked at the last bits of Cheerios with a tiny, ceramic sound.

Taylor's phone buzzed. He dug around in the couch cushions for it and grinned.

Hangover cure: 6 raw eggs beaten in a glass with a shot of Worcestershire sauce. My dad used to swear by it.

It was Julie. No one in the magical world would be texting him about hangover cures.

Thanks for nothing, Meadows, he typed back.

Last night... They'd been sitting at the bar, knocking back glasses of that excellent wine, when she'd turned to him with that mischievous smirk. "See? It's not so bad slipping the bodyguards and living a real life."

Taylor snorted. "Oh, so I haven't lived. Is that what you're saying?"

"Been spoiled, maybe." She shrugged. "Lived? I'm not so sure."

Spoiled. The word sat sourly in the back of Taylor's mind, and he decided he didn't need to watch *Pretty Woman* for the eighty-first time. He turned off the TV and jumped to his feet, sending the firebird fluttering from the window.

He hurried to the bedroom, switched his t-shirt and boxers for jeans and his favorite black sweater, then strode from the suite and across the beautiful green lawns surrounding every building in the keep. Avoiding the high tower in the middle of the keep, Taylor headed instead for a small door in one of the battlemented walls.

A guard stood at the doorway. He raised his eyebrows. "Your Highness? Did you wish to be taken somewhere?"

"No, thank you." Taylor brushed past him with a grin. "I want to take myself somewhere."

He pushed the door open and followed a flight of stairs into the vast underground parking garage. Waving a hand, he triggered the lights. The long fluorescent strips turned on, bathing the garage in a cool white glow. They shimmered on the smooth, stern lines of long flat hoods and slanting windshields that oozed both speed and money.

Taylor smiled and turned to the row of keys hanging on the wall beside him. He selected one, delighting in the *chink* of metal on metal. "I'll show her who's spoiled," he whispered.

Julie hurried around her apartment, packing away the handful of groceries she'd bought on her way home. She straightened the photograph on her nightstand of her, Mom, and Dad standing side-by-side by the statue of Balto in Central Park. Julie, wearing purple braces, had had to stretch her arm out to grab a selfie. Dad had his arm around Mom. He looked slender and tiny next to her like he always did. His gentle smile lifted his stubbled cheeks.

"Missed you today, Dad," she whispered, touching the picture. Then she grabbed the car keys and hurried toward the door.

Hat wriggled indignantly off the hook where Julie had hung him and flopped onto the kitchen counter. "Excuse me, are you going to leave me up here?"

"Aw, Hat, c'mon." Julie spun Genevieve's keys around one finger. "I took you with me to Mom and Ernesto's house."

"Your stepfather is an insufferable dolt." Hat sniffed. "Lillie Griswall, on the other hand, is a charming old pistol, and I like her."

Julie sighed. "The food's getting cold while we argue. Okay, you can come." She reached for him.

Hat scooted from her grasp. "It's okay. I'm teasing. You're still allowed a private life, you know."

Julie raised an eyebrow. "What? That's news to me."

Hat scoffed and made himself comfortable on the counter.

"I'll be back early. Lillie doesn't go to bed late." Julie patted Hat's crown. "See you later."

She clattered downstairs into the garage and retrieved two plastic bags, promisingly hot and heavy with Chinese food, from Genevieve's passenger seat. Hooking one bag over her elbow, she clumsily locked the car and strode to Lillie's back door. "Lillie!" She knocked. "It's me!"

"Come on in, dear!" Lillie called.

Julie couldn't help gasping as she stepped into the living room. It was all but unrecognizable. The coffee table had been cleared of debris except for a beautiful photography book. The TV was off, and there was even a vase of fake flowers on the nearest bookshelf. Julie made a mental note to get Lillie some real ones.

Even the pets looked better. The cat was sitting on the arm of the sofa, purring magnanimously. Julie tickled Pookie, the dog, under the chin.

Lillie's cheeks were faintly pink, and she patted her hair, which had been combed and squashed into a bun, even though some hair already hung loose down the back of her neck. "I know you said you wanted to help tidy the kitchen, dear, but then I thought I'd make a go of the living room, and we'd tackle the kitchen another night. You must be tired after this week."

Julie set the bags down on the coffee table and smiled. "It sounds perfect to me, Lillie."

The old lady's face cracked with a wide grin. She petted the cat's fluffy back, causing the purring to grow louder. "You brought Chinese, huh? Did you bring hot sauce?"

"Plenty of hot sauce!" Julie assured her.

Lillie bustled toward the kitchen. "I'm getting some root beer. Why don't you turn on the TV? I've already got the movie all set up."

Julie sank onto the couch, ignoring the cat hairs that stuck to her dress, and grabbed the remote from the coffee table. She was unsurprised that the film Lillie had chosen was *Baby Driver*. Smiling, she unpacked the Chinese food boxes on the table while Lillie shuffled back into the living room.

"Have you seen it?" Lillie asked, squinting at Julie as she set the soda bottle and two glasses on the coffee table. "Is it any good?"

"Well, it's got a lot of action and car chases."

Lillie beamed. "I was hoping so."

Julie laughed, and Lillie settled on the couch beside her. The old lady pressed the play button on the remote as Julie shoved a healthy amount of fried noodles into her mouth. *Take that, aloe vera juice.* Rosa had poured her a glass at the lunch table, of course.

Lillie's eyes widened as the movie started: a shot of city buildings, panning down to street level, then a glimpse of a sleek red bumper. "Subaru braking system!" she breathed. "This is gonna be good!"

Julie giggled into her noodles as *Bellbottoms* from Jon Spencer Blues Explosion began to play, its loud chords ringing through the living room. Chopsticks in one hand, a box of fried rice in the other, Lillie bounced on the couch. "My, I do love this tune!"

They had just reached the part where the red Subaru skidded through its first high-definition handbrake turn, and Lillie was about to hop off the couch, yelling excitedly, when the doorbell rang. Julie was trying not to choke to death on laughter and noodles as the dog darted back and forth, barking loudly.

"Whoo-hoo! Go for it, boy!" whooped Lillie.

The doorbell rang again. Julie reluctantly set down her noodles. "You expecting someone, Lillie?"

Flopping back onto the couch, Lillie paused the movie, looking disappointed. "I'm not, dear. You?"

"No. Let me go see who it is." Julie patted Lillie's shoulder. "Then we'll get right back to it."

"Okay, honey." Lillie's grin returned, slurping some root beer as though already tired from her exertions.

Julie padded over to the door on her socks and opened it a fraction, keeping one hand flat against it just in case. A guy wearing a FedEx cap squinted at her. "Sorry to trouble you, miss. I've been ringing the bell for the upstairs apartment."

Julie relaxed, letting the door swing open. "How can I help?"

"I'm looking for a Miss Julia Meadows. You wouldn't know her, would you?"

"That's me."

"Great." The FedEx guy held out a large envelope and a clipboard. "Then this is for you."

Julie blinked, taking the envelope. The paper was thick and heavy, with decorative designs on the corners and her name on the front in what looked like real gold leaf.

"Please sign here, miss." The FedEx guy gestured with the clipboard.

Julie tried not to think about the last time she'd had to sign for something. She signed her name and wandered back into the living room, perplexed as she turned the envelope over.

"What is it, dear?" Lillie asked. Her little dog had jumped onto her lap, and she scratched its ears. She saw no sign of the cat.

"It's a letter. No idea why I had to sign for it." Julie sat down beside her.

Lillie ran a hand over the paper. "Ooh, fancy! Reeks of rich."

Julie read the name on the return address. *Mr. J. Nox.*

"Friend of yours?" Lillie raised an eyebrow.

"Yes, actually." *At least, I think so.*

"Well, go on then, dear. Open it!"

Julie carefully slit the envelope with a blunt knife, even though it felt weird tearing something so nice, and pulled out what looked fancy enough to be a diploma certificate but turned out to be an invitation on thick cream-colored paper with elegant lettering and embossed gold leaf.

Julius Nox
requests the honor of your presence
at the handfasting ceremony of
his son, Malcolm Nox, and
Cassidy Consta
on the twenty-first of May, two thousand twenty-one
at four o'clock in the afternoon
Nox Residence
Staten Island, New York City
New York
Dress code: Black tie.
Dinner will be followed by dancing.

"What's a handfasting ceremony?" Lillie asked.

Julie jumped. She hadn't realized her landlady was reading over her shoulder and felt nervous as she scanned the invitation again. Still, there was no mention of anything paranormal. Lillie was still in the clear.

"It's the first step toward something like a marriage, I think." *A traditional ceremony for vampires*, the orb added in her mind.

"Fancy!" Lillie smiled. "Black tie, huh? I smell a shopping trip in your future."

Julie shook her head, her eyes lingering on Cassidy's name. "This is terrible news."

"Terrible? Why?" Lillie's brow furrowed. "I hoped with your new job, you'd be able—"

"Oh, no, not the shopping trip, Lillie." Julie smiled, resting a hand on Lillie's knee. "That's okay. It's just…well, this is a friend of mine, and this girl isn't right for him. Not at all!"

Lillie chuckled. "Let me guess. You *are* right for him?"

"It's not like that." Julie's cheeks reddened. "Cassidy is a real bitch!"

Lillie chortled. "Oh, fix it next week, dear." She picked up the remote. "Let's watch some driving!"

Julie put the invitation aside, grabbed her noodles, and sank into the couch as the squeal of tires and horns blaring filled the living room. Beside her, Lillie was laughing—warm, full, genuine laughter that made Julie smile.

New York City was filled with supernatural beings. Her mom saw something of Dad in her, and Lillie was a real firecracker.

Who knew, right?

It was a relief to arrive at work *without* the not-so-impending death threat hanging over her head.

Surprisingly for the early hour, Julie had to search for an empty spot to park Genevieve. She found one way back in the parking lot and eased Genevieve in. She got out of the car, eyeing the flaming chariot in the spot to her right to ensure the gently rippling fire surrounding it wouldn't damage Genevieve's paint.

Satisfied, she turned to head into the building and almost collided with the head of the IT department.

Julie hopped out of the way before the inevitable happened, and she smiled apologetically. "Sorry. I didn't see you there. Qbiit, right?"

The troll glared at her. "Don't play innocent with me, Meadows. I'm on to you."

AUTHOR NOTES RENÉE JAGGÉR
WRITTEN NOVEMBER 3, 2022

Thank you for reading through to the back!

Here we are at the start of a new series. Sorry for the long break. I was trying to learn some new things about writing, and it took longer than I thought! If you've read any of my other series, *Callie Hart, Werewitch*, or the *Reincarnation of the Morrigan*, I thank you and welcome you back. For those of you who are new, a bit about me…

I grew up in Los Angeles and now live in a small town in Arizona. It's just me and my dog Josephine; she is a Labradoodle. Or something. I'm really not sure since she's a rescue, but that's as close as I can come. Did you ever wonder who rules the world? It's her. She's with her grandma right now because…

I'm not in Arizona. I'm in Scotland <insert Highland Fling here>. In my last author notes, I said I desperately missed chips (French fries) and curry sauce. I can now tell you that it *is* possible to eat too many. My kingdom for some rice or noodles!

And I have discovered that haggis is actually good…if you can take the taste of organ meats. I like pate, so it was easy for me. Mostly, it tastes like really nicely spiced lamb. Before, I had some vegetarian haggis, and it tasted like I imagine carpet sweepings would, although I lack the culinary expertise to state that definitively. However, this time, I had some veggie haggis at a place I trust, and it was good too! It's a whole new world. If you get brave enough to try it, don't do it at some random place. But it's worth it!

I am slightly indulging another passion I found here: tablet. Some people would call it fudge, but it's not really that. It comes in many flavors, all made from sugar and condensed milk and butter, and you know you're going to hell (or to the clothing store for bigger clothes) for eating that second piece, but jeez! It's so good!

I have hung out with friends since I've been here and seen lots of autumn leaves and migrating geese and other birds. I see the seals in the harbor every day, and the resident swans and their babies, who are just fledging out in white now after their summer brown. Life is good! That's what I came here for. I am writing this as the sun comes up, which hasn't been normal on this trip so far. Of course I couldn't sleep last night. I have a "do" tonight and will be up until all hours. Sigh...

This series will be nine books, and I have another coming right after that is set in—you guessed it—Scotland. No haggis will be harmed in the making of that story. I hope you enjoy this story as much as I did writing it! I think my new approach worked, but y'all will have to be the judges.

As always, thank you to my proofreaders! They make my books the best they can be.

I hope you enjoyed the beginning of Julie's journey! Follow her as she learns about herself and her new world.

Until we speak again, I hope your skies are sunny and your days are filled with happiness and good books!

Renée

AUTHOR NOTES MICHAEL ANDERLE
WRITTEN NOVEMBER 2, 2022

Thank you for not only reading this book but these author notes as well!

Is this your first time reading a Michael Anderle book?

If it is, welcome! Why don't you get comfortable and stay a while?

If it isn't, welcome back! Get comfortable, and I'll make sure there is plenty of hot chocolate.

Why this story?

The genesis of Para-Military Recruiter occurred while I was traveling by plane between Las Vegas, NV and Cabo San Lucas, Mexico. My wife and I missed our connection in Los Angeles and had to grab a room for the night to pick up a plane the next day.

I was pissed.

It was mid-July 2022, and I was aching to get down to Los Cabos. I had been in Europe for almost a month and, for work reasons, hadn't been able to go to Cabo for months and months.

Right when it looked like I was going to get a break and relax a little...*I was stuck in Los Angeles.*

My wife was raised in and around Los Angeles, so for her, it was a *HOLIDAY*!

I know better than to complain…much. Well, I'm learning how to keep my mouth shut as a husband. It's taken a while. I'm occasionally wise. Not always. Not often, if I'm honest, but occasionally.

I tried to see the bright spot.

Which is that there ARE a lot of great Mexican food places in Los Angeles, so I jumped on Yelp after we got the motel room, and Judith was good to try a place.

A Uber later (and oh my, God, the traffic! How can it take so long to go three miles?) and we hit a really old Mexican restaurant and enjoyed ourselves.

For those interested, here is where we went: http://www.zacatecasmenu.com

One long Uber trip back and a stay overnight, badabing, badaboom…back on a plane. It wasn't that straightforward, but I'll save you from listening to my whining.

During that time, I came up with this idea. I'll share the original overview I wrote.

PROJECT: Para-Military Recruiter

Julie Meadows must recruit new members to the Official Para-Military Agency (OPMA) or die trying. Frankly, her boss is hoping she fails (or quits) as both require a mind-wipe.

He doesn't like humans knowing about paranormals.

The time is present day. Our main character, human Julie Meadows, is down on her luck when a letter arrives in the mail.

She has been drafted!

Not sure how this could be (she has two flat feet, right?) Julie goes to the offices listed on the DRAFT notice and is dropped into a world that shouldn't exist.

Imagine the scene from MEN IN BLACK when J comes into the office for the first time and sees all these aliens that shouldn't exist. https://www.youtube.com/watch?v=4YUQ4bRHfwo).

Except they are a bunch of paranormals instead of aliens.

As a human, she isn't supposed to be there.

Unfortunately (for Julie), she has two options. She can work in the Military Liaison for Acquisition of Soldiers(MLAS)as a recruiting officer or be killed. She can no longer unsee what she shouldn't have seen in the first place.

Renée and I have a LOT of stories with Julie, Taylor, and Hat coming at you. Please consider sharing with two (or twenty) friends about this fun little series if you like it.

I'm off to go find my own version of Hat.

Who doesn't want a magical hat that can turn into anything? I know I do.

Chat with you in the next book.

Ad Aeternitatem,
Michael Anderle

MORE STORIES with Michael newsletter HERE: https://michael.beehiiv.com/

BOOKS FROM RENÉE

Reincarnation of the Morrigan
Birth of a Goddess (Book One)
The Way of Wisdom (Book Two)
Angelic Death (Book Three)
A Cold War (Book 4)
A Battle Tune (Book 5)
Broken Ice (Book 6)
A Torn Veil (Book 7)
Sins of the Past (Book 8)
The Wild Hunt Comes (*coming soon*)

The WereWitch Series
Bad Attitude (Book One)
A Bit Aggressive (Book Two)
Too Much Magic (Book Three)
Were War (Book Four)
Were Rages (Book Five)
God Ender (Book Six)
God Trials (Book Seven)
The Troll Solution (Book Eight)

BOOKS FROM RENÉE

Winner Takes All (Book Nine)

Callie Hart Series
Thin Ice (Book One)
Cold Blood (Book Two)
Feelings Run Deep (Book Three)

BOOKS BY MICHAEL ANDERLE

Sign up for the LMBPN email list to be notified of new releases and special deals!

https://lmbpn.com/email/

For a complete list of books by Michael Anderle, please visit:

www.lmbpn.com/ma-books/

CONNECT WITH THE AUTHOR

Connect with Michael Anderle

Website: http://lmbpn.com

Email List: http://lmbpn.com/email/

https://www.facebook.com/LMBPNPublishing

https://twitter.com/MichaelAnderle

https://www.instagram.com/lmbpn_publishing/

https://www.bookbub.com/authors/michael-anderle

Printed in Great Britain
by Amazon